"Frasier has perfected the art of making a reader's skin crawl. . . . [An] exceptional thriller. . . . Frasier's characters are not only fully realized, but fascinating to boot, and she evokes the dark, mystical side of Savannah with precision and skill." —*Publishers Weekly*

"Has all the essentials of an edge-of-your-seat story. There is suspense, believable characters, an interesting setting, and just the right amount of details to keep the reader's eyes always moving forward. . . . I recommend *Play Dead* as a great addition to any mystery library." —Roundtable Reviews

Sleep Tight

"Anne Frasier hasn't wasted any time establishing herself as a master of the serial killer genre. . . . Gripping and intense. . . . Along with a fine plot, Frasier delivers her characters as whole people, each trying to cope in the face of violence and jealousies." —*Minneapolis Star Tribune*

"There'll be no sleeping tight after reading this one! A riveting thriller guaranteed to keep you up all night. Laced with forensic detail and psychological twists, Anne Frasier's latest intertwines the hunt for a serial killer with the personal struggles of two sisters battling their own demons and seeking their own truths. Compelling and real—a great read."
—*New York Times* bestselling author Andrea Kane

"Guaranteed to keep you awake at night . . . a fast-paced novel of secrets, lies, and chilling suspense."
—*New York Times* bestselling author Lisa Jackson

"Enthralling . . . there's a lot more to this clever intrigue than graphic police procedures. Indeed, one of Frasier's many strengths is her ability to create characters and relationships that are as compelling as the mystery itself. . . . Frasier's well-rounded characters will linger with readers long after the killer is caught." —*Publishers Weekly*

Hush

"A deeply engrossing read. *Hush* delivers a creepy villain, a chilling plot, and two remarkable investigators whose personal struggles are only equaled by their compelling need to stop a madman before he kills again. One warning: Don't read this book if you are home alone!"
—*New York Times* bestselling author Lisa Gardner

"Well-realized characters and taut, suspenseful plotting. It will definitely keep you awake to finish it. And you'll be glad you did." —*Minneapolis Star Tribune*

"With *Hush*, Anne Frasier slams into the fast lane of the thriller market and goes to the head of the pack. This is far and away the best serial killer story I have read in a very long time. It is packed with intense human drama, strong characters, and a truly twisted bad guy. Frasier's tale is fast and furious. This one has Guaranteed Winner written all over it."
—*New York Times* bestselling author Jayne Ann Krentz

"Anne Frasier has crafted a taut and suspenseful thriller driven by a villain guaranteed to give you nightmares . . . [ends] on a chilling note you won't soon forget."
—*New York Times* bestselling author Kay Hooper

"I couldn't put it down. . . . Engrossing . . . scary. . . . I loved it."
—*New York Times* bestselling author Linda Howard

"A brilliant debut from a very talented author—a guaranteed page-turner that will keep the reader riveted from beginning to end."—*USA Today* bestselling author Katherine Sutcliffe

"A wealth of procedural detail, a heart-thumping finale, and two scarred but indelible protagonists make this a first-rate debut." —*Publishers Weekly*

Other Books by Anne Frasier

Hush
Sleep Tight
Play Dead
Before I Wake

PALE IMMORTAL

Anne Frasier

AN ONYX BOOK

ONYX
Published by New American Library, a division of
Penguin Group (USA) Inc., 375 Hudson Street,
New York, New York 10014, USA
Penguin Group (Canada), 90 Eglinton Avenue East, Suite 700, Toronto,
Ontario M4P 2Y3, Canada (a division of Pearson Penguin Canada Inc.)
Penguin Books Ltd., 80 Strand, London WC2R 0RL, England
Penguin Ireland, 25 St. Stephen's Green, Dublin 2,
Ireland (a division of Penguin Books Ltd.)
Penguin Group (Australia), 250 Camberwell Road, Camberwell, Victoria 3124,
Australia (a division of Pearson Australia Group Pty. Ltd.)
Penguin Books India Pvt. Ltd., 11 Community Centre, Panchsheel Park,
New Delhi - 110 017, India
Penguin Group (NZ), cnr Airborne and Rosedale Roads, Albany,
Auckland 1310, New Zealand (a division of Pearson New Zealand Ltd.)
Penguin Books (South Africa) (Pty.) Ltd., 24 Sturdee Avenue,
Rosebank, Johannesburg 2196, South Africa

Penguin Books Ltd., Registered Offices:
80 Strand, London WC2R 0RL, England

First published by Onyx, an imprint of New American Library,
a division of Penguin Group (USA) Inc.

First Printing, September 2006
10 9 8 7 6 5 4 3 2 1

Copyright © Anne Frasier, 2006
All rights reserved

Excerpt from the *Kalevala* on p. xi taken from *The Kalevala: An Epic Poem after Oral Tradition* by Elias Lönnrot, translated from the Finnish and with an Introduction and Notes by Keith Bosley (Oxford: Oxford University Press, 1989).

 REGISTERED TRADEMARK—MARCA REGISTRADA

Printed in the United States of America

for Martha

From the Author

On a road trip from St. Paul, Minnesota, to Milwaukee, Wisconsin, I stopped for breakfast in a Black River Falls café and happened upon a conversation between two men about the Wisconsin town of Tuonela, where they claimed a vampire once roamed the streets.

I introduced myself and asked if they'd mind telling me more. They fell silent, looked at each other, then grudgingly continued. The story they told was so outrageous I decided they must be having fun at my expense. They'd probably meant for me to overhear their conversation; I was their entertainment for the day. Tuonela didn't exist, and we all know vampires don't exist.

In the car, I pulled out an atlas and was surprised to find a town called Tuonela on the map. If you were to draw a triangle by connecting Wausau to La Crosse to Portage, Tuonela would be somewhere in the center on the Wisconsin River. That area of Wisconsin was settled by Finns, and if you're up on your Finnish mythology and the *Kalevala*, you'll know that *Tuonela* means "land of the dead" in Finnish.

That left me to ponder about the men and our conversation, and about the vampire they'd referred to as the Pale Immortal. Had they been telling the truth after all? Was I now included in a secret only a handful of people knew? I have no answers to these questions. All I know is that day in the Black River Falls café the men told me the town often vanishes, and many don't believe it even exists. In case you think I'm making this up, dig out a map of Wisconsin and try to find Tuonela. Ninety percent of the time it won't be there.

Anne Frasier

Plenty have got there
few have come from there
from Tuonela's dwellings, from
The Dead Land's ageless abodes.
—The Kalevala, *Elias Lönnrot*

Or liker still to one who should take leave
Of pale immortal death . . .
—*John Keats*

Chapter 1

The car moved through the night, the two occupants staring silently out the windshield as the road unfolded before them.

They'd been traveling for over twenty-four hours, with only a few stops for gas and a bathroom. Food amounted to what packaged snacks could be grabbed while waiting in line to pay.

What had begun as desert and interstate had given way to narrow two-lanes that twisted through rural Midwest woodland and pasture unveiled in the yellow headlight beams. The landscape looked foreign.

At least to Graham Yates, who was used to millions of stars and a sky that stretched from horizon to horizon. His eyes couldn't get used to hills that blocked the sky, a curved road that hid what was ahead, and fog that clung to low areas.

The passenger window was open a crack, and the smell that came in reminded him of the tropical forest he'd once visited at a science museum. Or the compost bin at one of the schools he'd gone to. Like rotting plants and wet dirt.

How much longer?

Were they almost there?

He wanted to ask, but she wouldn't answer anyway. She hadn't said anything to him since they'd left Arizona. That was okay. Silence was better than yelling.

A second after she turned off the wipers, the windshield became covered with mist that he'd finally figured out was dew. She couldn't get rid of it. So weird. It just kept reappearing.

Graham had a plan. He'd had a lot of time to think—once he'd come down from a fairly major high. When they got there, he would run away.

What kind of plan is that? That's no plan.

Knocking her out and stealing the car—that was a plan. But he wasn't a violent person. Even after all she'd done to him, he couldn't hit her. And knowing her, being hit would just send her into a rage. She'd come at him spitting and hissing, adding a new element to an already bad situation.

Never make the situation worse than it already is . . . .

He wasn't afraid, he told himself, heart pounding. He wasn't afraid of anything. Not even death, which he'd been thinking about a lot lately, even before she'd dragged him into the car. What kid a few days away from his sixteenth birthday didn't think about death?

The thought of dying was one of the only things that gave him comfort. It meant there was a way out. And as long as you knew death was waiting, you knew this could end.

At four fifteen A.M., they arrived in the town of Tuonela, Wisconsin.

Their car was the only one on the street. House shades and curtains were pulled tight. Everyone was asleep, unaware of the drama just outside their doors.

So quiet.

And still. Almost as if nobody really lived there.

Tuonela was a place Graham had been threatened with ever since he could remember.

If you aren't good, I'll send you to Tuonela. You don't want to go to Tuonela, do you?

The threat was always delivered in a tone that implied the worst. Tuonela was a bad place. Tuonela was a horrible place. Tuonela was the troll under the bridge.

Last year Graham had seen a car wreck. A really bad car wreck. The man inside had been impaled by the steering column. Graham hadn't been able to stop staring. Just before he died, the guy had opened his eyes and looked directly at Graham.

That's how Tuonela had always seemed. Like looking at something terrifying. But now that they were here, the place didn't live up to the image of horror in Graham's head. *This* is Tuonela? he wanted to ask.

It was what some old lady might call quaint. Old-fashioned, maybe. It reminded Graham of a toy train village he'd played with as a little kid. Not his village, but a neighbor's. Some kooky guy who wore an engineer cap and had his basement set up with all sorts of train stuff.

They pulled to a stop in front of a dark house with a straight sidewalk that led to a porch and front door. Two faint streetlights gave off a blue haze. He could barely make out tree branches spread above the roof, and what looked like black, misshapen bushes littering a yard surrounded by a short fence.

He wouldn't give her the satisfaction of tears. He wouldn't even look at her, because that's what she wanted. She wanted him to cry and beg and tell her he'd be good. That he was sorry.

They'd played this game before, and he was done playing.

He grabbed the handles of his giant backpack, opened the passenger door, and tumbled out, slamming the door behind him. From somewhere a dog barked. It was a hollow, distant cry, given with only half a heart and coming from another world.

Before she could come after him, he walked down the sidewalk in the direction of the house.

Behind him the car was thrown into gear, the gas pedal tromped to the floor.

He could feel her anger radiating from the confinement of the car. She was pissed that he hadn't begged.

He looked.

He couldn't stop himself.

A slow turn of the head; then he was watching the ancient Oldsmobile chug away from the curb, watching it lumber down the street. Red brake lights appeared as the car squealed around the corner and disappeared from view.

Graham listened until the sound faded.

Would she come back?

She always came back.

Run! Hide!

He looked at the house again.

Now that he was closer, now that his eyes had adjusted, he could see that it sat low and kind of spread out. He didn't know shit about houses, but this was nothing like the houses in Arizona. This one was rough stucco and dark wood beams, two small windows up above in what looked like an attic.

Run! Run away! What happened to your plan? Remember your plan?

Where would he go? He didn't have any money. He was hungry. He'd hardly slept in forty-eight hours. He was cold.

It was his fault. He'd broken the rules. He'd stayed out all night drinking and smoking pot. He deserved to be punished.

Not like this. He was finally old enough to understand that no kid deserved this.

All his life he'd been accused of exaggeration, even lying. But he always told it like he saw it. If that was lying, then he was a liar.

He approached the house. He walked up the bowed wooden steps, his footfalls echoing. The air was thick, like breathing water. He was aware of the smells again: damp earth and green plants.

He raised his hand, then paused, his finger an inch from the button, his heart pounding in his chest and head. Hell had doors. He knew that. And if you left one hell, what was to stop you from stepping into another?

What else could he do? He was a thousand miles from anybody who might help him.

His brain wasn't working. He couldn't think. Couldn't decide what to do. He was past the point of tears and drama. All he wanted was a bed.

Get some sleep. Get some food. See what happens here first. See if it's as bad as she always said it would be; then decide.

An image of the car wreck popped into his head again. There had been terror in the man's eyes. The guy had seen the other side.

Graham rang the bell. When nobody answered, he knocked. Softly at first, then harder. Two minutes later he walked to a window, cupped his hands to the glass, and tried to see inside.

Chapter 2

The narrow redbrick streets were shiny with dew as Evan Stroud made his way home, hands clenched deep in the pockets of his coat, collar flipped up to deflect the damp wind. Above him the sky was black, without a single star or sliver of moon.

He was used to taking long strolls in the middle of the night. Night was the only time he came close to feeling normal.

He checked his watch and was surprised to find that morning would be arriving soon. This had happened before, his inability to account for a large block of time. Were the occurrences getting more frequent?

Evan continued his climb up the steep sidewalk out of the river valley.

The town of Tuonela was perched on a hillside, the tall Victorian homes clinging to rocks and outcroppings as if afraid to commit to a deeper foundation.

He'd been reluctant to leave his house ever since the break-in, but in the end he'd refused to give up these few hours of freedom just because someone was morbidly curious about him.

Sometimes he thought he should move from Tuonela. But where would he go? Here everybody was used to him. He didn't have to explain anything, and for the most part people accepted him. He might be a freak, but he was *their* freak.

At first he hadn't noticed anything missing after the burglary. Then, little by little, he realized some odd items were not simply misplaced, but *gone*. He couldn't locate his hairbrush. His favorite black T-shirt was nowhere to be found. The coffee mug he used every day? Gone too.

They were stealing pieces of *him*. The intruder or intruders hadn't been caught, and no suspicious fingerprints had been found.

He'd lived in Tuonela his whole life, but suddenly everyone seemed to have the same idea: *Let's stalk Evan Stroud.*

The publication of his books usually brought about a small flurry of interest that quickly whimpered and died. But the last one, a collection of history, tales, and speculation about Old Tuonela, seemed to have stirred up an extra helping of crazies.

Some people actually knocked on his door asking to come in and visit. Or would he sign their book? Could they take a photo with him? But others snooped, and some even took digital images that they later posted online with ridiculous captions like, *Stroud shopping in a dark grocery store. Stroud in his backyard at three A.M.!*

The backyard shot had been a blur, with some un-recognizable person stepping forward and looking behind him with the famous Bigfoot stride and pose. Evan supposed it could have been him, but it was impossible to tell, so why bother? Just some blob taking a stroll. But the very ambiguity seemed to give it credibility.

The photos were bad enough, until some of his uninvited guests, like the ones from the other night, broke in. They wanted proof that he was what some said he was. A vampire.

Evan rounded the turn that would take him to his front door. The soles of his shoes rang hollowly. With his house in sight he stepped from the sidewalk to the grassy area near the curb. What a concept: having to sneak up on your own damn house. But often thieves returned. He wanted to catch them in the act.

He heard a sound. Someone was on the porch, bent at the waist, tampering with a window.

Evan unbuttoned his long coat and reached inside, his fingers coming in contact with the butt of the handgun he'd taken to carrying since the break-in. At first he'd thought the weapon was an overre-action, but now he was glad he had it.

The lights on his street were different from the lights on the other streets in Tuonela. These lights were incandescent blue, and didn't contain harmful UV rays. In the glow of those blue lights Evan saw a kid, a teenager with gold, wildly curly hair straightening away from the window, turning to look at Evan with dismay.

The kid put up his hand as if to deflect a blow. Or a bullet.

Evan remembered the gun and sighed. He returned the Smith & Wesson to the shoulder holster, but didn't close the snap.

A vampire wannabe.

"Are you back for more?" Evan demanded.

This was a violation of his sanctuary, the only place he felt safe. But what could he do? Put up a twelve-foot razor-wire fence? He felt alienated enough from the world as it was. "Are you the idiot who broke in here the other night? Did you forget something?"

The kid didn't answer. Or maybe Evan didn't give him a chance. Later, when Evan replayed the incident in his head, he would wonder.

"Not very good at this, are you?" Evan demanded. "You should have come during the day. When I was asleep in my coffin. Don't you know anything about vampires?"

The kid pivoted, ducked, and leaped off the porch. Three strides took him through a stand of shrubs and beyond the scope of the streetlights.

Evan wasn't letting him off that easy. He switched from visual to audio, listening to the kid crashing through shrubbery and underbrush, following the sound of movement through the darkness.

Evan had the advantage; he knew the terrain. And he could see pretty damn well at night, proof that people could adapt and make up for other physical limitations. He would at least have the satisfaction of scaring the hell out of the asshole.

Evan catapulted himself over the low fence, coat-tails flying. He paused for a direction check. From the right came the sound of someone moving through dead leaves in the wooded area to the east of his house. Evan sprinted after him.

It had been raining off and on for days. The ground was soggy, and tried to suck the boots off his feet. In the distance he heard a splash.

Evan could just make out the kid struggling from the stream. He slipped and slid, finally dashing up an embankment to disappear from view. A second later Evan heard him let out a cry of alarm, followed by the sound of a body falling and tumbling, accented by snapping twigs and rustling brush.

Evan waded through the water, then climbed the steep terrain.

The kid was shoving himself to his feet. Before he could get fully upright, Evan quickly covered the short distance and tackled him. Breathing hard, Evan pressed the kid to the ground, a knee to his back, one of the kid's hands twisted between his shoulder blades.

"I could kill you right now," Evan said. "Is that what you want? I could drain every drop of blood from you." *And grind your bones to make my bread.*

No answer.

Evan pressed harder. "Are you a member of the Pale Immortals? Did they send you? Is this some kind of initiation?"

The Pale Immortals were a gang of kids whose name paid homage to a previous resident named Richard Manchester, aka the Pale Immortal, who'd terrorized the town and slaughtered its residents. Some claimed Manchester had killed as many as a hundred victims, drinking and bathing in their blood. In the panic of the time, in the mass exodus from what was now called Old Tuonela, records had been lost, so no one really knew the death tally.

"What're you talking about, you weird-ass?"

The kid was shaking with fear. But he'd called him a weird-ass. Had to give him credit for guts. Or stupidity.

Evan relaxed his grip.

Was that a sob? Was the kid *crying*?

He released the boy's wrist and removed his knee from his spine. "Come on. You're okay."

"Fuck you."

The teenager looked up, his face splattered with mud, his eyes haunted while he tried his best to sound defiant. Even though the boy had run like hell and put up a strong fight, he looked fragile.

Now Evan felt bad. As if he was the one who'd done something wrong.

Here the kid had been prowling around his house, getting ready to break in—probably for the second time—and Evan was the one who suddenly felt like shit.

"Come back to the house. We'll find you some dry clothes and get this sorted out. Call your parents. Have them come and get you." If the boy didn't cause any more trouble, Evan wouldn't contact the cops.

In one swift motion the kid lunged and pushed Evan backward, then just as quickly jumped away.

It took Evan a second to realize the boy had his gun. And that he was raising it.

To his own temple.

Evan saw the bleak determination in the kid's eyes; he had every intention of pulling the trigger.

Time slowed.

Tick, tick, tick.

Evan may have shouted; he wasn't sure. He kicked, hooking his foot around the kid's ankle. The teenager was flung backward and crumpled to the ground at the same moment the gun discharged. The echo of the gunshot ricocheted from hillside to hillside.

Evan dropped to his knees. He checked the boy for signs of an entrance wound, but couldn't find any. Had the bullet missed? Had he hit his head? Or passed out?

Evan pressed two fingers to the boy's neck. Even though his face was as pale as a corpse, his pulse was steady. The scene replayed in Evan's mind as he tried to grasp what had just happened.

The boy stirred. His eyes opened, and Evan let out a relieved breath. "Jesus Christ, kid. What the hell?"

The teenager didn't seem surprised to find that he wasn't dead. Live, die—it was all the same to him; that was obvious. "Are you Evan Stroud?" he finally asked.

"Yes."

"I have a message for you."

If it was anything like the one he'd just tried to give him, Evan didn't want it.

"I'm Graham."

"Graham?"

"Are you going to pretend you've never heard of me?"

Choose your words with care.

Evan had no idea who he was, but he didn't want to set him off again. The kid was staring at him with a directness Evan couldn't recall seeing in many adults. He also noticed that the night was fading.

The kid spoke again. "Your son," he spit out, as if the words left a rotten taste in his mouth. "I'm your son."

Evan fell back on his heels.

Punctuating that announcement, sirens began to wail from somewhere in the distance. As Evan listened they drew closer, then trailed off, heading toward downtown Tuonela, from the direction Evan had recently come.

Chapter 3

The siren shut off with one final squawk.

Damp wind blew down the collar of coroner Rachel Burton's jacket as she stood on the edge of the Tuonela town square. Hands in her pockets, she regarded the nude body of a female victim lying in a shallow ditch parallel to the road, a few feet from the base of a maple tree. If memory served Rachel correctly, it was one of those varieties of maples that turned a glorious shade of electric red in the fall. Right now it was leafing out, even though it was only early April. But enough of that. Enough of trying to distract herself from the horror in front of her.

The victim had been tossed like so much garbage. The scene reminded Rachel that no matter how the people of Tuonela tried, they couldn't ignore their history any more than London could ignore Jack the Ripper.

The headlights of two squad cars were aimed at the body, along with the beams of three flashlights. No one spoke. The only sound was the steady *clang, clang, clang* of a metal toggle against a flagpole in the center of the square. Nobody seemed to know what to do. Rachel sensed they were all waiting for her. She'd seen a lot of death, so it was only natural that they'd look to her for guidance.

"Who found the body?" she asked.

"We were on patrol," said a young male officer. "We circled the square twice before I saw it."

"Let me borrow your flashlight."

He passed it to her. She took a few steps closer, aware of the cold dew seeping through her sneakers. The victim's throat had been sliced. She directed the flashlight beam to the ground around the body.

No sign of blood.

Dying was often the only way people left Tuonela. Rachel had noticed that about the same time she'd started grade school. But Rachel had made it a point to get out. When she was little and people asked what she wanted to be when she grew up, she always said a doctor or teacher or nurse. "But not here. I want to be somewhere else. Somewhere far away." The adult asking the question would look baffled and chalk it up to weird things kids said. But Rachel had been serious. You had to fight the desire to stay. That had always been her goal: Get the hell out of Tuonela.

She'd made it as far as Los Angeles. Which was almost as far as a person could go without a boat.

Just keep going until the land stops.

She thought she'd gotten away; she really did. But then her mother became ill, and Rachel took a leave of absence from her job as coroner to come home and help her father. When her mother died, she was offered the combined position of county coroner and medical examiner. It was unusual but not unheard-of for one person to have both jobs. Especially in a place with few deaths and no murders. Even though she was only thirty-two, even though she'd been one of the best coroners in L.A. County, she'd decided to stay in her hometown.

Truth be told, she'd been getting tired of the relentless crime in L.A. But L.A. wanted her back. And in L.A., she could distance herself. This . . . this atrocity in front of her was almost like discovering you had a serial killer in the family.

Every few weeks she got a call from her old boss, telling her how things had fallen apart since she'd left, and asking what it would take to convince her to return. She knew she should go. Even her father seemed to understand that.

"Don't stay here for me," he'd told her more than once.

But it wasn't just her father keeping her here; the town had finally gotten to her. Her excuse to remain in Tuonela was that it was nice living in a town where the only deaths she saw were due to car accidents, hunting accidents, and natural causes.

Right.

Here was a violent murder in the heart of one of the most bucolic settings on earth.

"Could someone get my kit from the van?" she asked.

After putting on a Tyvek suit and slippers, she photographed the body and the surrounding area.

Her father, Police Chief Seymour Burton, came up beside her. He smelled like the cigarettes he pretended to no longer smoke. "The killing didn't take place here," he said.

She felt reassured by his quiet presence. Very few people could carry off being cool, but Seymour managed easily. He was James Dean if James Dean had lived to be seventy.

"No," Rachel agreed. "The body was dumped."

"And I'm guessing by an amateur. A first kill."

"But why dump a body in the middle of town?" she asked. "Almost seems the killer wanted her to be found."

"Or panicked," Seymour said.

"Local?" Rachel mused aloud. "Or someone passing through?"

A nearby officer was listening. "Gotta be somebody passing through," he said with conviction.

Seymour eyed the officer in that slow way of his. "Why's that?" he asked, even though it was obvious he already knew the answer.

"Nobody here would do such a thing."

Seymour looked from the officer to the body. For a moment he didn't speak. "Don't ever think it couldn't be a friend or neighbor. Most homicides are committed by people who know the victim. Our job is to find out who may have wanted to kill her. We'll start with relatives and friends and go from there." His voice was smooth and placating, not in the least condescending. The officer nodded and ducked his head.

"Let's finish up and get the victim out of here," Rachel said. It bothered her that the young woman was lying there nude for all to see. That kind of blatant exposure was different in a small town, where there was little anonymity. In L.A. she wouldn't have felt the need to hurry and cover the body.

"Anybody recognize her?" Seymour asked.

"I . . . I think she goes—I mean, *went* to school with my son," an officer said. "Mason and Enid Gerber's kid."

There was a murmur of agreement.

They put up numbered crime scene cards.

The grass hadn't been packed down. There were no tire marks.

Two officers spread a plastic sheet on the ground next to the victim. On top of the sheet they placed a body bag. Rachel had wrestled with a lot of dead bodies, and they weren't known for their cooperation. Once the victim was in place, Rachel zipped the bag and attached an evidence seal.

Dan, Rachel's assistant and the closest Tuonela had to a crime scene investigator, began vacuuming the grass in hopes of finding some small piece of something.

From her kit Rachel pulled out a tool shaped like a small shovel. She crouched above the area where the body had been lying. Using the tool, she scraped and dug, depositing clumps of grass and dirt into an evidence bag.

"What are you looking for?" Dan asked.

Rachel was aware of her audience: patrol officers standing in a semicircle, watching, waiting.

"Blood."

"And . . . ?" Dan prodded.

"Ground's too wet to tell."

"I can take care of that." He poked around in the evidence kit to lift out a plastic spray bottle of luminol, normally used indoors to expose trace amounts of blood. Dan had probably been waiting months for a chance to use it.

He sprayed the area in question, then produced a small, battery-operated black light. Nothing. He sprayed again, then tested with the light.

Still nothing.

He looked up at Rachel, silently communicating his dark thoughts, sharp black bangs slanting across his forehead.

Dan was a native. Except for a couple of years interning at a forensic lab in Madison, he'd lived in Tuonela his entire life. Although hardly more than a kid, he understood the significance of the missing blood when you lived in a town that meant land of the dead, a town where the Pale Immortal had once walked.

Behind her, Rachel heard the metallic snap of a lighter and turned to see her dad taking a deep drag from a cigarette, his eyes unfocused and troubled. Was he thinking what she was thinking?

This, on top of a recent theft of blood from the hospital, wasn't proof of anything, she told herself. And not the time to verbalize her own concerns. "I'll know more once I've examined the body," Rachel said.

Normally she would have gone to her apartment and cleaned up a bit. Had some coffee and probably some breakfast, most likely at Peaches, because she hated to cook.

But she wasn't going to expose herself to the public with this horrific homicide having just taken place. People would stare. They would ask questions. They would be afraid. And she had no way to alleviate their fears.

She went directly to the morgue. It was the best place to hide.

Chapter 4

It was every guy's nightmare.

A kid showing up at your door, calling you Dad. Worse, a mentally unstable kid who'd just tried to kill himself with your own gun. Right in front of you.

The kid—Graham—was sitting at Evan's kitchen table, eating as if he hadn't had a meal in a week. Evan figured the least he could do was feed him.

Graham had changed into dry clothes. He'd washed his hands, but his face and curly hair still bore traces of mud.

In the adjoining living room, beyond the bookcase divider, thick black curtains were pulled tight, the room illuminated with low-wattage incandescent bulbs. Evan was used to the murkiness; Graham didn't seem to notice.

It was strange as hell to have somebody sitting at his kitchen table, invading his space and filling the room with an alien presence, but certainly much more peculiar to have a teenager claiming to be his son.

"Your mother . . ." Evan began, fishing for information, yet not wanting to set the boy off. Evan needed details if he was going to be accused of being somebody's dad.

Graham looked up from his bowl of cereal. He wiped milk from his mouth with the back of his hand. "Lydia. Everybody calls her Lydia."

Lydia.

That's what Evan had thought. He pushed the box of cereal closer, but Graham shook his head. "You say she dropped you off, then left?" Evan asked.

"Yeah. She always threatens me with you. Like, 'If you don't straighten up, you're going to live with your father.' We've driven partway here before."

To think that this poor kid had been carrying around some mental image of his father, yet there wasn't a man out there thinking about Graham. "What was different this time?" Evan asked.

"I didn't beg to go home."

"Where is home?"

"Arizona."

"That's a long drive."

"Thirty hours straight."

Years ago the same road had brought Lydia Yates to Tuonela and then taken her away. She'd been one of those girls who'd slept with half the boys in high school. She and her mother had breezed into town one day during Evan's senior year. All the guys had been infatuated with Lydia. She'd been beautiful, and they hadn't yet learned how to be discerning and pick up on clues that would have told them to give her a wide berth. Lydia's mother got a job tending bar at one of the local dives. Lydia used to run her own little operation, tempting classmates with free liquor and sex. She'd most likely had a serious mental problem. Back then they just figured she liked to do it. A lot.

It had been a temptation boys couldn't resist. They knew it was wrong, but told themselves it was just this one time . . . .

Lydia mesmerized them all. She had been exotic and exciting, and Tuonela rarely saw anything exotic and exciting.

When she ended up pregnant, she'd pointed a finger at Evan.

At that time his parents had been comfortable but not wealthy. His father was a cop, his mother a substitute teacher. That was when Evan's illness was diagnosed and before medical bills began draining them of their savings. They'd suggested a paternity test, but Lydia had refused.

Then one day Lydia and her mother were gone. Just packed up and left, which led many, Evan included, to speculate that the pregnancy had been a fabrication. Evan didn't give her much thought after that, because by that time his illness had taken hold. Their coming together, his loss of virginity to someone who'd meant nothing to him, had left him feeling sick and ashamed. He was just glad she was gone.

Now that he thought about it, Lydia marked the beginning of the end of Evan's childhood and life as he'd known it. Strangely, he'd forgotten her existence until now.

So she'd stuck to her story about Evan being the father. At least she'd recognized the need to come up with an explanation for the kid's sake. She couldn't very well tell him she'd slept with half the town and hadn't a clue who the father was.

A kid's life shouldn't be so messed up.

Evan had no idea how to approach the father issue. Graham had just tried to kill himself. Better not to say anything for now. He knew nothing about talking to kids anyway, especially suicidal ones.

Graham's spoon hit the floor with a clatter. It took a few seconds for Evan to realize he was asleep, chin on his chest.

"Come on." Evan grabbed the boy by the arm.

He led Graham through the living room, around a maze of books, down a hall to a small bedroom Evan used mostly for storage and overflow.

He'd grown up in this house. The bedroom had been his at one time. After Evan's mother died and his father retired early and moved to Florida, Evan bought the place. It needed a lot of work, and at one time he'd thought he would take on the restoration, but that idea had lost steam and pretty soon was forgotten like lots of other thoughts.

The twin bed in the corner was stacked with leather-bound antiquarian books and boxes of manuscripts, notes and research from past projects or future projects. The room smelled stuffy and dusty, like old leather and moldy, yellowing paper.

Imagining the room through Graham's eyes served to underscore for Evan the reclusiveness of his own existence. He wasn't yet thirty-five, but the room looked like it belonged to some old fart who spent his days shifting piles of history around while wondering where the time had gone.

Once Evan cleared the bed, Graham tumbled forward onto the mattress, grabbed a pillow, and hugged it to himself. A second later he was out. Evan dug a comforter from the closet, straightened Graham's legs, covered him, and left the room.

Back in the kitchen, Evan prepared a cup of tea and sat down at the table.

Was Lydia at it again? Was this another attempt to extort money? Had she read a recent article about him? Did she know he was fairly successful?

Evan picked up the phone and called the police to see if Graham had been reported missing. He could be a runaway, for all Evan really knew.

"We'll have to look into it," said the male officer on the other end of the line. That was followed by a click of computer keys. "Nothing jumping out at me. No Amber Alert or national announcement. In the meantime, I'll connect you to Social Services. At the very least, we have an unattended juvenile on our hands."

Evan was connected.

"All we can do is lock him up until we get this figured out," a woman told him.

"Jail? That seems unnecessary. Can't you find someone to take him in temporarily?"

"Nobody wants to take in a boy that age, Mr. Stroud. No telling where he's been or what he's done. Would you be able to put him up until we find his mother?"

"Out of the question.".

"Then we'll dispatch an officer to take him off your hands."

"Now?"

"Someone should be there within the hour."

"He's asleep."

"Please make sure he's awake and ready."

"Can't you wait until he wakes up on his own? The kid's exhausted."

There was a long pause. Then, "Certainly, Mr. Stroud."

She seemed too agreeable.

Evan worried that Graham might try some other method of killing himself, so he kept looking in on him, hovering nervously in the bedroom doorway. Making sure he was breathing.

He looks nothing like me.

Does he?

No, he looked like Lydia. That's who he looked like.

Evan thought about what it must have been like having Lydia for a mother. What a head fuck.

He stared at Graham again, searching for but seeing no family resemblance.

He wasn't his kid. He couldn't be his kid, Evan told himself.

Chapter 5

Using a pair of medical scissors, Rachel Burton snipped open the evidence seal she'd attached to the body bag while in the town square.

Tuonela's previous autopsy suite had been located in the hospital basement. When a family-owned mortuary closed, the town council purchased the current property in hopes of tempting a medical examiner to become a permanent part of the community. At the time Rachel was offered the position, the only requirement she'd insisted upon was a decent air-exchange system. But decent didn't translate to quiet.

She pulled down the clear visor.

Another part of the package had been a place to live. The mortuary was a sprawling Victorian with scalloped gingerbread siding, turrets, and copper fascia that had turned green. Rachel had the third floor. She liked being up high. She liked being able to look out over the town, especially at night when the lights were on. Another plus was having the entire building to herself except for occasional help and the bodies that came to visit.

She began the visual description, dictating into a microphone. "Rope burns on the ankles. Cuts on the wrists and jugular."

The young girl had already been identified by her hysterical parents as sixteen-year-old Chelsea Gerber.

So sad. So incredibly sad . . .

After the visual, verbal description, and observations came the external exam.

When Rachel was in medical school, she'd quickly realized that her reaction to dead bodies was different from those of her fellow students. Some classmates were repulsed. Many commented on how it seemed that once death came to visit, it left behind an empty vessel. Like an old shoe someone had once worn.

It wasn't that way for Rachel . . . .

She found some straight dark hairs, complete with hair follicles, stuck to the body. Gerber was blond. She collected tissue scrapings and took photographs, numbering and labeling as she went.

The nails and cuticles were lined with blood. Rachel dropped cuttings into a small collection bag. She put the clippers on the metal tray near her elbow and held the young girl's hand.

Hands always got to her. Children's hands. A young man's hands. An old man's hands. Didn't matter. Hands were personal.

This hand held hers with unnerving urgency. Even in death, Chelsea seemed to be clinging to life.

A half hour into the internal exam, Rachel had confirmation of what she'd suspected in the square.

Every artery, every vein was lying as flat and white as a tapeworm. Chelsea had been strung up by her ankles and drained of blood like some slaughtered lamb.

Rachel let out a heavy sigh and sat down on a stool, trying to make sense of her discovery.

It was a chillingly familiar MO. An old case had involved exsanguination and a craving for blood. A very old case. A hundred years ago, in the ghost town that was now called Old Tuonela, a killer known as the Pale Immortal had walked the streets. When darkness fell, children were rushed inside. Doors and windows were locked up tight. Some claimed that the Pale Immortal had bathed in blood, and that blood had flooded the streets until the ground became saturated.

Even after the Pale Immortal's reign of terror ended, people were afraid. His death had come too late. A miasma of fear had grown over everybody. Many claimed the ground was cursed, and so a mass exodus had taken place. Every single person relocated to a new development five miles from the old one. A better location, they claimed. And prettier, on a bluff overlooking the river. Why had anyone settled at the old place, in such a dark valley? It didn't make sense.

Let's pretend Old Tuonela doesn't exist. Let's pretend we always lived here, in the new place.

Even though a hundred years had passed, many locals still liked to pretend Old Tuonela wasn't just beyond the outskirts of town where the softly rolling hills ended abruptly, the valleys became dark and deep, and the roads turned back on themselves. But for Rachel, Old Tuonela was a presence that couldn't be ignored. You could feel it, feel the connection between old and new, like an umbilical cord that hadn't been severed.

Years ago, a developer from Chicago bought the ground of Old Tuonela with plans to turn it into a resort. A place where the wealthy could escape Chicago for the weekend. Where they could shop and eat and sleep in quaint inns. When he couldn't get financial backing, he put up a FOR SALE sign and left, moving on to a new project. The FOR SALE sign was still there. The only habitable house was being restored by the owner's son, who'd recently been through a tough time and needed a place to heal and pull himself back together.

And the current Tuonela? New people came but rarely stayed.

At first they were drawn by the charm of the cobblestone alleys and brick streets, by the church spires and dark thickets of trees. But a town that appeared quaint from the outside quickly turned threatening, with undertones that made strangers uneasy and paranoid. A darkness lingered here. A darkness that spoke to Rachel, that spoke to the people who belonged.

Over the years there had been campaigns to infuse Tuonela with new energy and life. A fall harvest tour. A May Day parade. Shopwindow displays through those dark days of December. Efforts always failed. And now there was a movement under way to rename Tuonela—because what had begun as a tribute to Finnish mythology had turned into a tribute to a murdering madman. But a name change wouldn't help.

There was an unspoken feeling that celebration was wrong. That too much noise might wake up something that should remain asleep.

Superstitious nonsense, Rachel told herself as she got to her feet and turned to get the camera. She was a rational person. Rational people didn't think such thoughts. But maybe rationality or superstition didn't matter in this case.

Imitation was the sincerest form of flattery.

What had triggered the renewed interest in the Pale Immortal? The release of Evan Stroud's most recent book?

There seemed to be two camps in town: those who were proud to have a local author writing about their history, and those who thought he should keep his mouth shut. That he was exploiting a tragic past.

From behind her came a sound that registered in another area of her brain, separate from the noise of the exhaust fan. Like air escaping. Like an indrawn breath.

Rachel swung around to see the dead girl's head turn slowly in her direction, her eyes wide open and staring. The hand Rachel had been holding earlier reached for her in an imploring gesture. Rachel let out a gasp. She took a panicked step back. The face changed, became that of another woman, one Rachel remembered from childhood.

Victoria.

Rachel's arm jerked and struck the tray, knocking the stainless-steel autopsy tools to the floor.

And then the vision was over, as if it had never happened.

Chelsea Gerber's eyes were closed, her chin directed toward the ceiling, her neck positioned on the autopsy block just as Rachel had left her.

Rachel ran blindly across the room and through the heavy swinging doors. Outside in the hallway she collapsed with her back to the wall, her chest rising and falling, her heart slamming.

In that instant she was reminded of why she'd become a coroner.

To face her fear.

The only way to defeat it is to meet it.

As a young child she'd seen people who weren't really there.

Her parents hadn't been overly concerned about her playmates until they realized these weren't your garden-variety imaginary buddies. Rachel was actually hanging out with dead people. The recently deceased of Tuonela.

Once Rachel moved away she was no longer visited by the dead. And as time passed, she came to rationalize her visions as delusions caused by some forgotten childhood trauma. She must have seen photo obituaries in the newspaper. She must have read the names or heard her parents mention them. All easily explained once you really thought about it.

Yet the girl in the room behind her was dead. Very dead. There could be no doubt about that. Which meant it was happening again.

Chapter 6

Graham woke up confused and disoriented. It was dark, and his heart was thudding the way it did whenever he had a falling dream.

He thought backward, and a wave of bleak despair washed over him as his memory returned. He shot from the bed and felt around in the dark until he found a switch that he flipped on, illuminating the small space with dim light.

He was in some kind of storage room, maybe an office, cluttered with shelved books that overflowed in piles on the floor. The windows were covered in black fabric that looked like it had actually been glued to the glass. His mouth tasted rotten, and he could smell himself. He hadn't taken a shower in a long time, and he'd been doing some serious sweating lately. . . .

He opened the door and looked down the hall, spotting a bathroom.

He'd become an opportunist by necessity. He knew most things were fleeting, and you had to take what you could get when you could get it.

He grabbed wrinkled but clean clothes from his

pack, moved silently down the hall, slipped into the bathroom, locked the door, and quickly stripped.

Don't think, he told himself once he was in the shower. This wasn't the time to think. He had to stay strong, stay tough.

He scrubbed himself and washed his hair. The warm water felt great, comforting. Dried off and dressed in wrinkled jeans and black long-sleeved T-shirt, he opened the bathroom door, a cloud of steam billowing out.

Evan Stroud was waiting for him in the living room, standing near the front door, a coffee mug in his hand.

He's so pale.

Like the vampire he'd claimed to be last night?

You should have come during the day. When I was asleep in my coffin. Don't you know anything about vampires?

He'd just been trying to scare him. Graham knew Stroud had a disease called porphyria, an allergy to the sun. He'd seen stuff about the illness on TV. A couple of little girls who could go outside to play only at night.

Graham hadn't thought about how white a person's skin would get if he never went outside. If he never even walked from the house to a car when the sun was shining.

"I never meant to fall asleep," Graham said, still feeling groggy. The dim light didn't help any.

"I called Social Services," Stroud said. "Someone will be here to pick you up soon."

"And then what?"

"They'll send you back to your mom, or find another place for you to live."

Graham nodded fatalistically. He wasn't surprised.

When he was little he used to daydream about meeting his dad face-to-face. In those daydreams his dad shed a few tears of joy in honor of the touching reunion.

"I'm not going back to her," Graham said. "I'll be sixteen soon. I'll become emancipated. Kids do that." He didn't know how, but he'd read about it. You had to find a lawyer, and you had to get some papers signed. "Why are you looking at me like that?"

"They don't emancipate kids who are a danger to themselves."

"Are you talking about the gun?" He waved his hand as if to diminish the act. He'd forgotten about that little episode.

Just think. If the gun hadn't been knocked away, we wouldn't be having this conversation.

This was pissing him off: Evan Stroud standing there, pretending he wasn't his father, yet at the same time preaching to him and bossing him around.

The phone rang. Stroud answered it, talking in quiet tones. When he hung up, he turned to Graham. "Get your things together. Someone will be here in a half hour."

Graham pivoted and strode to the bedroom, where his backpack was lying on the floor.

Stroud had washed and dried his muddy clothes.

For some reason that gesture made Graham's throat tighten and his eyes burn. He grabbed the folded clothes and crammed them in his backpack. He zipped the pack and slipped his arms through the padded straps.

It wasn't a regular pack. It had been made for traveling, and he'd shoved a lot of stuff inside when he'd left Arizona. He was able to carry almost his entire life on his back. The only thing he regretted leaving behind was his vinyl collection.

What would she do with that? Throw it away? Take it to Goodwill?

"Thanks for all your help," he told Stroud once he was back in the living room. Would Stroud catch the sarcasm?

"I'm not your father."

"Right. She said you'd say that. But that's okay, you know. I don't care. We're strangers. You don't mean anything to me, and blood doesn't matter. I mean, being related doesn't mean shit. In fact, it gives somebody permission to treat you any way they want. That's all. I didn't want to come here. I didn't want to meet you. She made me."

"Do you always do what you're told?"

"No."

With that, Graham opened the door and stepped outside. After the darkness of the house the brilliance of the sun was blinding. He blinked rapidly, then leaped off the porch.

He heard footsteps behind him, and looked over his shoulder in time to see Stroud coming after him.

What . . . ?

Graham had figured he'd stop at the door.

But he was coming. Just like any other guy. Just like somebody who wasn't allergic to the sun.

Graham turned and ran. A quick pause at the gate; then he was fumbling for the latch.

Lift. Pull. Run.

Graham could run like hell, but his pack was heavy. Maybe forty pounds.

"Wait!"

Graham turned in time to see Stroud drop to his knees, cupping both hands to his forehead. Graham stopped. He watched for a moment, then let his pack crash to the ground.

Stroud kept curling up, until his head was to his knees.

Like Superman exposed to kryptonite.

Or a vampire.

Graham hesitated, then ran back through the gate, slipping his hands under Stroud's arms. He dragged him toward the house. "Come on!"

Stroud managed to get his feet under him. With Graham supporting him, they staggered up the steps and over the threshold. Stroud dropped to the floor and Graham slammed the door, shutting out the light.

Heart pounding, Graham stared in horror at the man writhing at his feet. "Are you gonna be okay?"

Was he dying? Right in front of him?

Graham took one step closer. Then another.

Stroud's hand lashed out and locked around his ankle, fingers digging into his flesh, his arm all taut muscles and veins.

Like a clawed hand from a grave . . .

I could kill you right now. I could drain every drop of blood from you.

Graham tore away from him and ran—out the door, down the sidewalk, through the gate.

Grabbed his pack and hauled ass.

He headed for the cover of nearby trees and the wooded area he already had a relationship with, ducking under branches that snagged his T-shirt and caught on his backpack. Five minutes into his escape, he paused briefly to listen.

His pounding heart and harsh breathing drowned out everything else. Chest rising and falling, his breath creating a cloud in the thick air, he finally picked up on the sound of birds. From somewhere far away, water trickled. Then came the faint hum of traffic. Not heavy traffic, but an occasional vehicle.

He braced his legs and gave the backpack a heave and an adjustment; then he began running again: over a hill, then down a steep incline, his boots slipping, heels leaving deep parallel gouges in the muddy bank as he skidded to a stop at the bottom to land three feet from a two-lane road that twisted into hillsides topped with trees that were just getting leaves.

He risked a glance over his shoulder, half expecting to see Stroud floating toward him through the trees, blood dripping from fangs.

A small blue truck appeared around the corner, heading downhill.

Graham pivoted to face the oncoming vehicle.

Continuing to walk backward, he stuck out his thumb.

The vehicle showed no sign of slowing, so he threw a little more into his performance. Pouring on the charm, he bent one knee while giving an exaggerated thumb gesture and a good-ol'-boy smile.

The truck flew past, a girl at the wheel.

Red brake lights followed by white reverse lights. Then the little Chevy S-10 hummed backward in a squiggly line.

"Hop in back!" the girl shouted through the sliding rear window.

It was starting to get dark, and from his angle he couldn't get a good look at her. All he could tell was that she had short blond hair and was about his age.

What the hell was she doing? A girl alone, picking up a hitchhiker on the road? Hadn't she ever heard of stranger danger?

He slipped the pack from his shoulders, tossed it into the bed of the truck, and followed. At least she had enough sense not to invite him into the cab.

She tromped down on the gas pedal, tires spinning on gravel as she shot back onto the road. She tossed more words at him through the window and over her shoulder. "Where you going?"

He scooted closer to the opening. "Where do people hang out in this town?" He was so hungry.

"The mall." When he didn't respond, she added, "Or a café called Peaches."

"That sounds good."

They picked up speed; he had to shout to be heard above the sound of the wind. "Just drop me off as near as you're going." Maybe he could panhandle for cash, or Dumpster dive for food if he had to. "I feel like I'm in confession."

"What?" She shot him a glance.

"Confession!" he shouted, pointing to the sliding window. She was probably Catholic. He'd probably just offended her.

She laughed, focusing once more on the road. "Well, then—confess!"

If she really knew about him, would she be repulsed? Scared? Feel sorry for him? He could be wrong about her, because people surprised you. She could have as much darkness in her life as he did. Because you couldn't always tell by looking at somebody.

Acting as though he hadn't heard her, he dug into the top section of his pack, pulled out his sweatshirt, put it on, and leaned back, arms crossed.

The tension left his body for the first time in days. He was free. At least for now.

In a short space of time the sun had disappeared completely, and darkness had fallen like a curtain. Strands of his hair whipped about, stinging his face, and he was riding in some girl's truck. Some girl he didn't know, heading to someplace called Peaches.

He tipped back his head and looked up at the stars that were forming above him in the black sky. His heart swelled, and at that moment he was glad the bullet hadn't hit him.

This was what it was about. These moments that crept up on you out of nowhere and whispered mysterious, unformed promises that made you want to live for something you didn't even know existed.

He was so caught up in the drama of his own thoughts that he didn't come back to land until the truck stopped. Dazed, he looked around and realized they were in town, parallel-parked at a meter.

He gave himself a mental shake, got to his feet, and vaulted from the truck. A door slammed, and the girl came around the tailgate to stand beside him.

He dragged the pack across the bed and hefted it over the side, resting it on the top of one foot. "Thanks for the ride."

She was average height, dressed in black ankle boots and black tights, a black skirt, and a black sweater with tiny white buttons down the front and some kind of pink flowery thing on one shoulder. The flower and her lips provided the only color he could find.

He inhaled something sweet, and dragged his gaze away.

Three feet behind her was a tree, its bare branches laced with tiny white lights. Beyond that was a movie theater with a curved art deco sign, the *H* and *R* burned out. He suddenly got the same feeling he'd had seconds earlier when he was looking at the stars.

This is a taste of real life, he thought. *This is what real life feels like.*

"I'm going to Peaches, too."

Yeah. Maybe he nodded slightly. He wasn't sure.

"They have these great mochas."

Ten minutes ago he'd been starving. Now food seemed trite and irrelevant.

She took a few steps away, then paused to look at him over her shoulder. "Coming?"

He picked up his pack and followed her into a huge two-story house that had been converted into a café. Before they reached the door he could smell coffee.

She ordered a large café mocha with almond syrup and whipped cream, then looked at him in expectation.

"I'll just have a glass of water."

She eyed him a moment, then turned back to the kid behind the counter and ordered a packaged sandwich from the glass case. While she waited for her order, Graham took his water to an empty table in a dark corner. Peaches had lots of dark corners.

The floors were wooden and scraped down past the stain and varnish, and the ceiling above Graham's head creaked as people moved about in rooms upstairs.

He leaned his pack in the corner and sat down on a yellow wooden chair that wiggled loosely. A CD was playing on the café's sound system. Some old Wilco song he couldn't quite place but that was intensely familiar. The music made him feel homesick. Graham wanted to go home, back to Arizona, where he had friends. But that was a bad idea. *She* was there.

It would be best to go someplace where nobody knew him. Not a cold place, since he might have to sleep outside. He should head south. Maybe into the

Carolinas. Maybe Georgia even. The ocean. Yeah. He'd never seen the ocean.

The girl plopped down beside him with a tray. The sandwich had been cut in two. She gave him half of it on a small plate. "I can't eat the whole thing," she explained.

He didn't even check to see what it was. He just picked it up and took a bite. Then another.

She dabbled a wooden stirrer in her drink, and scooped up some whipped topping. "My name's Isobel."

"I'm Graham." He glanced around for a napkin, then wiped his mouth with the back of his hand. "You should be more careful," he told her. "You shouldn't pick up strangers."

"I don't. I mean, I've never picked anybody up before."

"Why me?"

"You looked like you needed help. Like you were in trouble." Pause. "And that little dance you did closed the deal."

"Yep." Finished with his half of the sandwich, he leaned back in his chair, crossing his arms over his chest. "Just call me Mr. Funny Man."

With both hands she lifted the giant coffee cup to her face. "So, what's your deal? You just move here?"

"Just passing through." How lame. He was spouting dialogue from some old movie.

She asked him the normal questions, like where he was going and where he'd come from. He replied with lies and evasions, which made him feel guilty.

He probably didn't need to lie. Nobody was looking for him. Certainly not his mother. Evan Stroud? He wouldn't be trying to find him. And Social Services was always glad when someone was no longer a problem.

The door opened and a guy in a brown sweater and dark jeans stepped inside.

"Uh-oh." Isobel checked her watch. "That's Mr. Alba, my drama teacher," she said in a voice that indicated she'd been caught. "He's normally pretty cool, but he's getting a little bent because the play is in two weeks and nobody's learned their lines."

Graham had had teachers like him. The ones who were young and cool and wanted the kids to like them.

Alba cast a glance around the room. "Isobel," he said as soon as he caught sight of her. "I thought that was your truck outside. You're late. Play practice has already started." After delivering that announcement, he turned to leave, almost running into a tall, thin guy of about twenty-five who was stepping inside. There was a flash of recognition between the men, followed by hello.

"I gotta go." Isobel gathered up her things.

Just a girl. A normal girl with a normal life. Graham pivoted in his chair, dug in a side pocket of his pack, pulled out a CD, and handed it to her. "Here."

She didn't move.

"Take it," he insisted. "For giving me a ride. For the food."

She smiled and took it. "Take care of yourself," she said, without looking at the CD.

She probably didn't like music. She probably wouldn't listen to it. "Thanks."

Then she was gone.

He stared at the door for a long time. Then he looked down and realized she'd pushed her uneaten sandwich and large café mocha with almond syrup and whipped cream in front of him.

He ate the rest of the sandwich and drank the café mocha. It was so sweet it made his mouth sticky and his head thick and fuzzy. The tall, thin guy had taken a seat in the back. Graham stayed in the dark corner, watching people come and go, trying not to think of the girl, Isobel. Wondering if she'd like the CD he'd given her. Wondering if she'd ever even listen to it. Or ever think about him again.

A group of hard kids came in, dressed mostly in black. A little punk, a little Goth, with heavy, unlaced boots that made a lot of noise when they walked. They had sloppy tattoos, along with weeks of dirt ground into the lines in their skin.

Graham could smell them. It was the kind of sour BO that made your eyes water. They reminded him of some of the faux homeless he knew in Arizona. Kids who came from rich families and liked to play at poverty. Usually you'd find one or two real homeless kids in the mix.

One of them ordered a sandwich and several glasses of water while another raided the tip jar, pocketing several bills. They paid with the stolen money, left a stolen tip; then the entire group went pounding up the wooden steps to whatever was up there.

A few minutes later Graham followed and found them lounging on old couches and chairs, smoking cigarettes and playing checkers.

"Is there a blood bank around here?" Graham asked. "I need to make some quick cash." You usually had to be seventeen, but most places didn't care. They were just glad to get the blood.

The kids looked from one to another, then burst out laughing.

What the hell was wrong with them?

"Not permanent," one of the kids finally said. "Once a week they set up in the VFW hall." He pulled at the scraggly soul patch on his chin, then pointed at Graham. "But, hey, I know a place where you can make some quick bucks. Easier than givin' blood, and it pays better. All you have to do is stand there and let some perv take pictures of you."

The tall, thin guy came up the stairs. His hair was straight and slanted across his forehead. One of the hard kids called him Dan.

"You know cops found a body in the square?" Dan asked. "You hear about that?"

There was a lot of head nodding. A lot of, "Yeah, bummer." "That's sick." "That's too bad."

"Chelsea Gerber," Dan continued in a way that seemed to be more than just passing information.

"Who would dump a body in the middle of the square?" someone asked.

"The cops are thinking somebody really stupid," Dan said. "I think so too."

"Or maybe really smart," Soul Patch said. He pointed at Dan. "You ever think about that?"

"They find any clues?" asked one of the other kids, a tall blond with flame tattoos on his forearms.

Dan glanced at Graham. "You know I can't talk about the crime scene. But they seem pretty sure it's somebody who lives in Tuonela."

"When'd it happen?" Graham heard himself asking.

"Really early this morning. Before daylight."

This morning. Stroud had appeared out of the darkness this morning. "Do you have a lot of murders in Tuonela?" Graham asked.

"A long time ago we used to." Dan finally made direct eye contact with him. "But until recently nobody'd been murdered here in a hundred years."

Chapter 7

The van's headlights barely penetrated the heavy woodland as Rachel Burton drove up the twisted road that led to the south side of town. The labored climb always reminded her of a recurring dream, one in which she drove straight up a sharp hill, only to plummet down the other side once she reached the precipice. Even though the dream was cartoony and unrealistic, it never failed to scare the hell out of her. She'd always considered it a metaphor for life's struggles, but she was sure Freud would have had a different interpretation.

The town of Tuonela was divided by deep ravines, shallow creeks, and steep hills. There was often no easy way to get from point A to point B. When glaciers had crept across North America, dipping down into Wisconsin to smooth away the jagged peaks and sharp edges, they'd only skimmed areas of Juneau County.

Rachel hadn't experienced any more visitations, although last night she'd jumped at her own reflection in the window glass, but every time she turned around she braced herself for the unwanted. It never came. Now, almost twenty-four hours later, she was beginning to wonder if she'd imagined it. Deep down, she knew better.

It was just past seven o'clock and already dark. She would be glad when the time changed. She'd never cared for standard time.

The van struggled skyward, the headlight beams shooting at the stars before the vehicle crested the hill to level ground. Here the roads were flat and fanned out to follow deep hollows that led to rows of bungalows built in the twenties.

Rachel hadn't been to this area of town for a while, and she found herself confused by changes like new fences and landscaping, by trees that had grown and trees that were gone. Other things were the same, yet not the same. Kind of like a puzzle put together in a slightly different configuration.

She turned down Benefit Street.

Unlike the other well-lit areas of South Hill, Benefit Street was illuminated with softer bulbs that gave off a bluish hue. She pulled to a stop in front of a dark house, cut the engine, and got out. The ornate metal gate still creaked when she opened it. For a brief moment she half expected to hear a dog bark. But no, Finn was dead and gone.

She was on a quest—a quest for the grave of the Pale Immortal.

Up the walk, up the wooden steps.

Had the doorbell ever been fixed?

In the dark she ran her hand across the molding that surrounded the door, feeling for a button. Just as she found it, words came out of the darkness from the corner of the porch, causing her to jump.

"Enfant terrible."

Recognizing the voice even after so many years, she swung around, heart pounding, barely able to make out the undefined shape of Evan Stroud. She heard a creak and realized he was sitting in the porch swing that hung from the ceiling by chains. How many times had she sat there herself?

Enfant terrible.

A name he'd given her, a name that had come from one of her more volatile childhood phases of unattractive stomping and sullenness.

Their fathers had been cops together, and their mothers had shared after-school child care. There had been a period when they seemed to be together more often than apart. Evan was two years older, and had spent most of the time teasing Rachel, treating her like an annoying kid sister. She'd spent most of it trying to hide a schoolgirl crush. Young love. Crushes were foolish, and yet so devastatingly powerful. There had been a time when she would have died for him.

Then Lydia Yates came along.

Rachel would never know if Lydia's appearance changed the course of both their lives. What would have happened if she hadn't shown up in Tuonela? Would Rachel and Evan have parted anyway? Or would their relationship have blossomed into more? To her young mind, Evan had betrayed her with Lydia. Broken her heart.

The air was damp and cold. A shiver went through her.

"Want to come inside? Have something warm to drink? Some tea?" he asked.

Had he lived in darkness for so long that he could see in it? Had his eyesight compensated?

They went inside.

She shut the door behind her and followed him across the living room to the kitchen, sitting down at the round table as if she'd done it every day for the past seventeen years. In the center of the table was a copy of the *Tuonela Press* and the front-page color photo of her standing near the coroner's van. The depth of field was amazing. Behind her, just as clear as anything in the foreground, she could see a body wrapped in heavy black plastic being slid into the back of the van.

Evan filled a teapot with water and placed it on the gas stove. He was dressed in jeans and a wrinkled, untucked shirt, the sleeves rolled a couple of turns. The shirt was white with fine gray lines running through it.

It looked as if he cut his own hair, maybe holding up clumps and slashing away with a razor until there was nothing left but a point.

He probably can't go to a barber, she realized with shock. Such a simple thing, but he couldn't do it. So he chopped at his own hair in front of the bathroom mirror.

The kitchen was cast in low light. She couldn't see him clearly, but she detected a weakness in the way he held his body, the way he leaned against the stove with his shoulders slightly hunched. Were those dark circles under his eyes? Or shadows caused by poor lighting?

"I'm sorry about your mom."

She nodded. "I got your card."

"I would have come to the funeral. . . ." His words trailed off.

She'd seen his name in the visitation book and knew he'd come to the funeral home in the evening. Her mother had never cared much for Evan after the Yates fiasco. Maybe she'd felt betrayed too.

"How's your dad?" she asked.

Evan's dad had had a breakdown and retired early, while Rachel's father went on to become chief of police.

"Loves it in Florida," Evan said. "Golfs every day. Keeps trying to get me to move down there, but I tell him it's too sunny."

"I can see where that would be a problem."

"I like your short hair," he told her.

She touched some strands that barely covered her ears. It was shorter than his hair, but close to the same shade.

"Darker than I remembered," he added.

"That's deliberate."

He placed a mug in front of her and a canister of tea bags. His hand trembled. He saw that she saw, and curled his hand into a fist, then eased himself into the seat opposite her.

"Are you okay?"

"I'm fine." Elbows on the table, he rubbed his forehead, then let out a harsh laugh. "Just a little under the weather. It's my own damn fault. My own stupidity. It'll pass."

Since he was obviously uncomfortable, she steered the conversation away from his health. "I'm surprised your dad left." He was one of the rare few to leave Tuonela.

"He's not sentimental. And I think he needed to get away."

"It's not sentimentality that keeps people here."

"No?"

"Why are you here?" she asked.

"It's easier to be here. Why did you come back?"

She thought about the life she'd had beyond Wisconsin. She thought about returning home, thought about how her heart had begun to pound when she got within sight of Tuonela. The way it smelled, the haze that enveloped the landscape—it crept into your bones.

"This feels real," she said softly, surprised that she would reveal so much. "I like the sense of belonging. Of familiarity." Or at least, she had until last night.

He must have seen the hesitation in her face. "But you don't want to be here . . . " he suggested with a question in his voice. "You wish things were different."

She broke eye contact to draw her finger around a pattern on the tablecloth. "Yes," she whispered. She'd always been able to talk to him. How had she forgotten? Not forgotten, but deliberately locked away. It seemed so foolish now. Childish.

But she'd *been* a child. They'd both been children.

She'd never told him about the dead she saw. Nobody but her parents had known about them.

The teapot whistled.

"I'll get it." She rose to her feet. "Stay where you are." She almost touched his shoulder in a reassuring gesture, then stopped herself just before making contact. She crossed to the stove, shut off the flame, and filled their mugs. "Milk? Cream?"

He shook his head, and she sat back down.

He removed a tea bag from the container and unwrapped it. "I have tea sent from England. The new shipment hasn't arrived, and I'm running low, so not much of a selection."

Ordering tea from another country was his way of bringing a little bit of the world to him. She understood that. "What about this?" She picked up an ornate silver tin from the center of the table.

"That's loose tea I found in the back of the cupboard. Something my dad left. I tried it a few times, but it's pretty bad."

She pulled off the lid. It was one of those weird, exotic teas with flowers and herbs and maybe even pieces of dried mushrooms. She took a sniff and recoiled. It didn't smell horrid, just surprising. Earthy and musty. She replaced the lid and handed the container to him. "That isn't something I'd want to drink, but then, I don't know anything about tea."

He stared at the canister. "I was going to throw it away, but I might have to resort to drinking it if I run out."

"Don't get rid of the tin," she said. "The tin is beautiful."

He put it down, then leaned back in his chair. "What are you doing here, Rachel?" His shift made the angle of the light change, accentuating the indentations in his cheeks.

He was sick. He was living some Russian tragedy.

She felt an ache deep inside, and she thought of the seventeen years that had passed since she'd last seen him. Such a long time . . .

She was glad she'd come. She would come back again, even though he couldn't possibly help them with the murder case.

"Stop it," he said.

"What?"

"Stop feeling sorry for me."

Sympathy was replaced by irritation. "This is who I am. When I see someone who is pathetic, I feel sorry for him." Heat raced up her face. She couldn't believe she'd just said that. It was so easy to revert back to bratty, nasty childhood habits.

He laughed. *Laughed.*

"I'd better go." She got to her feet, the chair scraping the floor.

"Oh, come on. Don't leave." He grabbed her arm. She could feel every one of his fingertips. "You just got here." He looked up at her, the pale column of his throat exposed. "Stay and entertain me. Drink your tea. Your English tea." He smiled in the most beguiling way.

He let go of her arm.

Should she mention the reason for her visit? But her silence would be sheltering him, treating him as if he were different.

"I see you've been reading about the murder." She sat back down.

His house was so quiet. You could hear the clock ticking. She remembered coming here when she was young, running in, dropping books on the couch, and racing to the refrigerator. Evan's mother would sometimes be baking cookies. His dad would come up out of the basement smelling like hot metal and gun cleaner.

"I've been kinda busy today, but I read a little about it," Evan said.

"We've contacted the Wisconsin Division of Criminal Investigation. They requested a copy of the case file. Also the state police will probably send someone down to ask questions and basically get in the way of any investigating we're able to pull together on our own."

He let out a snort that said he understood her problem.

It was an old story: People who didn't live in Tuonela weren't interested. If anyone did come, they would be nothing more than a pain in the ass.

Rachel's dad was interviewing Tuonela residents, focusing closely on the group calling themselves the Pale Immortals.

Vampire clubs were common in L.A. Most of the people involved were a bit on the geeky side and into harmless role-playing, although some actually drank blood. Tuonela's Pale Immortals were just a bunch of kids, but Seymour was keeping them on his list.

"I thought you might be interested in helping," Rachel said.

Evan frowned, puzzled. "I'm no detective. I can't even leave the house during the day. What's this about?"

"There's more to it than your average homicide. Something that wasn't in the papers." She paused for effect. "The body was drained of blood."

That got his attention. "The Pale Immortal?"

"Same MO. With your background in folklore and knowledge of the Pale Immortal, I thought you might be able to help us."

"You think he's returned?" He smiled. "Risen from the grave?"

"Of course not." She made a face that said his words were ridiculous. At the same time she tried to push aside the fears she'd had last night in the morgue. "Someone might be imitating him. So we need all the information we can get."

He held out both hands so she could see how badly he trembled. "I'm weak as a kitten. That happens when I'm exposed to sunlight."

"We just need information. With the research you've done . . . Maybe with enough information we can predict the killer's next move, if he has a next move."

"I'll do what I can." He picked up a pen and began to doodle on the edge of the newspaper.

"In your research, did you come upon any clues to the whereabouts of the Pale Immortal's grave?" She leaned forward, elbows on the table. "Some people say the body was burned. Others believe it's buried in Old Tuonela."

"Why are you looking for the grave?"

"We figure anybody so obsessed with the Pale Immortal would also be obsessed with finding his grave." Not many clues had been left at the crime scene. Her hope was that they might find clues at the grave of the Pale Immortal. Offerings. Trinkets. Flowers. What did vampire worshipers leave for vampires?

Evan clicked the pen. "Some people think a dummy grave was created in Old Tuonela, and that the real grave is in the corner of a farm field."

That made sense. Years ago dummy graves were commonly used for criminals. Otherwise, families of the victims would dig up the corpse, tear it to shreds, and burn it in order to keep the soul from finding peace.

Evan tossed down the pen. "But my research has led me to believe it's in Old Tuonela. Do you know Jacob Johannsen? He died a few years ago, but he claimed his father dug the grave for the Pale Immortal. And when they were done an oak tree was planted over it."

"Why a tree?"

"To keep the Pale Immortal from rising up."

"I've never heard that."

"Jacob seemed pretty sure it was in Old Tuonela. In the graveyard next to the church, but you know how these stories are. Most of the history I've gathered on Old Tuonela isn't history at all, but tall tales and fabrications."

"Still, it should be looked into."

"Don't go out there by yourself."

By herself? After last night she didn't want to go out there period.

The dark basement with cement-block walls smelled faintly of a sewer and a lot of mold.

This would be over soon.

The camera flashed again, blinding him.

Graham hadn't gotten a good look at the guy—he was pretty sure that was intentional. The man with a digital camera had answered his knock on the unlit basement door wearing some kind of fishing cap pulled down to meet the top of silver aviator glasses with blue lenses.

Kind of the fishing-hat bandit meets the Unabomber. Pervs were never cool. Pervs never had any sense of style. Not that Graham had known a lot of them, but he watched the news.

"Come on."

The perv had motioned for Graham to follow him down the wooden stairs into a dark hole. Graham had known it was stupid, but he went with only a second of hesitation.

And now Graham stood naked in front of a tripod and camera while the guy snapped away. It should have been awful. It should have been degrading. But it was so weird and stupid that Graham had to stifle the laughter that bubbled in his throat.

"Turn around."

Graham complied. *I aim to please.*

Click.

Flash.

Had Isobel listened to the CD he'd given her? If so, had she liked the Sonic Youth song, "Diamond Sea"? It was a little darker than most of the music he listened to. He tended to lean toward songs that were light and upbeat, passing over music that made him sad and put him in a dark mood. A young heart could take only so much.

"Turn around."

He turned again.

Had she liked the line about the kids dressed in dreams? He loved that. *Loved* it.

The man stepped away from the camera. "I can't pay you the full hundred dollars."

"Why not?"

"The scars."

"What difference do a few scars make?"

"I don't want to see them. They make me uncomfortable. I'm not into any of that sadomasochism shit."

"You said a hundred bucks."

"You said there was nothing wrong with you."

"There isn't. Come on, man. I need the money."

"Okay. Listen. There's one way you can make it up."

"How's that?"

"Ever do it with a man before? I'll wear a rubber. I'll make it quick."

It was another one of those this-can't-be-happening moments. Graham had been having a lot of them lately.

Everybody had a line they wouldn't cross. Graham

had just reached his. But the scary thing was that
he'd actually thought about it for a quarter of a
second.

Graham quickly pulled on his jeans. Forget underwear. Sockless feet shoved into unlaced boots. He
grabbed the rest of his stuff. "Fuck you."

He ran, leaving with no money.

Chapter 8

Rachel tucked the hardback copy of *Terror Twilight* under her arm, pressed the metal security bar, and stepped out of the public library. Like most buildings in Tuonela, the library had been built on a steep hill. Across the street was St. Paul's Church. The steeple appeared to be falling over as the sky pressed down upon it.

Rachel could smell earth and new grass, a scent she associated exclusively with Tuonela, even though she was fairly certain grass grew other places. It was unusually warm for early April, so warm she'd left her coat at home, the sun's rays penetrating the back of her black short-sleeved top.

On the way to the van, she stopped near a tall, moss-covered stone wall, pulled out her cell phone, and keyed in Evan Stroud's number. "I just picked up your new book at the library," she said when he answered.

"You should have told me you wanted one when you were here last night."

"That's okay."

"Return it. I'll give you a copy."

"That's *okay*."

"I don't like library books. They've been imprinted with the previous readers. And they smell. Not like paper, but like people. I want my books to be clean."

"I'm sure Mrs. Douglass would love to hear you talking that way about her library books. If I remember correctly, you and I spent a lot of hours at the library. I don't recall you having a dirty book problem then."

"It's a more recent development."

Ah. If he could see better, his sense of smell was probably also more acute.

A teenager came rushing around the corner. He was tall, with curly golden hair, wearing jeans and a long-sleeved black T-shirt. He almost ran into her.

"Sorry," he mumbled, putting up a hand as if to steady her. He made eye contact, then quickly glanced away.

It looked as if he'd been crying.

Rachel watched the boy as he strode down the hill, his movements heavy from a large canvas pack he carried on his back.

"Rachel?" came Evan's voice from the cell phone.

"I gotta go. Talk to you later." She disconnected and hurried down the hill after the kid. "Hey!"

Half a block away, he stopped and turned.

She continued to walk toward him, but more slowly now, because she didn't want her movements to come across as threatening. "Are you okay?"

His mouth opened in alarm. He gave a little launching hop, spun around, and took off, running like hell. At the intersection of Church and Jefferson the light was green, and traffic was coming from both directions. He slowed and took a right, skidding around the corner.

Rachel hurried down the hill, but when she reached the intersection there was no sign of the boy.

Her cell phone rang. She expected Stroud, but it was her dad.

"I made arrangements to meet Phillip Alba at his home near Old Tuonela late this afternoon so I could have a look around the place," he said. "But I've had something come up and I haven't been able to get in touch with him. Would you have time to run out there? Just have a look around. Take Dan with you."

Weakness flooded her arms and legs. Old Tuonela was the last place she wanted to go.

"Rachel? You still there?"

She pulled in a deep breath. "I'm here."

"I lost you for a minute. Did you hear what I said about Alba? He has play practice tonight, so he's making a special trip to meet with me."

"Yeah, I heard. I can do that."

Sure, she could. Going to OT was exactly what she needed to do. A chance to prove that what had happened with Chelsea Gerber's body had been nothing more than an illusion caused by poor lighting, or low blood sugar, or fumes. . . .

She told him good-bye and disconnected. She pulled up her phone book, found Dan's number, and pushed the call button. She got his voice mail and left a message, telling him to call if he wanted to ride to OT with her.

Two hours later, when she hadn't heard back from him, she headed to Old Tuonela by herself. It was probably better this way. If she freaked out, there would be less explaining to do.

Her parents didn't know it, but Rachel had sometimes ridden her bike the five miles to Old Tuonela. A foolish thing for a young girl to do.

She turned off a narrow, unmarked asphalt road to an even narrower gravel drive. Getting there wasn't easy. You had to know the way. If you didn't know Old Tuonela was back there hidden in the hills, you'd never see it. Which was perhaps why the original settlers had chosen that spot.

When she reached a rusty FOR SALE sign, she turned left and headed up a steep rutted lane leading deeper into heavy woodland.

You could feel it before you got there: the change in the air. It became heavy and seemed filled with static electricity. Maybe that was one of the things that had drawn her as a kid.

She drove over a shallow, rocky stream and finally came to a stop in an open, treeless area. In the distance, a dark two-story house stood outside the boundaries of Old Tuonela. This time she was prepared for the fear that overcame her. It didn't surprise her or make her weak, but it fluttered insistently in her belly.

A conditioned reaction, that's what it was. A childhood fear and fascination revisited.

This was where her dad had said to meet Alba. She checked her watch. She was ten minutes late. Had he been here already, gotten tired of waiting, and left? But she hadn't met another vehicle. And there was only one way in.

Rachel got out of the van.

She'd parked downhill from the house, which made the building tower over her. No one knew for sure, but some said the two-story house, made of dark stone chiseled from a quarry that no longer existed, had been built by Richard Manchester, the Pale Immortal. It stood in a cleared area on top of a small knoll. There were a few ragged shrubs near the house, but not a single tree.

Sometimes Rachel agreed with the people who thought Old Tuonela's rotting buildings should be demolished and burned, all trace of its existence wiped out. But others felt the town should remain undisturbed, that something bad might be released unless the place was left alone.

An old fear crept into Rachel's head. What if the ground itself was cursed and imprinted by the evil done there a hundred years ago? What if their ancestors had been right to walk away and not look back?

Phillip Alba's parents were from Chicago. As outsiders, none of them had believed the superstitions that surround Old Tuonela. They bought the OT property and began restoring the main house. When they couldn't stir up interest in their plans to turn OT into a tourist village, they packed up and moved on. Rachel had never met Phillip Alba, but he was the talk of Tuonela.

As a graduate student he'd been involved in a horrendous bus accident. He'd been the only survivor. His girlfriend had died. His best friend had died. A tragic story. His parents told him he could recover in Old Tuonela, finish the restoration, and keep an eye on things in case any buyers showed up.

His parents were idiots. Who would send someone to such a place of a horrors to get over a tragedy?

Damn. There she went again. Believing all the hype and superstition.

Go see for yourself that nothing's there.

Old Tuonela was a scary campfire story, a flashlight under the chin.

Off in the distance, treeless grassland met dark woodland. The woodland was surrounded by a fairly new fence. Rachel climbed the locked gate, her feet landing solidly on the other side.

She looked back toward the van. Still there. She hadn't passed through some invisible barrier, she noted wryly. She began walking in the direction of Old Tuonela, staying between the ruts left by horse-drawn wagons and buggies.

She'd been twelve or thirteen when she'd ridden her bike here. She would lean it against the fence, then slip between the loose strands of barbed wire that had surrounded the place then. One time she'd scratched her back. When her mother asked how it had happened, she'd lied. She'd rarely lied to her mother, but it had been a compulsion, just like riding her bike to Old Tuonela had been a compulsion. Girls on the cusp of puberty did weird things, had strange ideas.

Old Tuonela's pain and loss and tragedy had spoken to her, and she had responded.

The lane opened up.

Suddenly there was the town, or what was left of it. The buildings looked as if they were growing out of the ground. They had sunk over the years, slanted, decaying, shrouded in vegetation. Except for the flour mill at the opposite end of the street, most of the structures were being devoured by moss and creeper vines, the wood beams rotten and mushy. Roofs had caved in, and what was outside had come inside.

Rachel spotted the church with its crumbling bell tower. The stone wall surrounding the adjoining graveyard was only a couple of feet high, and she climbed over easily.

Hidden in the grove of hickory and cottonwoods was a tree that could have been an oak. She knew an oak leaf when she saw one, but this tree hadn't begun to leaf. Dead? Dying? It appeared to be blighted, the trunk dark with sap and crawling with ants.

If there were graves in the graveyard, she saw no evidence of them, no traditional markers. She supposed flat rocks covered by tangled grass and weeds could be lurking underneath. Wooden markers would have disintegrated long ago.

Nothing appeared disturbed. There were no signs that anyone had visited recently. She paid particular attention to the areas around the base of the tree in question. Just grass and weeds. Just earth and stones.

She pulled out her cell phone. Two bars . . . three bars . . . .

She punched in Evan's number, hoping to ask him

for suggestions. It rang twice, then went dead. She checked the signal. Nothing. She redialed but it didn't connect, so she dropped the phone back in her pocket.

She heard the drone of bees and the twitter of birds, the faraway trickle of water.

Old Tuonela made the hair on your arms move. It was a place where an incredibly evil man had butchered children and drunk their blood.

But sometimes, like today, the town didn't seem so bad. It could almost appear peaceful.

Darkness was falling.

She clicked the green light on her watch dial. She'd been there over an hour.

A faint sound came from inside the crumbling stone church. Almost like a voice. Or a whisper.

Female.

Human.

Rachel froze. Her scalp tingled. The air around her suddenly seemed thick and close and smothering.

Run!

Instead she moved slowly toward the church. Weeds brushed the legs of her jeans, and the soles of her sneakers made a *shh-shh-shh* sound against the flagstones.

She shoved her shoulder against the church door, managing to get it partly open.

The interior was black, with vague outlines that looked like pews. A rectangular room with plaster walls and a woodstove.

What was that across the room?

A form.

A woman.

Victoria.

She was lying in something made of metal. A zinc tub.

Victoria had long, beautiful hair. Victoria was of another age.

Slowly the woman stood.

Rachel heard water splashing. But it wasn't water. Somehow she knew it wasn't water. Victoria reached for Rachel with one hand—just as Victoria had reached for her in the morgue, in a sorrowful, imploring, helpless gesture.

She wanted Rachel to come inside the church.

This was why she should have stayed in California. The dead didn't appear to her in California.

Victoria was still calling.

Don't do it.

Don't go in there.

Turn and leave. Act like you don't see her.

Rachel fled.

Now that she was in motion, now that her body had finally responded, she ran like hell. Her feet flew over the ground, and somehow she didn't trip. Branches slashed her arms and face, but she didn't care.

She wasn't in great condition, and her lungs quickly became raw, her breathing loud. Still she hurtled herself forward into the darkness.

A shape appeared directly in front of her.

She veered to the right. Hands grabbed her.

"Hey!"

A male voice.

Hands holding her arms.

"Hey, hey, hey! What's going on? Why are you running? I'm sorry I scared you. You just came plowing into me."

It took her a moment to realize this was a real person.

"Are you Rachel?" he asked. "I'm Phillip. Sorry I'm late. I got hung up at school."

The presence of another person had an immediate calming effect on her.

He put an arm around her shoulders, guiding her, and they began to walk from the woods toward the gate, which she could see was ajar. "Old Tuonela was built on a fault line," Phillip said, in what seemed a poor attempt to distract her. "Did you know that? Did you know that we could have a bigger earthquake here than anything San Francisco has ever seen?"

"I try not to think about it."

They had reached her van.

"You scratched your face." He wiped a thumb across her cheek, then showed her the blood. His car was next to hers, running, parking lights on.

He was one of those intense artist types. Probably raised by a nanny in a suburb of Chicago. Not that Rachel held it against him, but she suspected that kind of upbringing created another form of alienation.

She could easily imagine him as a college student, writing obscure poetry and attending open-mike night. He would have worn a black turtleneck and horn-rimmed glasses. Very serious. Very mysterious.

His hair was shaggy and longish, which added to the Dylan Thomas quality. People in Tuonela spoke highly of Phillip Alba. They thought he was doing a great job with the children and the plays.

"Did you see something in there?" he asked.

"Like what?"

He watched her closely. "I don't know. Why were you running?"

"I just got spooked, that's all."

"What were you looking for?"

"A grave." Bit by bit she pulled herself together.

"What kind of grave?"

"The grave of the Pale Immortal. Have you heard any rumors? About it being somewhere in OT?"

He shook his head. "Nothing other than the possibility. But I was also told he was buried somewhere else."

"I've heard that too. Probably right. If you see any signs of anybody snooping around, call Chief Burton."

"Will do. But I get the idea you were looking for something specific. Were you?"

Normally she wouldn't have been so free with information. But she was still shaken, and she felt that they now had a bond. He'd rescued her. "Some people think he was buried under an oak tree in the church graveyard."

"*Under* a tree?"

"The tree was planted over his grave. To hold him down. To keep him from rising."

"Oh." Phillip nodded and smiled. The kind of smile outsiders smiled, because she was talking silly stuff. Outsiders didn't believe the Tuonela myths. Hell, *she* didn't believe the myths.

"Did you find it?" he asked. "The grave?" He was joking with her.

"No. I think I found an oak tree, but no grave."

"Would you like to come inside a minute?" He jabbed a thumb toward the house.

She was about to say yes when a pair of headlights appeared in the lane. Rachel recognized Dan's car. He pulled to a stop, cut the engine, and jumped out.

"Hey." He looked from Rachel to Alba, then back to Rachel. "Sorry. I just got your message."

"Why didn't you call me?" she asked. "You could have saved yourself a trip."

Dan ran a hand through his hair, elbow high, one hand at his waist. "I don't know."

"I'm just getting ready to leave. I'm sorry you drove up here for nothing."

At that moment another set of headlights appeared, the twin beams vanishing and reappearing, bobbing with the rough terrain.

"Jeez," Alba said under his breath. Apparently he wasn't used to so much company.

As Rachel watched, the vehicle topped the last rise and pulled up behind her van. The door opened and Evan Stroud stepped out. He wore a dark, unbuttoned coat. "I saw you tried to call me. I had the feeling you might be out here." He hovered near the car, then slowly moved in her direction, as if he were unwilling to step far from his vehicle. "Is everything okay?" He glanced toward the woods and the heart of Old Tuonela, then quickly back. "Is that blood?" He pointed to Rachel's face.

She put a hand to her cheek. "I ran into a branch."

Now that Evan was there, Alba didn't seem nearly as interesting. She felt bad about that. Even the woman in the zinc tub had taken a backseat. Her visions were like that. Once they were gone, they never seemed real, like something she'd watched on TV when she was almost asleep. She didn't know what caused them, but they came from her. They couldn't be real. How could she—a coroner, a medical examiner—believe otherwise?

Evan's cell phone rang, but he ignored it. Her cell phone rang and she noted she had a strong signal this time. It was her dad. "If you see Evan," Seymour said, "tell him we have the kid."

"Kid?"

"The kid claiming to be his son."

That was the last thing she'd expected to hear. "I'll let him know." She disconnected. "I really have to get going," she told Alba.

His son. Evan's son. What was that all about?

Rachel remembered the boy she'd seen that morning outside the library. He'd been crying, and he'd looked different. You could usually tell when somebody wasn't from Tuonela. There was nothing to put your finger on; it was primal, the way animals from the same litter knew one another and could sniff out strangers.

"Are you Evan Stroud?" Alba asked.

Rachel had assumed they knew each other. She found it strange that they'd never met, considering

Evan had written a book about Old Tuonela. Alba extended his hand and introduced himself.

"That was my dad on the phone," Rachel said. "He wanted me to tell you they have your son at the police station."

That produced a long silence.

"You mean the kid *claiming* to be my son," Evan finally said. "Big difference." But he moved toward his car as if the kid meant more to him than he was willing to admit.

They all slid into their vehicles. In a caravan, they headed in the direction of Tuonela, away from the land of the dead.

Chapter 9

The jail cell was tiny, with a toilet and sink right there in the open so anybody could watch. That was probably so you didn't try to hang yourself in secret.

The cell actually had a window—probably because the entire building was old. The barred window was so high that Graham couldn't see out, even though he'd jumped several times. The cement-block walls were full of writing. How did people write stuff? You had to have a pen to write. Nobody let Graham have anything. No wonder that guy—de Sade—wrote stuff with his own poop. It was all he had.

Graham had been there only three hours, but he was about to lose it.

He hadn't done anything. He'd been hanging out in the square, but it was more of a park. What was illegal about that? A public park.

The cop who'd pulled up said it wasn't allowed, then asked for ID. Loitering and unattended juvenile was what they got him on. How lame was that?

One of the cops who'd been in on the arrest appeared outside the barred cell. He was young and kind of shy. "Need anything?" he asked. "Water? Something to eat?"

Graham shook his head. They weren't supposed to be nice to him. He didn't want them to be nice. Were they up to something? "What day is it?"

"Thursday."

"No, I mean the date. What's the date?"

"April eighth."

Graham's birthday was tomorrow.

The young cop left, then reappeared a half hour later. He unlocked the cell door and held it open. "Chief Burton wants to see you in his office."

Was this a good sign or a bad sign?

Chief Burton was old and thin, and reminded Graham of somebody's grandfather. He wore a gray suit that matched his gray hair. The thin fabric hung from his sharp shoulders. He reeked of cigarette smoke and fried food. In an office with wood-paneled walls and no windows, he motioned for Graham to take a seat on the opposite side of his desk. He smiled, and Graham relaxed. A little.

"So . . ." Grandpa pulled out a metal lighter, lit a cigarette, shut the lighter with a loud snap, then leaned back in his chair. "I hear you've been in a little trouble."

"I didn't know there was anything wrong with hanging out in a park."

"There are several things wrong with that. You were sleeping. We don't allow sleeping and loitering in the park."

"How do you not loiter in a park?" Should he

have been selling hot dogs or something? "Can't somebody take a snooze in the park?"

"Let me put it this way. You can take a nap—but you can't settle in for the night. Doesn't matter." He waved his words away. "You're underage. Fifteen-year-olds can't live alone."

"I'm sixteen." Almost.

"Sixteen-year-olds can't live alone either. That makes you an unattended juvenile. Another concern: Someone was murdered in that park, not far from where you were sleeping, just two days ago. And since perpetrators often return to the scene of the crime, you chose a particularly bad place to set up camp."

He paused to take several deep puffs from his cigarette, then tucked it into a large glass ashtray. "If I had a grandson your age, I wouldn't want him in the park. We're lookin' out for you, Graham."

"Ummm. Okay." The room was small, and Graham's eyes were burning from the cigarette smoke.

The chief stubbed out his butt, then started hacking away.

Why don't you just quit smoking? Graham wanted to say. *You're telling me I'm stupid for sleeping in the park when you're killing yourself?*

When the guy finally stopped coughing, he acted as if nothing had happened. "Unless you *are* the perpetrator." He leaned back in his chair. "You hit town the same night the murder took place."

"What?" Graham's heart began to pound. "What does that have to do with anything?"

"Maybe nothing." Burton shrugged.

"You think I *killed somebody?*" That was insane! He'd thought his life couldn't get any more screwed up, but apparently he was wrong.

"Personally, I don't think you killed anybody, but that's not to say you aren't a suspect. Your badly timed arrival makes you suspicious."

"But I was at Evan Stroud's. Ask him."

"We did. He told us the approximate time you showed up on his porch. Hours after the murder took place. Where were you before you went to Stroud's? Do you have an alibi?"

"I was in a car. We were driving to Tuonela. Me and my mom."

"Unfortunately we can't find her. We have no proof of what you're telling me."

Did that mean he was going back to jail? He couldn't do that. Maybe this guy was just messing with him. Trying to scare him into confessing, if he had anything to confess.

"Here's what I'd like you to do," Burton said. "Since we can't find your mother, we've made temporary living arrangements for you until we can locate her."

Social Services. But not jail.

"During that time, which hopefully won't be long, you have to go to school. We can't have you piddling around all day, doing nothing."

He shrugged.

"Good." Burton smiled.

They both got to their feet.

The old guy put an arm around his shoulders,

giving him an encouraging pat. "No matter how bad things seem, they always work out."

Someone had left Graham's pack in the hallway. He picked it up, and the chief walked him to the door. Outside, a car was parked at the bottom of the wide marble steps. Next to the vehicle, dressed in a long coat topped off with dark glasses, even though it was night, stood Evan Stroud.

Graham's stomach did a flip-flop.

"Go on." The old guy gave him a gentle shove.

There was nowhere to run. He was at the police station, for dog shit's sake. If he took off, they'd have him in a second. They'd put him back in jail, where he'd soon be writing his name in stinky letters.

Like a robot, he moved jerkily down the steps toward Stroud.

"Here's the deal," Stroud said once they were in the car driving away. "You can stay at my place while we get things figured out. I'll take DNA samples and send them to a lab so you can see that I'm not your father. So you can have some closure."

"You don't have to do this." Graham didn't want to stay where he wasn't wanted. He had pride.

"It's all right. I want to help, but I can't monitor you. I can't follow you around and make sure you're going where you should be going. Tuonela is small, and everybody knows everybody's business. If you ditch school, I'll find out."

"Okay. Okay."

Graham didn't know if it really was okay. He was exhausted. The only sleep he'd gotten was the one night/day he'd spent at Stroud's. And the deal about the DNA, maybe that was a good thing. Maybe Stroud would believe him once and for all. Maybe the guy would step forward and take some responsibility.

Chapter 10

Graham sat at the table studying Stroud. When he turned around, Graham quickly looked down, watching as the guy slid two fried eggs from the spatula to the plate in front of him. Next came toast and orange juice.

Stroud took a seat. "Gotta have a good breakfast before you go to school."

Would a vampire say something about a good breakfast? Would a vampire even *fix* breakfast?

Graham picked up his fork. Keeping his chin low, he glanced through the hair that curled across his forehead. Stroud looked pretty normal except for being so pale.

Graham took a bite. Then another. And suddenly he was embarrassed by his own stupid thoughts.

The old guy from the police station picked him up.

They hadn't even given him a chance to get some decent sleep. Stroud had driven him to his place, where Graham got what seemed like five minutes before Stroud was standing over his bed, waking him, telling him the chief would be there soon to take him to school.

Maybe it was some kind of strategy to break him down with sleep deprivation.

Move along, son. Just move along. Nothing to think about here.

The car was old and big and kind of floated over the streets, the chief leaning back in his seat and steering with one finger. The ashtray was overflowing with butts. He must have put out a cigarette before Graham got in, because it was still hazy inside.

It took maybe five minutes to get to school. It was close enough that Graham could have walked, but they wanted to keep an eye on him. They wanted to make sure he didn't take a detour to Arizona along the way.

The boat of a car docked at the curb. A wide sidewalk led past a flagpole, up a set of steps to double doors.

Graham's stomach lurched.

He was sick of being the new kid. His mother never stayed in one place for more than a year at a time. He didn't even know how it felt not to be new, not to always be on the outside, not to be defined by being from somewhere else.

The building was brick. Sprawling, with a flat roof. Classes must have already started, because nobody was around.

The chief hacked away, holding a fist to his mouth. When he was done, he said, "They're expecting you." He talked fast and breathlessly, as if wanting to get the words out before his next coughing spell. Graham's mother smoked, so he knew all about the morning coughing fits smokers had. "I talked to Principal Bonner this morning and explained the situation. She said she'd have everything ready when we got here. Want me to come in with you? I can."

"No." Graham opened the door and slid across the seat. "I can handle it."

"I've made arrangements for my daughter to pick you up. Right here, at exactly three fifteen. She'll be driving a white van. You'll be here, won't you, Graham?"

Ordinarily he would have said yes while silently saying no. But he liked this old guy. Why'd he have to be so nice?

"Yeah. I'll be here."

"Good." The old guy smiled and gave him a wave. "Take a right once you step inside."

He didn't pull away. Instead he waited for Graham to walk up the sidewalk, past the flag, and through the double doors.

The school smelled of books and bodies and whatever they used to clean the floors; it made Graham's stomach drop again.

The old guy had been right: They were waiting for him in the office. A secretary greeted him with a tight, phony smile that meant she'd been there too many years and now hated every kid ever born, but was trying to hide it because deep down she knew it was wrong to hate so indiscriminately.

She gave him his schedule. She gave him a map. She gave him his locker combination and lunch tickets.

"Who paid for this?" Graham asked.

"Mr. Stroud."

'Bout fucking time.

"Your first class is English, with Mr. Richards. Room 102. Down the hall and take a left."

Graham took the printed schedule and looked at it. What was he doing here? "Thanks."

"On second thought, I'd better come with you." She left the safety of the counter, and side by side they walked down the hallway.

Strips of kraft paper had been taped to the walls and were covered with handwriting from colored Magic Markers. It wasn't until they passed a locker with a cluster of flowers and stuffed animals on the floor that he realized the display was a tribute to the dead girl.

They stopped in front of room 102. It was probably a good thing the secretary had come along. At this point he would have taken off.

She reached around him and opened the door. "Go on."

He stepped inside the doorway and halted. She followed. "I have a new student for you, Mr. Richards."

A million eyes turned to stare.

The teacher was in the front of the room, one leg dangling over the corner of his desk. "Take any empty seat."

Everything was a blur of embarrassment and self-consciousness. Graham hated being the new kid. Fucking *hated* it.

Frantic, he spotted an empty seat and shot

straight for it, quickly sitting down. The kid in front of him gave him a half smile and slid back around. A sound of mass movement—and the class was once again facing forward.

Graham sat there and waited for his heart to quit pounding.

It took a long time.

He had no idea what the teacher was talking about. He didn't care, but vaguely came to attention when the man showed up beside him. Just as suddenly a book appeared on his desk.

Why did schoolbooks always smell like puke? Could anybody explain that? Was it because someone had puked in them? Or was it the ink? The paper? Or did he just associate it with puke? He'd never been able to figure that out, and anytime he ever mentioned it, nobody seemed to have the answer.

Something soft hit him in the back of the head, and a crumpled piece of paper landed on the floor. He ignored it. Another one hit him. He slid around in his seat, ready to throw somebody the finger, when he spotted Isobel sitting in the back of the class. She gave him a little wave, pointed to him, pointed to the floor, then lifted both hands, palms up, in the pantomime question of, *What the hell are you doing here?*

But she was smiling. Looking kind of happy and surprised at the same time.

He smiled back and shrugged his shoulders. *Beats me. Just fell out of the sky.*

Someone cleared his throat—a sound meant to get

Graham's attention. It took him a second to realize the teacher, Mr. Richards, was politely trying to get him to turn back around and listen.

Didn't want to chew out the new kid.

Graham faced front, but spent the rest of class intensely aware of Isobel sitting several seats behind him.

She was waiting for him in the hall after the bell rang. "What are you doing here?" She was dressed in another black skirt, pink tights, and a pink sweater. Her hair had a couple of yellow plastic barrettes in it that almost went with the messenger bag over her shoulder.

Standing next to her, he remembered he was wearing the clothes he'd slept in last night. He hadn't taken a shower; he wasn't even sure when he'd last brushed his teeth.

That self-awareness was like a rug being pulled out from under him. It was hard enough talking to a cute girl when you didn't stink.

He looked down at the floor. "It would take a long time to explain." His words sounded curt and impatient, as if she bored him and he wanted to get away. He hadn't meant to sound like that.

"Oh." Her smile faded and she took a step back. From her expression it was obvious she was trying to figure out what had just happened. "Okay."

"Graham!"

He turned to see the hard kids from Peaches lumbering toward him. Travis, the one with the soul patch, who'd told him about the pervert, held out his hand. Graham reached to shake and Travis smacked his palm. Graham hated that shit. "What are you doin' here, man?" Travis asked.

"Decided to stick around for a while."

"Cool. You should come with us after school."

"I can't."

"Then later. Tonight."

"Ah . . ." Graham looked over his shoulder. Isobel was gone. He spotted her in the distance, her blond hair standing out in the mob of kids moving down the hall, away from him. "I don't have any money." It was true, and better than having to admit he couldn't leave the house.

"You don't need money," Travis said. "We cruise looking for shit to do, or we just hang out at Peaches."

Today was Graham's birthday. A guy should be able to do what he wanted to on his birthday.

Rachel pulled her van to the curb across from Tuonela High School and cut the engine. It wasn't the same high school she and Evan had attended. This was the "new" school, having been built ten years ago.

Kids poured through the double doors, and she kept her eyes open for someone with curly blond hair. Tall. Kinda lanky, her dad had said. And kind of a smart-ass.

Pretty soon she spotted a kid with wildly curly hair striding toward the van. He looked a little lost as he eyed her vehicle. With a jolt of recognition, she realized he *was* the boy she'd seen downtown near the library.

She waved through the windshield.

He crossed in front of the van to climb in the passenger door. "He said a white van. He failed to mention that it would say 'County Medical Examiner' on the side."

Yep. Smart-ass.

She pulled away from the curb. "My dad likes to keep people guessing."

The smart-ass was nervous, long, thin fingers tapping against a spiral notebook. But he was trying to appear calm, cool, bored.

She gave him a quick glance. Her dad was right: He didn't look like Evan. Nothing that stood out, anyway. He was almost pretty, with that head of hair, clear skin, nice cheekbones. Like an angel. But then, Lydia had been so beautiful people had stopped to stare at her on the street.

"Are you the medical examiner?" Graham asked. "Or do you just work for him?"

Not only was she female, but she'd never dressed the part of medical examiner, preferring jeans and T-shirts. "I'm him."

"So, you do autopsies?"

What about his voice? Was it anything like Evan's? Graham's voice was deep and young, with a little bit of a drawl and a slow delivery that were indicative of the South. But he didn't have what she'd call a Southern accent.

"I'm the coroner *and* the medical examiner," she told him.

He nodded. "That's cool."

Kids were into blood and guts now. Not like when

she was in high school, when girls fainted over dissected frogs. She'd always suspected the fainting was an act, put on for the sake of the boys, who loved it.

Graham looked over his shoulder. "And you carry the bodies around in here?"

"It's not *nearly* as glamorous as it seems."

What would Evan do if Graham ended up being his child? What then? When he'd denied his existence his entire life? "How was school?"

It didn't escape her that she'd been dropped into the version of the life she'd daydreamed of having with Evan years ago—sans the death mobile and vampire lifestyle.

"It's a school." He shrugged. "They're all the same."

"Do you need anything before we head to Evan's?"

He thought a moment. "I'm kinda hungry."

She hadn't been talking about food; she'd been talking about school supplies. "How about stopping at a café?" She could use a cup of coffee. It occurred to her that he was stalling, that maybe he wasn't looking forward to seeing Evan.

She braked for a red light and took the opportunity to inspect her passenger again. He might have been beautiful, but he also looked delicate, as if he needed a week of good meals and decent sleep. His eyes beneath the curls had dark circles under them.

Thrown away.

How did it feel to be thrown away? Passed off to a stranger? And what if Evan wasn't his father? That might be the bigger question here. What would happen to this child?

She spotted a poster on a nearby wooden electrical pole. A MISSING poster with a photo of a young woman. Rachel made a right turn and pulled to the curb to get a closer look.

Karen Franklin. Twenty-six years old. Rachel vaguely remembered hearing about the girl's disappearance on the news. Last seen at a bar in a town about a hundred miles north of Tuonela. She'd been missing for three weeks.

Any similarity between this missing-persons case and Chelsea Gerber's murder? Not really, other than the fact that both victims were female. Still, she'd run it past her dad. He was waiting on lab results, and seemed to be putting too much faith in DNA. Understandable. He wasn't used to dealing with homicides, and she hated to tell him that DNA evidence wasn't all it was portrayed to be on television. Some people, even law professionals, were under the impression that DNA could solve anything.

And if DNA was found in the samples from the Gerber case? Then what? Collect DNA from every person in town? It had been done before in smaller communities. You couldn't force people to participate, but peer pressure was a big factor in a place like Tuonela.

Her dad needed to look into this. Make sure his suspects hadn't been in Summit Lake, Wisconsin, on the date the woman vanished.

*　　　*　　　*

Evan slipped on a pair of dark glasses. With one finger he parted the heavy living room drapes a crack. They should have been here by now. School had let out twenty minutes ago.

He dropped the curtain and regarded the portable phone in his hand. Should he call Rachel? See if everything was okay?

Wait a little longer. Maybe Graham had to talk to a teacher or the principal. Maybe there was a traffic jam at the school.

The portable phone rang. He jumped and answered it.

"We stopped to get something to eat," Rachel said. "We'll be there in fifteen minutes."

Evan crossed the room to the kitchen table and picked up the DNA paternity test kits Rachel's father had dropped off earlier. "I've got plans for him once he gets back."

He heard a lot of background noise. Music. People talking. The sound of dishes. He imagined them sitting at a table in some sunny window.

"Fifteen minutes," she repeated before hanging up.

They made it with time to spare. Evan was impressed.

Graham came bursting in, smelling like coffee and chocolate and onions. When you lived in isolation, your nose became sensitive to such things in much the same way cigarette smoke became obvious once bans were put in place. Olfactories sorted out the unfamiliar and ignored the rest.

Graham closed the door and tossed a stack of books on an overstuffed chair. That was followed by the sound of Rachel's van pulling away. Evan experienced a brief moment of disappointment. He'd hoped she'd come in. But he and Graham had things to do.

"Chief Burton dropped off the DNA test kits," Evan said.

"How long does it take to get the results?"

"Five to ten days."

Okay. Evan knew this was going to be weird. He'd been mentally preparing for it all day. But now that the time had come, it was even weirder than he'd expected. And awkward as hell.

But this was the best way. He couldn't come right out and tell Graham that yes, he'd had sex with his mother. Once. And they'd used a rubber. At least twenty other guys in town had also had sex with her. He seriously doubted they'd all used condoms.

She'd been a nymphomaniac.

You didn't tell a kid that either.

The results were going to be tough. Apparently Graham had thought of Evan as his father his entire life. Now what little order that false knowledge had brought him was going to be destroyed. But at least he would know the truth.

"Start by rinsing your mouth," Evan said. "You don't want any food particles in the sample. Then you have to rub the swab between the gum and cheek, fairly roughly, but it shouldn't hurt. Back and forth. I'll set the timer for twenty seconds."

Graham rinsed and spit in the sink. Evan handed the packet to Graham, and picked up the other one for himself. Simultaneously they tore open the packets and pulled out the swabs.

With his free hand Evan set the stove timer.

Standing facing each other, the two men stuck the swabs in their mouths and began rubbing vigorously back and forth.

Twenty seconds was a long time when you were doing something like taking a DNA sample. Evan had the urge to turn away, give himself some privacy, but he needed to watch and make sure Graham took the sample correctly.

The bell finally rang.

They both removed the swab.

"Wave it in the air." Evan demonstrated. "Let it dry a little."

They stuck the swabs in the individually supplied packets, sealing the ends.

They did a second test. Evan had come up with the idea of a backup test in case Graham didn't believe the results. Two negatives couldn't be disputed. He would send the kid off with no doubts.

After finishing the second packet, they attached the labels. Everything was boxed and ready to mail. "FedEx will pick it up in the morning," Evan said.

"I'd like to go somewhere tonight," Graham announced. "Do something."

"You mean, like, to a movie?" Evan asked, surprised but intrigued by the idea. "We could do that." He could slip past what ultraviolet lighting they might have in the lobby. God, he hadn't been to a movie in years.

"No, I mean by myself. Well, not exactly. I want to meet with a study group. Downtown at Peaches."

Evan thought about the gun incident. He couldn't quit thinking about the gun incident. The image of Graham pressing the weapon to his temple, his eyes squeezed tightly shut, would probably remain eternally etched in Evan's brain.

"We haven't been monitoring you closely all day just to turn you loose tonight. I'm responsible for you right now. How do I know you won't run away again?"

"I took off before because you called Social Services. And today . . . well, who wants to go to school? This is different. And why would I leave now? Don't you think I want to stick around to see your face when you get those back?" He motioned to the packages on the table.

Good point. "If you wait until after dark, I can give you a ride."

Chapter 11

Travis jabbed the shovel in the soft mound of dirt and looked at the sky. "It's getting dark. It gets dark here so fast. How does that happen? It's like it sneaks up on you."

Craig Johnson stood there watching like he was the goddamn king or something. "I don't care how it happens; I just want to finish and get the hell out of this place."

They were in the Old Tuonela graveyard, digging under a rotten oak tree.

"Maybe if you'd help dig it wouldn't take so long."

"Hey, I only had one shovel. How can we both dig with one shovel? And I did most of the digging when we dug him up. The ground was a lot harder then. My hands bled. You're just repotting him."

Travis wanted to point out that they'd dug him up in broad daylight too. None of this spooky nighttime shit. "Why don't we dump him somewhere?" He took a shovelful of dirt and tossed it angrily aside. "Why do we need to do this?"

"He wants him put back where we got him. Come on. Hurry up. Have you hit the coffin yet?"

"It's too dark to see. Get a flashlight."

"I don't have one."

Travis tossed down the shovel. "Fuck this shit."

"He wants him buried tonight."

"You do it then. I'm not your bitch. Or his. Why can't he do it?"

"You think he's going to get his hands dirty? Come on. Why don't you just admit you're freaked about being out here after dark?"

"And you aren't?"

"You're supposed to be a Pale Immortal. How can you be scared? Of this place? You should feel at home here. I don't think you're serious about this. I think it's just a game to you."

Travis had liked it better when it was just them. Just their gang. "If I wasn't serious, I wouldn't be standing here in the middle of fucking Old Tuonela digging around in a damn graveyard."

Brandon, who'd been leaning against the open trunk of the car drinking vodka from a bottle and keeping tabs on the body, suddenly became alert. "What's that? You see that? Those lights?"

"Lights?" Travis straightened. "You're drunk. You better hope to hell you saved some of that for me. I bought it."

"In the air. Over that ravine. See them? Two of them. Green. Don't you see 'em?"

"Yeah." Johnson took a few steps toward the car. "Floating around."

"Coming this way?" Brandon's voice sounded

like a girl's. Travis would laugh his ass off about that later.

"Are they coming this way? Shit! Ghost lights. That's what they are. My uncle told me about 'em. He saw some around here once. Ghost lights."

They scrambled.

Travis tossed the shovel in the trunk with the corpse. Brandon slammed down the lid. They piled into the car. Johnson fired up the engine and threw the vehicle in reverse. They shot backward, bouncing over rough ground to finally fly through the open gate.

"Stop!" Travis shouted. "We have to lock up."

The car pitched to a sharp halt. Travis jumped out, closed and locked the gate, dove back into the car.

Were the lights coming? He pounded the dash. "Go! Go!"

They hauled ass, tires spinning.

"We still have the body," Brandon said, out of breath. "He wanted him reburied tonight."

"We'll do it tomorrow." Travis looked over his shoulder. "We'll come back tomorrow and do it in the daylight. Nobody'll ever know."

Graham took a shower and put on clean clothes. He brushed his teeth. In his makeshift room he lay down on the bed thinking to just close his eyes for a few minutes . . .

When he woke up it was dark.

He fumbled around, turned on a light, and was relieved when the clock read a little after seven P.M.

Stroud was sitting on the couch in the living room with his laptop.

Graham knew he was a writer. He'd even looked up some of his books at the library. Graham wasn't much of a reader. The required reading of *Lord of the Flies* and *Beowulf* had pretty much done him in. Then again, maybe Stroud wasn't writing. Maybe he was a message board junkie. Or an eBay junkie. Placing bids on a Jesus pierogi. Or a nun bun.

Stroud gave him a ride downtown. "Do you have any money?" he asked, parking at the curb near Peaches.

Graham shook his head.

Stroud produced a ten-dollar bill and handed it to him.

"Thanks." What was he thanking him for? The guy had gotten off easy. He'd never paid a cent during sixteen years. "I can get a ride back."

Stroud reached into the pocket of his long wool coat and pulled out a cell phone. "Take this and call me if you need a ride. And remember, curfew on weeknights is ten thirty. And it's enforced."

Graham grabbed the phone and almost thanked him again before he caught himself. "I'll watch the clock."

Inside Peaches, the music was loud and pulsing. Portishead. He hadn't heard Portishead in a long time.

He quickly scanned the room, looking for a girl with blond hair. No sign of Isobel. He ordered hot tea. "And one of those things." He pointed through the glass case at some kind of cake. It could be his birthday cake.

"Apple Betty?" the girl behind the counter asked.

Betty? He looked a little harder. "Do you have anything with frosting?"

She craned her neck, then popped back up. "A cookie."

"Give me that Betty thing, I guess."

After paying, he took his order upstairs. That's where he found the hard kids, hanging out in the same place as before.

"Hey, how'd things go with the perv?" Travis asked, coming over to see what Graham had on his plate. His fingernails were painted black, and he was wearing eyeliner. His black hair fell in chunks around a face that was not really fat, but kinda puffy. More like a kid's face than a teenager's.

Travis had been filthy before, but now he had actual soil on his shirt and pants.

Travis broke off a piece of the cake and shoved it in his mouth. The two other guys behind him weren't paying any attention. One of them was asleep; the tall, skinny guy with short bleached hair had his back to them and was talking on a cell phone. His jeans were heavy with dirt.

"Not very well," Graham said. "He wanted to screw me."

A spray of cake shot out of Travis's mouth, followed by coughing and choking.

"Did you know about that?" Graham asked with accusation. "Did you know that was part of the deal?"

"Hey, man." Travis held up his hands. "I didn't know he was into that stuff. Swear to God. Well, I figured he was, but never heard about it being part of his little hobby. I've known a few guys who've gone there. None of them ever said anything about it." He put a fist to his mouth, his shoulders shaking. He was laughing now. He smelled like alcohol.

"Thanks." Graham walked over to a chair and plopped down.

Travis followed. "Dude, I'm sorry. I didn't know."

Graham picked up the heavy fork.

"Did you do it?" Travis asked. His eyes were bloodshot, and Graham realized he was drunk. "Did you let him fuck you?"

"Hell, no. I left without getting paid."

"Bummer. That's a real bummer. You should do something about that."

"Like what? Go to the cops?"

Travis laughed again, elbows bent, wrists slack. "Can you imagine? Going to the cops and saying, 'Hey, some old fart stiffed me out of my pay for nude shots.'"

Like he wasn't in enough trouble already.

"We should go over to his place and threaten him," Travis said. "Maybe rough him up a little."

"I don't do that kind of thing."

"He owes you money. When you go underground like that, you have to live by a different set of rules. The things out here don't apply."

"My own rules still apply. I don't beat up old farts, even if they're pervs."

"That's the best place to start," Travis insisted. "Who better to beat the shit out of?"

Why had he come here? To Peaches?

It hadn't been to see Travis and his buddies. Graham had been fooling himself with that excuse. He'd really come hoping to run into Isobel. Hoping to make up for the disaster in the hallway. Maybe even tell her it was his birthday . . .

"Here." He shoved the plate of apple crapple into Travis's hand, put his tea on a nearby table, and left.

His boots pounded on the wooden stairs; then he burst out the front door. Nobody around. A couple of cars rolled down the street.

With his hands jammed into the pockets of his black sweatshirt, he walked, head down.

Happy fucking birthday to me.

He wasn't proud of his self-pity, but sometimes it felt good to feel sorry for yourself. He walked with long strides, not looking up, finally finding himself in the square where he'd been arrested the other night.

He ran for the cover of a huge evergreen tree with branches that swept to the ground. Once inside their shadows, he paused in the darkness and caught his breath. As he stood there, something beyond the tree caught his eye. A flicker of light.

He parted the branches.

Far away was a cluster of small, shifting lights. Curious, he slipped from his cover and slowly approached the lights until he was near enough to recognize them as candles. Maybe fifty of them, some in glass, some just wedged in the dirt, the flames flickering wildly.

Behind the candles were stuffed animals and bouquets of dead flowers. A necklace. A letter jacket. In the center of it all was a photo of a pretty blond girl.

His heart did a swan dive.

It was the girl who'd been murdered. Then he realized this was probably the spot where her body had been found, and his heart took another dive. He'd heard kids talking about it at school, about how her body had been completely drained of blood.

Some even said Stroud had done it.

He stared at the picture. It was an eight-by-ten glossy. The kind kids had taken for graduation. She stared back at him, all perfect, with white teeth. She was the kind of girl who was prom queen, who dated the star football player. Lame shit, as far as he was concerned. But she didn't deserve to die.

Several candles had blown out. Someone had left a book of matches on the ground. He dropped to one knee, grabbed the matchbook, struck a match, and lit the candles.

Were you supposed to say a prayer?

He'd been to church a few times with friends, but he didn't know much about religion or praying.

"Good luck."

Good luck? That was all he could come up with? Kinda late for luck. *Have a nice trip. Sorry you're dead.*

Where did people go when they died?

He stared at the photo of the girl for so long that it suddenly seemed to change slightly. It almost seemed

that her eyes were really looking at him, seeing him.
And the smile . . . The smile was so personal and
real, directed at him. He caught himself responding
with a smile of his own.

He jumped to his feet. He tossed the matchbook
to the ground, turned, and walked away. Was he losing his mind? Did a person losing his mind know it?
Maybe not. Probably not. So thinking about it meant
you weren't crazy.

A car approached from behind, the sound barely
penetrating his consciousness. Then he gradually became aware of a vehicle intentionally keeping pace
with him, hanging back slightly.

He'd been warned about walking around at night.
Whoever killed that girl hadn't been caught. His leg
muscles tightened as he prepared to launch himself
into a mad run.

"Graham!"

Graham swung around to see Travis hanging out
the passenger window of a small green car. "Come
on. Cops'll kick your ass if they find you out past
curfew. Get in. We'll give you a ride."

Graham jumped in the backseat.

Someone was sitting in the dark corner opposite
Graham. He didn't say anything, and Graham figured he was high or asleep.

"We have a few minutes," the driver—the tall kid
with the bleached hair—said.

What was his name? Had Travis called him Johnson?

They headed away from downtown. Several

blocks and stop signs later they turned into a park that sat high on the bluff overlooking the river.

"Swing around where that stone wall is," Travis said.

The driver, who may or may not have been Johnson, stomped down on the gas, and they flew around the corner, skidding to a stop near a wall. The two bailed out. Graham stayed where he was.

Travis and the driver opened the back door, pulled the guy out of the backseat, and dragged him in front of the headlights.

Graham let out a gasp.

The thing they were wresting didn't look human. It was some kind of mummified mess dressed in an old-fashioned suit. Travis and his friend were laughing their asses off. They were drunk or high or both.

Where had they gotten it? Was it real? Or was it some Halloween decoration? Yeah, that's probably what it was. Had to be.

"Look." The tall, skinny guy started humping the body like a dog would hump someone's leg. "Humpin' the mummy," the tall kid said. "Humpin' the mummy."

They both crumpled into a fit of giggles. Inside the car, Graham let out his own burst of laughter.

A minute later, laughing so hard they could hardly walk or talk, Travis and the tall kid dragged the body to the wall. With one on each end, they began swinging it, each swing getting wider as they prepared to toss it.

'Wait," the tall kid said, breathless with laughter. "I have an idea. Put him on the wall. Yeah. Like that.

Now turn him on his side. Yeah." Giggling, they worked until they had him positioned just right, then stepped back to admire their handiwork.

"Oh, my God," they wheezed in unison, hands to their mouths.

Car lights appeared behind them. "Oh, shit!" They ran for the car, dove in, and pulled away. "Get the hell out of here!" Travis said, laughter bubbling behind his words.

The cell phone rang; Graham almost jumped out of his skin.

"It's ten thirty," Stroud said when Graham answered. "Are you still at the coffee shop? I'll come and pick you up."

"That's okay." Graham spoke rapidly. "I've got a ride. I'll be right there." He disconnected and leaned back in the seat, his heart beating fast.

Five minutes later they were pulling up in front of Stroud's house.

Graham had had enough of Travis and his pals for one night. Maybe for more than one night. He got out, slammed the door, and they peeled away.

Inside the house, Graham found Stroud sprawled on the couch, hands behind his head, wearing tinted glasses while he watched TV. Near the door was a pair of muddy leather boots—evidence that he'd been out.

Stroud paused the picture and tossed down the remote. "Have a good time?"

That called up an immediate mental image of the dead corpse Travis and his buddy had been dragging around like some toy. His mind moved backward, to the town square and the candles and the picture of the murdered girl, to Peaches and no Isobel. "Yeah. No. It was okay." He dropped into a big stuffed chair across from the couch, and his gaze automatically went to the TV screen. He wished he hadn't gone out at all. "What are you watching?"

"A documentary. But we can watch something else. Look in the cupboard over there. I don't have *Lord of the Rings* or *Harry Potter,* though. No *Batman* or anything like that."

What the hell did he have then? Graham wasn't really interested in a movie, but now he was curious to see what Stroud spent his time watching. And it kinda pissed him off that Stroud would immediately think he wouldn't want to watch something that was real. Okay, he had to admit a lot of that shit was boring, but some of it was pretty good.

He went to the cupboard and opened the set of double doors. Shelves full of DVDs. Some old movies like *Harold and Maude. Midnight Cowboy. The Godfather.* But most of them were documentaries and *National Geographic* travel–type things. Ireland. Scotland. Germany. France. Cities in the States like New Orleans and New York.

And then it hit him. Stroud couldn't go to any of those places. He would *never* go to any of those places.

Graham had never really thought of the restrictions Stroud's disease placed on him. He just imagined Stroud roaming around at night. Staying out of the sun. Slathering on sunblock and wearing long-sleeved shirts. But this was it. This was his world.

Where it started and where it ended, with not a lot in between. He traveled in his head. He sat on the couch in his living room while the world came to him.

Graham felt kinda sick. He wasn't sure why. Maybe because he'd been clinging to hatred of his father for so long. He'd imagined him having this great life without the responsibility of a kid. But his life was just as fucked up as Graham's. Maybe more.

At least most people could fool themselves into thinking something good was coming around the corner. Stroud couldn't do that. This was it. This house. The couch. The television. His Internet connection. Graham was standing in the center of Stroud's world.

Graham shut the cupboard. "What're you watching?"

"The *Up* series."

"What?"

"A documentary made for British television. It follows the lives of a group of people, reconnecting with them every seven years."

"I think I heard about that."

"This is 7 *Plus Seven*, the second in the series, but I can start it over if you want to see it."

"Nah, that's okay. I'll watch from here." He grabbed a pillow from the chair and stretched out in the middle of the area rug.

"I'd like to see the first one again anyway." Stroud ejected the DVD, popped in another, and sat back down on the couch. "It's kind of sad." After issuing that warning, he pointed the remote at the player and started the DVD.

Graham curled the pillow under his chin. "Like real life."

A half hour ago he wouldn't have guessed the night would end like this, with the two of them watching TV together. And that it would feel so un-weird. That it would feel normal and right. Not the boring kind of normal and right: the good kind.

Chapter 12

The ringing phone woke her. Rachel checked the readout on her portable handset. Her dad, calling from his cell phone. She gave him a groggy hello.

"A corpse has been found in the park," he told her.

Pressing a hand into the mattress, she scooted up in bed. "Female? Same MO?"

"Well . . . not exactly sure about either of those things, but from the way the body is dressed, you'd assume it's a man."

Only once had she seen a body so mutilated that they had to wait until the autopsy to determine the sex. "That bad?"

"Come and see for yourself. I told the officers on patrol not to touch anything until you get there. We're at City Park. Lover's Leap."

It was still dark when Rachel pulled to the edge of the steep brick lane with a hairpin curve and a stone wall at the bottom. But morning wasn't far off, which meant they would soon have adequate light. No need to bring in any generators.

She spotted her father's ancient green Cadillac—a gas-guzzling monstrosity, but he wouldn't part with it. Two white patrol cars were angled, their high beams meeting to best illuminate the body on the wall. She cut the van's engine and grabbed her evidence-collection kit.

Outside the van, her ears picked up the murmur of low conversation from a group of huddled officers. The air was damp, the bricks under her soles wet with morning dew. As she approached she smelled coffee. Someone had brought a thermos and was filling a mug. She spotted her dad in his gray fedora. He was off by himself, his back to the crowd, talking on his cell phone. She caught his eye; he gave her a quick wave and smile, then went back to his conversation.

One of the police officers spotted her. "Morning, Dr. Burton." They shuffled backward and parted, giving her a good view of the victim. Everybody was watching her, waiting for a reaction.

What the . . . ?

Someone stuck a flashlight in her hand. Without taking her eyes from the display, she moved forward.

The body had been carefully arranged. It was lying on its side, head resting against a palm, elbow down. The legs were crossed in what was meant to be a casual pose. Or possibly sexy. It was wearing a cap advertising one of the local gas stations. A few straggly clumps of hair. Dressed in a dark suit.

Now she understood why her dad had told her

the sex and MO couldn't be determined. The victim appeared to be a partially mummified corpse.

The clothing was very old. Shredded and rotten and crumbling.

"Is it real?" the cop with the thermos asked. "They can make things that look real. When I first saw it, I thought it was something someone maybe bought online. Don't think any stores around here would sell that kind of thing."

"Come on," another officer said. "You mean you haven't seen the mummies they sell at Grant's Gas and Go?"

Everybody got a chuckle out of that.

The mood was light, a little electric. Certainly none of the somberness that had accompanied the Chelsea Gerber murder. This was probably a sick prank. A prank that was also a felony.

Rachel bent at the waist so her face was a foot from the corpse. "I'm pretty sure it's real. Or rather, pretty sure it was a living, breathing person at one time."

"Freaky."

She straightened. "Let's treat this like any other crime."

The scene had already been somewhat compromised, since the area hadn't been effectively cordoned off, and care hadn't been taken in keeping police from walking over possible clues.

Her dismay must have shown on her face; suddenly one of the young policemen nudged his fellow officer, then pulled him back. Everyone else did the same.

Until the other night they'd never had to put into practice the lessons they'd been taught. And now, in all the excitement, they'd forgotten it all.

"I've had extra patrol on duty," Rachel's father said, coming up behind her.

"Anybody see anything suspicious?"

"Been pretty quiet. Nothing that stood out." He struggled to control a cough, reached inside his jacket, pulled out a nonfilter cigarette, and lit it. She managed to keep her mouth shut. Normally he didn't smoke in front of her, but he probably figured she'd find a fit of coughing even more disturbing.

She took a large number of digital photos, then almost as many more with her thirty-five-millimeter camera.

Dan showed up, skidding to a stop beside her. "Got here as fast as I could," he said breathlessly. He wore jeans, tennis shoes, and a brown jacket.

She gave him a couple of minutes to meet their new friend; then he was off to the van to return with a white sheet and plastic body bag. He spread the sheet on the ground, butting it up against the stone wall. They both snapped on latex gloves.

"I'll get the head," Rachel said.

She put her hands under the shoulders. Dan grabbed the ankles. They lifted.

"Whoops."

She looked up to see Dan holding a shoe in his hand. It took her a moment to realize that the shoe had a mummified foot in it, with a jagged piece of brown bone sticking out.

They placed the body on the sheet. Dan made a

feeble attempt to reattach the foot; the shoe and bone fell over. He tried again. Same thing, so he gave up.

Behind them someone let out a loud snort. That was all it took for everyone to burst into laughter.

Glancing up at Rachel, Dan finally placed the shoe and foot next to the body. "Sorry," he muttered.

They wrapped the body in the sheet so there would be no chance of losing anything between the crime scene and lab. The body was then placed inside the plastic body bag, zipped, and sealed with a chain-of-custody tag.

Rachel wanted to get out of there before the local paper got wind of the discovery. The *Tuonela Press* dealt mainly with church bazaars, high school sports, and the occasional spotting of a riverboat passing through town on the Wisconsin River, but editor Bonnie Stark had been hoping for a big-break story for the last twenty years. With Chelsea's death she'd gotten it, and this discovery would further excite her.

Rachel and Dan placed the cadaver on a gurney, then slid the collapsed gurney into the back of the van and slammed shut the double doors.

"Stay here and finish collecting the evidence," she told Dan.

"How're you gonna get him out?"

"I'll manage by myself or find somebody to help."

At the coroner's office, Rachel dragged the gurney from the back of the van, locking the legs in place. If the body hadn't been so dehydrated, she wouldn't have been able to manage by herself, but it didn't weigh much more than a small child.

She wheeled the gurney through the street-level doors, down a dark hallway to the elevator. In the basement she went directly to the autopsy suite, where she suited up and began the exam.

After unzipping the body bag, she parked the gurney beside the exam table, locked the wheels, then used the edges of the sheet to drag the body onto the stainless-steel table.

She opened the sheet with care, then got out her digital camera and began taking full shots and close-ups, focusing on the details of the clothing. Vintage, maybe early twentieth century.

The body had been dressed in a topcoat. Under that were a waistcoat and a white cotton shirt tucked into black wool trousers. Over the shirt, a pair of suspenders and a white silk scarf with a small design or insignia on it.

She took a Q-tip and wiped the surface of the shoe Dan had dropped. Patent leather. Didn't see that much anymore.

The pockets were empty.

She cut the pants away and unbuttoned the wool waistcoat.

White cotton tank top and briefs that stopped at the knee.

She cut through the underwear; the fabric crumbled under the scissors.

The body belonged to a male.

The clothing would have to be sent to a specialist

to prove authenticity, but Rachel was ninety percent sure she was looking at the real thing.

She cut the cotton undershirt, then carefully pulled aside the two sections of cloth.

The chest cavity had been opened at one time, either from an injury or an autopsy.

She brought the swing-arm light closer and picked up a magnifying glass. Leaning over the leathery corpse, she examined what had once been an outer layer of skin.

The edges were ragged, like torn paper. Some of the damage appeared to be fairly recent, the inner layer of skin lighter than the outer. But there was also evidence of old damage—areas of torn flesh and a broken rib cage from some long-ago trauma.

And the cavity where the heart should have been? Hollow.

Chapter 13

Rachel rang the doorbell, waited a few beats, then knocked. She heard something fall, then footsteps. The door flew open and Evan's voice came out of the darkness.

"Come on in."

She stepped inside and closed the door behind her. It was like entering a movie theater. She couldn't see a thing, and had to wait for her eyes to adjust.

A lamp clicked on, then another. Evan straightened, rubbing his head. He wore a white T-shirt and a pair of striped cotton pajama bottoms slung low on his hips. On his feet were black socks.

"I woke you."

He probably slept during the day. Her father had taken Graham to school, and she'd thought it would be a good time to talk to Evan.

"That's okay." His voice was sleep-slurred, and he seemed disoriented as he stood eyeing the rumpled couch where he must have been lying before she rang the bell. He bent and picked up a book from the floor, placing it on the end table. "I need caffeine."

Evan was already on his way to the adjoining

kitchen. Without looking back, he pointed toward an overstuffed chair. *Have a seat.*

She ignored his direction and followed him to the kitchen, putting her leather briefcase on a chair.

He filled a teakettle with water, and she went to the shelf where she'd seen Evan retrieve the coffee cups last time she'd been there. She grabbed two mugs and placed them on the table, then searched for tea in the cupboard next to the refrigerator. She found the ornate silver tin, opened it, and gave it a shake. "I see you haven't dumped this out yet."

Evan took the tin from her and replaced the lid. "Emergency rations." He put the container back in the cupboard and produced two tea bags from a small red box. "Haven't gotten my shipment from England yet."

"You know, I'll bet they have tea at the grocery store in Tuonela."

He smiled, unruffled by her teasing. "I'm not a tea snob." He paused to reconsider his words. "Well, maybe I am."

"There are worse things."

The kettle whistled. He turned off the flame, poured the steaming water, and sat down across from her.

"I came here to let you know another body was found, this time at City Park."

He looked up sharply. "Jesus."

While waiting for the tea to steep, she unzipped her leather briefcase and pulled out a digital print she'd made before leaving the office. "This body."

She passed the eight-by-ten to him. The photo

was one she'd taken before the autopsy, when the corpse was still dressed.

Evan studied the image. "At least we know he wasn't knocked off last night while out for his evening stroll."

"The heart was missing," she told him. "Normally I wouldn't think a missing heart so strange. Organs aren't always buried with the body, especially in cases of homicide or suspicious death."

"But . . ." He urged her to continue.

"The body is old. How old, I don't know. And while most of the damage to the chest cavity occurred years ago, some appeared fairly new."

Lost in thought, Evan got up from the table. He started to walk away, then seemed to remember his manners. "Back in a second." She heard him banging around in a room on the other side of the wall. Returning, he opened a manila folder, took out three yellowed newspaper clippings, and spread them on the table in front of her.

The articles described separate cases dealing with people who had dug up corpses they claimed were vampires in order to make and drink a protective broth made from the heart.

"Kinda like an inoculation, I guess." Rachel passed the newspaper back.

"It makes no difference if you believe the Bram Stoker version of Dracula," Evan said. "Vlad the Impaler existed. Countess Elizabeth Bathory existed. They drank blood. They bathed in it. Some people believe in vampires. And one way to keep yourself safe from a vampire is to drink a broth made from his heart."

"But where is the vampire? *Who* is the vampire? Who are they protecting themselves against? You? The Pale Immortals? Whoever killed Chelsea Gerber?"

"Hey, I'm just tossing out ideas here. I guess I'd rather be considered a vampire than your run-of-the-mill crazy." He slipped the clippings back into the folder. "Here's another thought. The heart of a vampire is sometimes removed and eaten in order to gain power."

"You mean by another vampire?"

"Or someone who fancies himself a vampire. I read about it in a book published in Romania in the eighteen hundreds. Some people also believe it will bring about immortality, or at least superhuman strength." He picked up the eight-by-ten Rachel had handed him earlier. "Do you have any more photos? Any close-ups?"

"I always take too many shots, but too many is better than too few." She dug into her case again, pulled out her folder, and passed it to him.

He let the folder fall open on the table and quickly glanced through the photos.

"What are you looking for?"

"This." He lifted out a five-by-seven and turned it around. A close-up of the white silk scarf. "See the insignia?"

He was talking about an embroidered design sewn with black and red thread on the edge of the fabric. "I thought that might be important. It almost looks like some kind of crest."

"Exactly." He seemed excited.

"Do you know what it is or who it might belong to?"

"No, but I'm fairly certain I've seen it before."

He shoved his chair back and got to his feet. "C'mon." He stuck the photos back in the folder, closed it, and tucked it under his arm. She double-checked to make sure she had her cell phone and pager, then followed him down the hallway to a large door stained a shade of deep brown. The varnish was thick and cracked, the doorknob glass.

An antique photo on the wall stopped her dead.

A woman lying in a zinc tub, one arm draped over the edge, her fingers trailing to the floor. She had long dark hair, some clipped on top of her head, some flowing and rippling around her shoulders. Behind her were two large narrow windows. Except for the tub and woman, the room was empty.

Victoria.

Rachel put a hand to her throat. "Where did you get this?"

"From an estate sale."

"An estate sale around here?"

"Lyndale's. Judge Lyndale was quite a collector. I'm not sure where the photo came from originally, or who the woman is. Nobody seemed to know its history, but I would guess it was taken somewhere in Juneau County in the early eighteen hundreds. Most of the judge's stuff was from the immediate area. Have you seen it before?"

"I don't think so," she answered vaguely, struggling to pull herself together. She was used to telling white lies.

"Maybe she's a relative of yours," Evan suggested.

A relative?

He shoved the door open with his shoulder. "It's just a woman taking a bath. Probably considered pretty racy for its time." He moved aside, and Rachel slipped past him, glad to leave the photo behind.

The space was one huge library in need of a librarian. It was part of the original house, with the same heavy woodwork and built-ins. The walls were painted a dark green that contrasted with orange sconces. An ornate cut-glass light hung from the center of the room. There were no windows.

"I didn't even know this room existed," she said. "I remember the door, but I always thought it was a closet." It was weird how you got certain things in your head when you were a kid, and it was hard to make your brain accept reality when you'd lived with a false notion for so long.

"My dad always hung out in here," Evan said. "He was interested in Old Tuonela before I was. He used to lock himself up for hours, going through articles and photos. It didn't look like this back then. I've accumulated so much . . . *stuff.*" He cast a glance around the room, then shook his head as if overwhelmed.

That must have been the time when people said his dad had gone a little bonkers from dealing with Evan's illness. Rachel was glad he was okay now.

"Have you ever thought about having someone come in to organize everything for you?"

"All the time, but I don't want to have to deal with somebody being in my house, and I'm also afraid I would never find anything again."

She could understand both of those concerns. She liked privacy, and didn't want somebody constantly around.

He plunged into the clutter. "I'm looking for a box of old newspaper articles, photos, and silver emulsion glass-plate negatives that were published by the *County Quill* in the eighteen hundreds. I bought the stuff when the *Quill* closed down and they auctioned everything. Someday I hope to get them cataloged with matching prints and negatives."

She cast a dismayed glance around the room at the stacks of books and magazines and newspapers. Most of the floor was covered, with only twisting paths leading through the dusty, leaning towers of chaos.

"Do you have any idea what the box looks like?"

He tossed the folder on top of a stack and surveyed the place. "I think it was gray. Or brown. About this size." He made a shape with his hands.

Fifteen by twelve?

"This deep."

Eight inches? "Okay." She moved forward, taking a long step to maneuver around several piles of newspapers. "One time in L.A. I was sent to a house where an elderly woman had died." She stopped and considered her path options in much the way of a mountain climber. "She was a hoarder, and had accumulated so much trash over the course of her life that we had to crawl over it with only about three feet between the top of the garbage and the ceiling."

"I'm not a hoarder. I'm a *collector*. This isn't trash; it's history."

"I'm just sayin'."

"That I'd better watch out?"

"Something like that."

"Hey, this could be it." Using both hands he pulled out a box. He would have made a lousy Jenga player. The stack collapsed, but he didn't seem to notice. He blew off the dust, wiped the box top with his arm, and set the lid aside. "Here we go." He glanced up, smiling. "Walked right to it. If somebody came here and organized this place, I would never have found it."

Sadly, he was probably right.

He found what he was looking for: a photograph of a man from the turn of the century, black-and-white, the edges curled. He handed it to her. "Look at the scarf."

The image was small, but it was the same embroidery as on the dried-up corpse's scarf.

"On the sale brochure, this was listed as a photo of the Pale Immortal," he said.

"How can you be sure it's him?"

"I can't. Not completely." He began searching the room again, this time heading straight for shelves that went from floor to ceiling, quickly pulling out a thick book. Bracing it against a stack on the floor, he lifted the leather-bound tome, finally settling on a page. "Manchester."

Rachel made her way to his side.

"It's the Manchester family crest," he said when she was near enough to see the black and red image.

It was identical to the design on the shriveled corpse's scarf.

They'd found the Pale Immortal. Only someone else had found him first.

Chapter 14

Graham stepped out of the school counselor's office.

What a waste of an hour. She'd spent a lot of time asking him if there was anything he wanted to talk about. When he kept saying no, she started on more direct questions, like how he felt about death and dying. And finally, "Do you still have thoughts about killing yourself?"

Who didn't? Who the hell didn't? Of course he said no.

"Are you a danger to yourself?" she probed.

He'd answered no to that question too, and he supposed it was the truth. Because right now he was in a holding pattern, waiting to see what would happen. You didn't think about killing yourself when you were waiting for your life to start. When you were thinking it might actually happen.

But don't hope, he warned himself. Hoping got you into trouble. You had to be prepared for the worst, then if the worst came it wasn't so bad. And if the worst didn't come, it was even better. It was like Christmas.

This is temporary. It will be gone soon, so don't start thinking this is your new life.

He went to his locker, dumped his books, and was heading for the cafeteria when he spotted Isobel through the huge windows that were really a glass wall around a courtyard. Kind of like the outdoor area in a prison, except this one had trees and landscaping. Isobel sat on a bench, head bent, concentrating on something in her hands. A few other kids were milling around not far away, talking and laughing.

Graham slipped through a heavy door, stopping a few feet from Isobel, hands in the front pockets of his jeans.

Click, click, click.

"Are you crocheting?" He used to know somebody who crocheted.

She glanced up, squinting against the sun. When she saw it was him, she immediately looked back down. "Knitting." She looped a piece of lime green yarn around a pink metal needle, then slid the top needle free.

Click, click, click.

The sound was hypnotic.

"The counselor's lame, isn't she?" Isobel said.

He plopped down on brown grass that was just beginning to show signs of turning green. He could smell the ground, and the sun felt good on his back. "You've been to her?"

"Twice. That was enough for me." She shrugged. "It was like Psych 101. Everybody falls into either this slot or that one."

He wanted to tell her he was sorry about the other day and the weird way he'd acted, but how did you bring up something like that? "Why were you seeing her?"

"My mom and stepdad are musicians. They travel all the time, so I get dumped on relatives and friends. Right now they're in Prague. Anyway, when I started school here last fall, they thought I should see a counselor to help me adjust."

"So who are you staying with now?"

"My cousin. She was away at college, but got mono and broke up with a boyfriend she'd had for four years, so she's living at our place, on the outskirts of town. They thought we'd be company for each other. Right. She doesn't leave the house. She just stays in bed all day, watching television, sleeping, or talking on the phone."

Here he'd thought Isobel probably had an apple-pie normal life.

"Are they in a band? Your folks?"

"Orchestra. It's kinda famous, ya know. It's called the Overland Symphony Orchestra."

He'd never heard of them, but he didn't know anything about that kind of music. He wanted to ask if she'd listened to the CD he'd given her, but didn't want to put her on the spot. And didn't want to know if she hadn't. Or if she'd hated it.

She resumed her knitting.

"What are you making?"

"A scarf."

He nodded. "Cool."

"Sometimes I make stocking caps, but I usually make scarves."

He watched for a little longer. He liked the sound and the movement and the color. "Could you—" He stopped.

"What?" She paused and looked up.

"Never mind."

"Tell me."

He squirmed inside, and wished he'd never started the question. But now he plunged forward. "Could you maybe teach me how to knit?"

"You're kidding, right?"

"No."

"So you can start a knitting club with Travis and that bunch?" she asked with a snort of sarcasm.

"I'm done with those guys. No, I just think knitting seems kinda cool. I'd like to try it."

Gripping the needles, she dropped both hands in her lap. Today she was wearing a black-and-white skirt and a black sweater with black knee boots. "Get some yarn and needles," she told him, "and I'll teach you. But don't buy little needles. You want something that will go fast to begin with; otherwise you'll get sick of it."

He smiled, leaned back on his elbows, and closed his eyes. Here was another of those moments. Those good moments. . . .

The bell rang and he realized he'd missed lunch.

His next class was biology. It went pretty fast, even though his stomach was growling and he was thirsty. After that was American history, another class he had with Isobel.

He sat a few desks behind her and to the right. Ten minutes into class the instructor set up the projector and turned out the lights so they could watch a film. Something about the Civil War.

The film was boring as hell. Graham had always suspected teachers showed those things so they could go into their little back offices and tinker around. Maybe play video games or pay bills.

The boredom was interrupted by the loudspeaker announcing an immediate assembly. The students were herded down the hall to the gym, where Principal Bonner stood at a microphone. She was a small woman who obviously liked red clothes and big gold jewelry. She hardly ever smiled, because being a principal was serious shit. And being a small woman who was also a principal was even more serious shit.

Graham and Isobel climbed to the top of the bleachers. From that vantage point, Graham spotted Chief Burton and Phillip Alba near the double doors.

"I know you've all had to deal with the loss of classmate Chelsea Gerber," the principal said. "So it comes with great regret that I must bring you more disquieting news." She drew in a breath. "Another serious crime has been committed in Tuonela. Early this morning a body was found in the park."

People looked at one another, fear in their faces. Some girls began to cry.

Bonner held up a hand for silence. "Fortunately

we didn't lose one of our own, but I'll let Chief Burton give you the details."

Burton crossed the gym and took the microphone. "The body found in City Park was most likely an incident of grave robbery."

That brought another gasp. Isobel looked at Graham, her eyes big. He glanced down at his shoes, then scanned the gym, spotting the Pale Immortals sitting in a row on the bottom bleachers, quiet and well behaved. Not far away, their backs to the wall, stood a group of teachers, their faces solemn.

"We think this latest case was perpetrated by someone with a sick sense of humor," Burton said. "Probably a prank—a cruel one, coming on the heels of the recent tragedy and heinous crime. We also feel it was done by kids. Maybe somebody at this very school. And kids like to brag. We want you to keep your eyes and ears open. If you hear anything suspicious, report it to Principal Bonner, to a teacher, to your parents, to the police."

He let his gaze pan the crowd from the top of the bleachers to the bottom. "We're here for you. We want you to be safe. We don't want anyone else hurt. Toward that end, we've put together phone numbers and safety guidelines for you to follow when you aren't at school. These will be passed out at the door as you leave the gym."

Some of the students glanced over their shoulders at Graham.

"What are they looking at me for?" he whispered to Isobel.

She leaned closer. "Because of your dad."

They thought Stroud had done it? *Oh, wow.*

But if Graham didn't know any better, he'd probably be thinking the same thing.

Chapter 15

Evan opened his laptop and clicked on the e-mail icon, his eyes quickly scanning the screen for important messages.

One was from the DNA lab.

His stomach dropped.

That was fast.

With labs springing up all over the country, it didn't take long to get results back, especially if the DNA wasn't related to a crime. Still, he was surprised to see the e-mail show up only seventy-two hours after he'd overnighted the samples.

His heart was hammering. He knew what the results would be. Now Graham would have proof. What would that do to him? To finally know that Evan wasn't his father?

He would be home from school in another hour. Should Evan tell him right away, or should he wait for the hard copy to arrive in the mail? That might be better, but Evan didn't like the idea of keeping the results a secret even for a few days. Graham had had enough secrets kept from him.

Evan took another deep breath—and opened the e-mail.

Test results: Match.

Evan read it again.

Match.

There had to be a mistake.

He grabbed the portable phone and dialed the lab's number. It took five minutes to get through to a real person, but it seemed like hours. Evan explained the situation, giving the woman on the other end his test number. "There has to be a mistake," he told her. "The samples had to have gotten mixed up."

"We test everything two times," she said patiently. She probably got a lot of calls like this. Irate fathers who were trying to get out of a paternity suit.

"Our test results are ninety-nine-point-eight percent accurate."

"Then I've somehow fallen into that two-tenths of one percent."

He suddenly remembered the second set of samples. In all of the confusion, he'd forgotten about it. *Whew.* At the time he'd thought he was being overly precautious. "You should have received another set of samples," he told the woman on the phone. "The processing number would have been one off."

"Hmm. I'll have to check on that and get back to you."

His laptop announced a new message.

From the Wisconsin DNA lab. He opened it. One word jumped out at him.

Match.

He stared at the screen.

How could that be? *How the fucking hell . . . ?*

"Hello? Hello?"

Staring at the wall, he lifted the receiver to his ear. "Thanks. I found what I was looking for." He disconnected.

In a daze he put the computer aside and got to his feet. His legs felt weak. Two seconds later he dropped back down on the couch.

How had this happened? Logically he knew girls could get pregnant even when a guy used protection. But when he wasn't the only guy, and it had been only once . . .

Lydia couldn't have really known he was the father. Her choosing the right guy must have been a coincidence. She'd just picked someone. He'd been a sperm donor. An accidental sperm donor, because he doubted she'd planned to get pregnant.

In his mind he saw Graham putting the pistol to his head, closing his eyes, and pulling the trigger. It was an image that had haunted Evan, but now it took on a whole new meaning.

How responsible was he for the despair that dwelled in Graham's young heart? But Evan himself had been a kid. Shortly before Lydia and her mother left town, he'd gotten sick. He'd put Lydia and what most people decided was a fraudulent pregnancy from his mind, not giving them another thought until Graham showed up at his door.

Evan couldn't absorb it. He simply couldn't absorb it.

Or make sense of it.

He had to move. He had to walk. Run. Get out of the house. He was suffocating.

He opened the front door; bright sunlight poured in. He slammed the door shut and pressed the fingers of both hands to his eyelids.

Trapped.

Over time he'd found ways to deal with his condition. He'd always been able to talk himself out of the panic that sometimes washed over him.

He paced back and forth, then strode to the library and searched through a large built-in bookcase until he finally found what he was looking for: bourbon.

He pulled off the stopper and sniffed the liquid, then took a swallow from the cut-glass decanter. Warmth slid down his throat to settle in his belly. He waited while that same warmth seeped into his bloodstream. He raised the container once more, paused, then slowly lowered it and put the stopper back in place. Bad idea. Graham would be home soon. He had to think about Graham and what he was going to say to him. What he said could resonate for years. For a lifetime. He had to get the words right.

Beyond the turmoil in his head he heard the front door slam. He returned the bourbon to the cupboard and left the library to find Graham standing in the middle of the living room.

He was staring at the laptop screen.

Finally he looked up. "It says 'match.'" He swallowed. "That means you're my father, right? Isn't that what it means?"

So much for easing him in gently. "Yeah."

"You really didn't know, did you?"

The length of half a room separated them, but Graham was picking up on Evan's bafflement.

"I thought you were trying to ditch responsibility, but you didn't even know."

Evan saw that Graham couldn't figure out how something like that could happen. Evan couldn't figure it out either. He was going to have to go from not having a son to talking to his son about sex. It was a big jump.

"Don't you know how babies are made?" Graham tossed his books on the couch. "I can explain it to you if you need some details."

Why, the kid was enjoying this! He was enjoying watching Evan squirm.

"Should we start with the male and female anatomy?"

"I can't go into this very deeply," Evan said. You didn't tell a kid his mother was a slut and had slept with half the guys in town.

"That's okay," Graham said. "I know what she was like when I was growing up. I can guess what she was like before I was born."

A perceptive kid. It made things easier.

Evan stared at Graham, remembering how he'd taken note of his light, curly hair and angular face. *He can't be my son*, he'd thought that first day. And now, *He is my son*.

Suddenly overcome with some emotion he'd never before experienced, Evan strode across the room, wrapped his arms around Graham, and hugged him.

Graham shoved him away and took three steps back. "What are you doing? Why are you hugging me? That's so hypocritical."

"How does hugging you make me a hypocrite?"

"You wouldn't have hugged me yesterday. When you didn't think I was your kid."

"That doesn't make me a hypocrite. I don't go around hugging people. If you brought over a friend, I wouldn't walk up and hug him."

Graham laughed sarcastically. "No, I guess not. And even if you'd known you were having a kid, would you have done anything differently? Really?"

Evan didn't know. "I wasn't much older than you are now. Think about that."

That got Graham's attention. He looked a little startled.

"This isn't going to be easy, but we'll get through it. We'll figure it out."

"So . . . what now?"

"I think you should continue to see the school counselor. Maybe twice a week if possible. At least for a while. I'll call and see what we can arrange. Maybe once a week we can both meet with her."

"No, I mean, what *now*? Am I staying?"

"No matter what happens, you'll always have a home here."

"No matter what happens? What will happen?"

"We have to find your mother. Legally she still has custody."

"But I'm sixteen."

"That doesn't matter." Evan paused. "Sixteen? I thought you were fifteen."

"I turned sixteen."

"When?"

"The ninth. The day after you sprang me outta jail."

Something else to feel guilty about . . .

After Graham was asleep, Evan went to the kitchen cupboard and pulled out the red box. Empty. What difference did tea from England make at a time like this? He had a son. A son he hadn't been aware of until recently.

Sick, confused and distracted, Evan prepared a cup of tea from the antique tin.

How could he have had a son all these years and never known it? How could he fix it? What did the future hold for Graham? And Lydia—where in the hell was Lydia?

He drank the tea.

When he was finished, he broke out in a sweat, his heart beating oddly in his chest. Had the shock been too much? Was he having a heart attack?

The room began to spin. He reached for the edge of the table, missed, and tumbled to the floor.

Consciousness slowly returned, and Evan found himself staring up at the ceiling, hyperaware of his body. He could feel blood pumping through his veins.

He rolled to his knees and staggered to his feet. Upright, he shrugged into his coat and left the house, plunging into the darkness of the streets, pulling the night air deep into his lungs.

One hundred years. Seventeen years. Death. Birth.

Rebirth . . .

He came upon a frat house that vibrated with music and light and loud voices. A girl drunkenly lunged out the front door.

"Kristin!" another girl shouted after her from inside.

Kristin waved her away with a floppy hand, stumbled and weaved ten feet, then fell forward on the ground. She spotted Evan in the shadows and started to smile, then stopped. "Hey. You're that guy." She pointed. "The vampire."

Alcohol and drugs took over, and she passed out.

Evan's ears picked up sounds. Voices and shuffling feet.

Coming toward him on the sidewalk was a group of kids—teenage males dressed in black clothes, their boots unlaced and dragging over the cement. As they drew closer there was a moment of mutual recognition. The Pale Immortals.

Chapter 16

Pain jerked Kristin March into unconsciousness, and she screamed.

"Shut her up! Shut her up!"

She sucked in air to scream again. Something was jammed in her mouth. Fabric. Rotten, stinking fabric.

"Screaming's not cool," said another voice.

"Nobody can hear her here."

The sharp pain in her wrist that woke her up now gave way to warmth.

Drip, drip, drip.

"Don't miss any."

Her head felt swollen; her arms were heavy, dead-weights. She tried to raise a hand to her face, but couldn't. Her fingers felt thick and fat as sausages.

Moving. Things were moving. Sick. She felt sick. But the fabric . . . stuffed in her mouth. What would happen if she vomited?

Swaying. Turning.

She opened her eyes.

Flickering lights. *Candles.* Dark shapes of people. She blinked. And blinked again. Things were messed up. Things weren't right. Everything was upside down.

Someone touched her. That started the swaying motion again. *She* was upside down. That's why her head and arms felt so heavy.

The last thing she remembered was being at a party. She'd done a keg stand. She was the queen of keg stands. Wasted. Staggered outside for some fresh air. She remembered seeing that guy. That vampire freak, Evan Stroud . . .

Now this.

Sleepy.

Getting sleepy. Couldn't keep her eyes open.

"Don't let her bleed out," one of the voices said. "We want to keep her alive, at least for a while."

Keep her alive. At least for a while.

Above her something creaked and groaned.

More from the disembodied voices: "How much do you have?"

Who was that? Somebody she knew?

"The bowl is almost full. Eight, ten ounces anyway."

"That's enough for now."

Fingers on her arm. Something wrapped around her wrist. Then they moved away.

Must be a dream . . . had to be a dream . . . bad weed. She'd always heard bad weed could make you see crazy shit. . . . Bad weed laced with something. Poison or something. Or a roofie. Maybe somebody slipped her a roofie. . . .

Open your eyes, Kristin.

Was that her voice? Didn't sound like her voice.

Open your eyes.

She forced her eyes open. She was so fucked up, so tired, and everything was upside down and dark. But she could see them. Standing in a cluster, drinking from a bowl.

Drugs and alcohol made you stupid. That's what her mama was always saying. Kristin finally believed it. Because it wasn't until that second that she put it all together. That she realized the buncha funky-assed white boys were drinking her blood. And wiping it on their faces and bare chests. The Pale Immortals, that's who they were.

Someone else showed up, but he was behind her, out of her field of vision. She could tell by his voice that he was an adult and the boss. He was angry about something. He lifted her arm, her wrist, and began sucking. . . .

Wake up, girl.
Kristin slowly came around.
Creak, creak, creak.
She opened her eyes.
Dark.
She listened, but all she heard was the creaking overhead.
They were gone.
With a burst of adrenaline, pissed and scared, she bucked and twisted.
Something cracked and gave. A second later she hit the floor, smacking her head, landing hard, the wind knocked out of her.
She recovered quickly and didn't waste any time.

The sound of the breaking beam would bring on the crazies, if any crazies were close. She tugged the fabric from her mouth—a sock—and untied the rope from her ankles. She didn't wait for shit. She just ran.

And she could run like hell.

Seymour Burton pulled into the hospital parking lot, cut the engine, and entered the building through the main doors. He'd gotten a call about a girl named Kristin March found wandering barefoot and half naked along the old highway outside Tuonela in the predawn hours by a farmer up early to check on his calving heifers. Seymour had already looked the girl up and found she'd been arrested a couple of times for underage drinking. Not a big offense, as far as Seymour was concerned, but drinking often led to other things kids that age weren't mature enough to handle.

Seymour met with the victim's doctor first. Best to have pertinent details going in.

"She's had a concussion," Dr. Ruth Ellison said when Seymour caught up with her in the doctors' lounge. The only people in the room, they sat across from each other, Dr. Ellison taking the chance to eat a bagel and drink some coffee. Behind Seymour, the soda machine kicked on.

"She can't remember much of anything between doing a keg stand and the farmer pulling up beside her in his truck and asking if she needed a ride. Upon arrival in the ER, she had a blood-alcohol level of point-oh-five. Says she was drinking before ten o'clock last night, so she was probably well over the limit at one time. The concussion alone could explain the loss of memory. A concussion along with drinking? Double whammy."

"Think she was slipped something?"

"You mean a date-rape drug? Very possibly. We're running more tests."

"The person who called me said her feet were a mess."

"Judging by their condition, I'd say she walked miles."

So she could have been anywhere. "And her wrist?"

"Ten stitches. One thing you should know about Kristin is that she's tried to kill herself a few times. Been under psychiatric care off and on. Antidepressants right now." Dr. Ellison sighed and looked at her coffee. "Kids have a lot to deal with these days."

"Any sign of rape?"

"No bruising, but we ran a rape kit on her anyway."

Seymour nodded. "So what's your medical opinion?"

"Attempted suicide."

"How does that explain showing up in the middle of nowhere?"

"She could have easily walked that far from the party. She was found three miles from Tuonela."

"Antidepressants have been linked to suicide in teens. Mix that with alcohol . . ."

With no evidence of rape, it made sense. And yet, another girl the same age as Kristin had been murdered and drained of blood . . . .

Seymour thanked the doctor, then went to meet Kristin. Her parents hovered anxiously nearby, looking sick, glancing at each other, brows furrowed.

Kristin was holding court, sitting up in bed, pillows behind her. Seymour got the idea she was enjoying the attention.

Now that they were face-to-face, Seymour remembered seeing her picture in the paper. She was a pretty girl with strong features. "You're the track star," he said. "What do you run?"

Kristin smiled and relaxed. "Fifty and one-hundred-yard dash."

"No relays?"

She shook her head. "Could never get the hang of passing the baton."

"I used to run distance," Seymour said. "And high jump."

She looked surprised.

"Believe it or not, they had a high jump when I was in school."

They all laughed, at ease now.

Seymour worked his way around to Kristin's ordeal. "Do you remember anything?"

"Just being at the party . . . I remember going outside. I got sick." She shot her parents a guilty glance. "I think there was a guy there. Yeah, there was. But I can't remember who."

"A guy? Someone your age?"

"An adult." She struggled to recall the incident. "I almost think he was around later . . . somewhere . . . ." She gave up. "Sorry."

"That's okay. Mind if I see your injuries?"

She held out her wrist. It was bandaged. "Ten stitches." Near the white bandages were a couple of bruises. Small. Round. About the size of someone's fingertips.

"Did you have these before?" Seymour asked.

She shook her head.

"What about your feet?"

Gingerly she slipped her feet from under the sheets. They were swathed in bandages. But it wasn't her feet that drew Seymour's attention. It was the rope burns on her ankles. He'd seen those rope burns before. On the body of Chelsea Gerber.

Chapter 17

Graham stared at his knitting needles with the intensity of a mind reader. Isobel had taught him to cast on, and now he was doing the real thing. He'd produced an inch of knit red yarn so far—soon to be a scarf. The small scrap had some holes in it, but Isobel had assured him that was normal for a first-timer.

"Do you think Ouija boards are real?" Isobel asked, not looking up from her knitting.

Graham couldn't knit and talk at the same time. He paused, needles in his hands. "I think it's a subconscious thing."

"But one time I used a Ouija board and asked it a bunch of things the person with me didn't know."

"But *you* knew."

"I wasn't doing it!"

"You didn't think you were. That's how the subconscious works."

They were sitting in the school's enclosed outdoor area, which had turned into their noon spot. Isobel sat on the cement bench; Graham was on the ground, legs crossed, shoulders hunched over his knitting. Even though it was almost seventy degrees, he was wearing a blue-and-gray-striped stocking cap Isobel had made and given to him.

He planned to have nothing more to do with the Pale Immortals. What they'd done was wrong, but they hadn't killed anybody, and he wasn't going to turn them in. He just wasn't going to hang out with them.

Life was good. It had been only four days since Stroud had gotten word of the DNA match, but already Graham wasn't looking over his shoulder as often. He wasn't constantly thinking some trickster was going to pull the rug out from under him.

He walked to school by himself, just like anybody else. He walked home, sometimes hanging around and talking to Isobel for ten or fifteen minutes after the last bell.

Except for his two visits with the counselor and one with Social Services, his week had been perfect. The counselor had to dredge up old shit Graham didn't want to talk about, like his life before coming here, and his relationship with his mother. The social worker had been more interested in the Evan part of his life. She'd wondered if Evan's disease and inability to leave the house would eventually make Graham feel resentful. She asked about his unusual lifestyle. She wanted to know if Evan slept during the day and was awake at night.

"It's the only way he can go outside," Graham had said with a shrug.

"Won't that become a problem for you? How can he take care of you if he's always asleep when you're awake?"

"I can take care of myself." Didn't she get it? Didn't she know his life was more normal now than it had ever been? Even if his biological father was considered a freak by half the town?

"Isobel."

They both looked up to see Phillip Alba looming over them, hands in the pockets of his brown corduroy pants. He was dressed in a black sweater, his hair wavy and dark.

"Don't forget play practice tonight," he said.

Two days ago Isobel had talked Graham into coming to play practice with her. Just to hang out, she'd said. But it ended up that they'd needed help with the set construction, so he found himself agreeing to lend a hand. Now he was part of the play crew.

"I won't." Isobel had stopped knitting to stare up at Alba with open admiration. It was obvious she had a crush on the guy, and Graham wondered if the sick feeling in his belly was jealousy.

"Just making sure." Alba flashed her a smile. He pulled his hand from his pocket, pointed, and addressed Graham. "Nice to have you with us." Then he left.

"Some people think the Ouija board is the tool of the devil," Isobel said, back to her knitting. The scarf she was making was purple.

Distracted, Graham watched Alba as he made his way through the enclosed courtyard. "I'm not sure I believe in the devil."

"You don't think people are evil?"

Oh, he *knew* people were evil. No question about

that. "I just don't think there's some red guy with a tail and horns running around."

Her needles stopped clicking. She looked up at him and laughed.

"So what do you think Tuonela's new name should be?" Isobel asked.

"You know it will be something nonthreatening."

"I like Shadow Falls."

"They'll never name it Shadow Falls. Too dark. Too spooky. The whole thing is stupid. You can't change something by changing the name."

The bell rang and they gathered everything up. "Stitch and bitch is over," Isobel announced with a laugh. She always said that, and she always laughed. He hadn't understood why it was so funny until she explained that knitting was something old ladies usually did.

"See you in American history." Graham jumped to his feet.

The rest of the day went quickly. When school let out Graham walked home, planning to head to the theater that evening for play practice.

The sun was low in the sky, and the day had cooled off so that the air was actually cold, and Graham was glad for the stocking cap. His mind drifted, and he had a slight smile on his face as he thought about Isobel.

Behind him a vehicle took the corner and headed in his direction. When it was almost even with him, it slowed, keeping pace. He looked, half expecting to see Rachel Burton, or maybe even Travis and his buddies.

It was a car he recognized, with his mother behind the wheel.

He froze; then his brain kicked in.

Run!

His leg muscles tensed. He pivoted and ran.

Sprinting through a yard. Slipping between houses, skidding down a hill.

She's coming!

He knew she was coming. No matter how fast he ran.

As he moved he dug into the front pocket of his jeans, his fingers coming in contact with the house key. His lungs were raw as he vaulted over the iron fence around his dad's yard. He sprinted up the sidewalk, taking the porch steps three at a time.

At the door his hand shook as he struggled to get the key in the hole. He finally made it, turned the key, and fell inside the living room, slamming and locking the door behind him.

A minute later the front door shuddered with ferocious, angry pounding. "Open up!" came his mother's voice. "I know you're in there!"

Evan, who had been sleeping, flew out of his bedroom. "What the . . . ?"

"It's my mother!"

Terror. She would make him leave. She would make him go back with her.

Evan moved toward the door.

"No! Don't open it! You can't open it!"

Evan opened the door and stepped back to avoid the sunlight.

Graham ran to the bedroom.

While Evan was trying to figure out what the hell was going on, Lydia charged into the living room, blinking at the darkness.

"Shut the door," Evan said.

She backtracked and slammed it. "Where's Graham?"

"I think you and I need to talk."

"I came to get Graham. I have no interest in talking to you."

She'd aged at least twenty-five years since he'd last seen her. She smelled like stale cigarette smoke. Her hair was shoulder-length, a curly medium brown with quite a bit of gray.

He had to keep reminding himself that this was the girl he'd known in high school, even though she looked nothing like the slim, beautiful, sexy Lydia.

"Let's talk about this."

"Talk about it?" She let out a harsh laugh. "Like you wanted to talk about it years ago? You have no right to discuss anything about Graham. Have you supported him in any way these past sixteen years? Have you even acknowledged his existence? No. He is my son, and only my son."

Something crashed in the other room.

Lydia turned to the sound, then marched to Graham's bedroom and forced open the door. "Get your things. We're leaving. Now!"

"No!"

Graham was lying on the bed, clutching a pillow, one knee drawn up to his chest, his eyes huge and glassy.

One thing was apparent: He was terrified of his own mother.

And with a realization that practically brought Evan to his knees, he knew Lydia was right: He had no legal hold over his son.

"We are going."

Graham could no longer defy a direct command. He scrambled from the bed and began to blindly gather his belongings, stuffing them into his large backpack.

"That's enough," Lydia said. "Let's get out of here. Right *now*."

Lydia led the way, both of them walking down the hallway. Graham didn't look at Evan.

She opened the door.

Evan moved fast. In a few strides he caught up with her and slammed the door closed before she could exit.

She did a double take, then struggled unsuccessfully to make her face expressionless. "What are you doing?" Unable to hide her fear, she lifted a hand to her throat.

"Graham isn't leaving here," Evan said, his voice quiet and low and threatening.

Chapter 18

Police chief Seymour Burton pulled the search warrant from his jacket and knocked on the front door of the one-story ranch-style home with yellow aluminum siding and white trim. When no one answered after a repeated series of knocks, Seymour stepped back and let his boys smash the lock on the hollow wooden door.

"Somebody go around the back. Make sure he doesn't try to get out that way."

Even though there was surely a special place in hell for child molesters and child pornographers, Seymour wanted to make sure Ed Wilson II would be able to visit a special place in prison first. They'd been watching him for months and had finally gathered enough evidence for a search warrant.

Seymour pulled out his Smith & Wesson, pushed open the door, and slipped inside. It smelled like cat shit, grease, and body odor. Like some old guy who hadn't bathed in a year and never did his laundry. Guess he had more important things to do.

The plastic shades were pulled down tight, and even though it was still light outside, the house was dark. Seymour shouted into the darkness, announcing their purpose.

Nobody answered. The house was silent.

Seymour nodded for the young cop named Abernathy to go past him. It didn't take long to determine that no one was upstairs. A quick scan of the basement revealed the same thing.

Abernathy opened a door that led outside.

"Nobody here," the other cop said, joining them in the basement.

Seymour silently cursed his decision to make a daylight raid. But they'd been tracking Wilson's habits, and it had seemed the best time to catch him at home.

In one corner of the basement was a bondage setup, with chains and black leather cuffs hanging from the ceiling. Nearby was a desk with a computer.

"Pack up the computer," Seymour said.

He snapped on a pair of latex gloves and opened a drawer. It was stuffed with photos: some five-by-sevens, but mainly eight-by-tens. All in color. Hundreds. Seymour went through them. All young nude boys.

He shuffled through the photos, looking for any faces that might be familiar. He found one.

Damn.

His cell phone rang.

It was Evan Stroud. He sounded a little wound up.

"Graham's mother is here," Evan said. "At my house. She wants to take Graham back to Arizona. Is there any way I can keep him in Tuonela? Somebody I can contact? Somebody who can help?"

Seymour stared at the photo in his hand, a full-frontal nude of Graham Yates. "Don't let him leave your house. I'll be there in less than an hour. I think there's a way we can keep him around for at least a few more days."

Seymour remained at the yellow house long enough to make sure evidence was being gathered correctly. Then he headed for Evan's, lighting a cigarette as soon as he got in the car. Once he was parked outside Evan's house, he finished his smoke, crushed out the butt in the ashtray, and grabbed the manila folder off the seat.

He was never sure why he'd become a cop. He hadn't been into authority. And he wasn't an excitement junkie. And he certainly didn't like giving people bad news or making them uncomfortable.

He took a deep breath and walked up the wooden steps to the front door. Evan must have heard him arrive. Before he could knock, the door opened.

The sun was down past the horizon, but the sky was still light. Seymour stepped inside and closed the door behind him.

The air was electric, saturated with tension and anger and fear. His own home life with his wife and daughter had been calm. There had never been much drama.

Seymour had always liked Evan. Now, seeing him with a new kind of desperation in his eyes, Seymour felt sorry for him.

He turned to the other person in the room. "You

must be Lydia Yates." Seymour held out his hand, and the woman reluctantly took it.

He remembered her. In trouble a lot. One of those girls who was always in heat, his mother would have said. Seymour had been a patrol officer then, and he'd caught her having sex on more than one occasion. At that time she'd seemed to have cast a spell over most of the boys her age. Looking at her now, he doubted she'd cast any spells in a long time.

"I don't know what this is about." Lydia dropped his hand and got back to her problem. "I came here to get my son. And now this asshole refuses to let me leave with him."

"I'd like to talk to Graham in private," Seymour told the two adults.

Evan motioned toward the hallway. "He's in the bedroom on the left."

Seymour walked down the hall. The door was ajar. He pushed it open, then closed it tightly behind him.

Graham sat on the edge of the bed, both feet on the floor, his fists between his knees. He gave Seymour a slight nod, then looked back down.

He wasn't crying right now, but he had been.

Seymour pulled a straight chair from a nearby desk, turning it around so he faced Graham. "I hear your mom is here to take you back with her."

Graham nodded.

"Do you want to go?"

Graham shook his head.

"That's what I thought."

Graham looked up. A minute ago his eyes had

been flat and dead. Now they held a spark of hope that didn't make Seymour's job any easier.

"Can I stay?" His voice was thick.

"I have a way for us to delay things. Long enough to get a judge in here to look at your case. Find a way for you to stay here at least part of the time."

"He's my dad. The DNA tests came back, and he's really my dad. That should help, shouldn't it?"

"I would think so."

But kids usually went to the mothers. That's just the way it was. And it wasn't as if Evan had had anything to do with Graham up to this point. Plus, with Evan's illness . . . the situation didn't look good.

Seymour opened the folder. "We just raided a house on Fifth Avenue, where I found this." He pulled out an eight-by-ten color photo.

Blood drained from Graham's face and he turned a pasty white. He broke out in a sheen of sweat, and his eyes began to roll.

Seymour jumped to his feet. "Put your head down."

The kid wasn't hearing anything; Seymour pressed Graham's head down until his body quit shaking and his breathing became a little more normal. Then Graham slowly sat up and wiped his face with the hem of his long-sleeved T-shirt.

"Do you want to tell me how this happened?" Seymour asked quietly, returning to his seat.

"I was broke. I was hungry. I ran into some kids who said a guy would pay me a hundred bucks for some photos."

"Who were the kids who told you this?" Seymour

pulled a small notebook from the breast pocket of his shirt and flipped through the pages until he came to a blank one.

"I don't know who they were. Just some kids."

"What did they look like?"

"I dunno. Guys. About my age. It was dark. I only saw them a little while. I don't remember."

Seymour didn't believe him, but he would let it go for now.

He'd spent a lot of time—years, actually—wondering why so many of today's kids were so messed up. Being a cop, he'd run into a lot of them who had no moral compass. Young sociopaths. But the percentage of young sociopaths had taken a huge leap over the past twenty years.

It was bad, really bad. And he was afraid there was no fixing it, because you couldn't go back. Right now it was cool to be shallow and ironic and heartless. But Graham wasn't like that. Somehow he'd managed to cling to some good part of himself.

"So you went to this guy's house, and he took pictures of you," Seymour said. "Did anything else happen?"

"What do you mean?"

Young girls never liked to admit to being raped, but boys were worse. They rarely offered the information without being coaxed. "Were you sexually molested?" Seymour asked.

"No!"

"Graham?" Seymour prodded, keeping his voice low and matter-of-fact.

Graham looked up. "I wasn't. I swear. Oh, he

wanted to. He told me he wouldn't pay unless I had sex with him. So I left. Without any money."

Seymour believed him.

"So now what?" Graham asked.

"We need to go down to the police station and file a report. Then we'll have to take your deposition."

That was the part of the process Seymour hoped to drag out so Graham would be forced to stay in town. "Sometimes it can take a little while to get that all set up. Have to find a stenographer and such."

Mary Pelton lived in town, and she was always eager for more work, but Seymour would just forget to call her for a day or two.

"Do you need to put me in jail? 'Cause if you do, I'm cool with that. I don't mind."

The kid would rather go to jail than be sent home with his mother. Seymour closed his small notebook and slid it back into his pocket. "You won't need to go to jail, but we'll have to get the judge's permission for you to remain here until the deposition."

Graham nodded.

"Right now we have to tell the two people out there what's going on, and why you can't leave town."

Graham went pale again. He swallowed. "Do they have to see the picture? I don't want them to see it."

Seymour got to his feet and slipped the photo back in the folder. "We should be able to avoid that."

The news wasn't taken well. Lydia screamed and said that kind of sick activity was exactly why she needed to get her son out of town immediately. Evan went whiter than his normal shade of pale. And even though Evan had hardly known Graham at the time of the photo shoot, Seymour could see he was feeling in some way responsible.

"Kids make choices," Seymour said. "Not always good ones. This was bad, but not nearly as bad as it could have been. And now, with Graham's help, we'll hopefully be able to lock this guy up for a long time."

"What are we supposed to do while we're waiting?" Lydia demanded. "I can't afford a motel."

"They can put you up downtown in the YWCA," Seymour said. "Tell 'em I sent you. Graham will have to stay here. Women only at the W."

She could see she wasn't going to win.

Seymour didn't like the thought of her hanging around town causing trouble, but there wasn't much they could do about that.

Chapter 19

For two days, Chief Seymour Burton used delay tactics until he couldn't use them anymore. Even though they'd been able to track down several other kids who'd been photographed by Wilson, they needed to get Graham's deposition.

Wilson himself was in jail after an anonymous tip led police to the river shanty where he was hiding.

Once the deposition was taken, the only thing left was for Graham's case to be reviewed. A Wisconsin judge couldn't officiate, since Graham and his mother were residents of Arizona, but Seymour was using the excuse that someone local had to decide whether or not the mother was responsible enough to take her son back with her to Arizona.

In the meantime, Lydia was staying at the YWCA and Graham was continuing to go to school, once again with an escort to and from, since it was highly likely his mother would simply pick him up and drive off.

Which was going to happen anyway, Seymour was afraid. They had no reason to keep him out of her custody. Once he was back in Arizona, Graham could seek out a lawyer and try for emancipation.

And Lydia wasn't lounging around, taking a vacation. She'd contacted the local paper, and they'd already run a story on her, making Evan Stroud and the Tuonela Police Department look evil. She was in communication with the state attorney and Arizona and Wisconsin child welfare offices, as well as the judge who would be reviewing her case. Seymour was afraid his delaying tactics had been exercises in futility, and given poor Graham hope where there wasn't any.

And Kristin March? No new evidence. No return of the girl's memory.

Seymour's phone rang.

It was the DNA lab from Madison.

"Got some interesting information for you," Kent, the lab technician on the other end, said. Kent was a friend of Seymour's, and worked at both the state forensic lab and private DNA lab.

Seymour sat up straighter, tucked his cigarette into the ashtray on his desk, and pulled a pad and pen close.

"You know how you asked me to keep an eye on those DNA samples?" Kent asked. "The ones sent to the lab for the paternity test? Listen to this. They matched the forensic samples collected at the Chelsea Gerber crime scene."

Seymour's heart did a little gallop. "Are you sure?"

"Yep. I'll send you a fax in just a minute."

Seymour thanked him and hung up. Jesus. He'd

only asked Kent to keep an eye on them so that they could unequivocally rule out Evan Stroud as a suspect.

Rachel's cell phone rang.

"We got a DNA match on the Gerber girl," her dad said when she answered.

His voice sounded odd. Strained. "Are you okay?"

He let out a deep sigh. "One of the specimens you sent in matched a DNA sample belonging to Evan Stroud."

She shut off the kitchen faucet and dropped into a nearby chair. She suddenly felt weak, and thought she might pass out. "There has to be some kind of mistake."

"I gave Evan two test kits. They both matched. I'm trying to track down the judge right now so I can get an arrest warrant. Heard he was out fishing, so it could take a while. . . ."

Arrest? Of course they would arrest Evan.

Where would they keep him? How would they get him to the jail? In the daylight? And beyond that . . . ?

A trial. Prison. He couldn't live through it.

"I'm sorry," Seymour said. "I know he's your friend. I know how hard this must be for you to hear."

Rachel didn't even know what she said, or if her reply made sense. As soon as they disconnected, she grabbed her keys and hurried downstairs to her van.

Ten minutes later she was pounding on the front door of Evan's house. When he answered, she stepped inside, slammed the door, and locked it. "We have to get you out of here."

"Hmm?" He was sleep-rumpled and groggy.

"The DNA samples you sent in for the paternity test? Matched samples collected from the Chelsea Gerber crime scene."

That woke him up. "Impossible."

"That's what I said, but that won't stop them from coming to arrest you."

"I have no reason to run." He looked baffled. "I haven't done anything."

"Think about it, Evan."

If he'd been anyone else—if he'd been someone in normal health—it would have been different. "They'll cart you away—in broad daylight. They'll put you in a cell with bright fluorescent light. Maybe even natural light. You won't live long enough to prove you're innocent. And it's not as if you're the most popular guy in town."

He stared at her for a long moment while her words sank in.

"You know how the legal system works," she went on. "You know how suspects are treated. Especially suspects who look damn guilty of murdering a young girl."

"Why do you think I'm innocent?" he asked. "I mean, if they have a DNA match. . . . That's considered irrefutable by some."

"DNA isn't the answer to every case. It's not the Holy Grail, even though it's been treated as such for the past several years." She was a coroner, an ME. She worked with facts, so she could hardly add that her gut was telling her he was no murderer. Or was it her heart?

They had to hurry. They could chitchat later. "I'll pull the van around to the side door and pick you up," she said.

"Where will we go?" She could see that the idea of leaving his comfort zone was sending him into a panic. "This won't work. I have no place to hide. And what about Graham?"

"We'll deal with Graham later. Right now we have to get you out of here. I'll take you someplace they hopefully won't think of looking."

"Where?"

"The morgue."

Her van wasn't exactly a vehicle of stealth, but at least it had been parked on the street in front of Evan's house quite a bit lately. There should be nothing unusual about today's visit.

The driveway sloped into a hollow, then leveled out to meet a low sidewalk that ran around to the back of the house. Evan owned the adjoining lots, which were woodland, and the layout created a secluded buffer zone; no one could see them from the road or from any nearby homes.

She drove up on the sidewalk, pulled the emergency brake, jumped out, and opened the van's heavy back doors. It was an industrial vehicle; the only windows were in front. The two seats were separated by a mandatory metal cage meant to keep cargo from flying into the passenger area.

She climbed in the back, snapped open a plastic body bag, and spread it out on the gurney, unfastening the zipper from top to bottom. Once everything was prepared, she returned to the house to get Evan. At the last minute he grabbed the antique tea tin and shoved it in his coat pocket.

He was bringing *tea*?

With a dark blanket draped over his head, he shot from the house and leaped into the back of the van. Rachel followed, shutting the door behind them.

"Lie down on the gurney."

Crouching, he pivoted in the small space, the blanket brushing the knees of his jeans.

"Here." She grabbed his arm and urged him down. Light poured in from the front; they had to hurry.

Grasping her plan, he quickly settled himself on the gurney. She zipped the heavy bag, leaving a gap of an inch near the top for air. "All tucked in."

"Snug as a bug." His words were light, but she could hear the underlying panic.

She slipped out the back, secured the van door, and locked the house. Once in the driver's seat she disengaged the emergency brake, threw the van in gear, and made a three-point turn. Then it was up the hill to the street, take a right, and haul ass to her place.

On the way there, she had a few minutes to think about what she was doing.

Aiding and abetting a murder suspect.

She hit three red lights and saw three people she knew. They all waved; she waved back. In order to avoid more people, stop signs, and traffic, she cut down the alley and followed it for five blocks, then pulled into the driveway and parking area of the morgue.

The sun was shining brightly, and there wasn't an inch of shade. She turned off the ignition and hurried to the back of the van.

Inside the darkness of the body bag Evan heard the van's doors open. He felt the gurney being dragged forward. Wheels snapped and locked into place. Sunlight pounded down from above, heating the plastic. He blinked; a beam found its way through the small airhole and pierced his retina.

He moaned and squeezed his eyes shut. The world swirled and slanted, the wheels beneath him turning.

In the blackness, sound and movement were his only grounding.

They paused. A door opened; then they were moving forward again, away from the heat of the sun into the shelter of a building.

The wheels rolled smoothly and silently over carpet; speed was impossible to gauge.

He chanced a look. Twin fluorescent bulbs burned into his brain. He quickly closed his eyes

The gurney stopped. "Evan?"

He ran a tongue over his lips, and was preparing

to answer when he heard a *ding*, followed by what sounded like an elevator door opening.

Someone screamed. "You scared the hell out of me!" came a woman's voice that didn't belong to Rachel.

"Sorry," Rachel said. "I forgot you were cleaning today."

"I didn't know you were in the building."

"Gotta get this one to the cooler. He's rotting as we speak."

"Autopsy?"

Rachel didn't answer; Evan presumed she nodded.

"Let me know if you want me to clean up the suite when you're done."

He was rolled forward; then a door rattled shut and the elevator began to move.

"That was Patricia," Rachel whispered, her voice close. "She cleans once a week. Guess we could have really scared the crap out of her if you'd moved."

He wanted to smile, but pain ripped through his spinning head.

"I'm taking you to the basement."

The elevator shuddered to a stop. They moved forward. Wheels clacked over cement, then tile, through swinging doors to come to what he hoped was the final destination.

Rachel unzipped the bag two feet, pulling back the sides to expose his face. Evan didn't like people seeing him when he was in the middle of an attack, and here she was, staring.

"Evan?"

She sounded scared. She probably thought he was dead. He could look like a corpse at times like these. That was the trick: to remain as still as possible.

Don't move. Don't breathe.

Then maybe the nausea wouldn't be as bad, and maybe the weakness wouldn't last as long.

"Evan?"

He struggled to open his eyes. Just to let her know he was still kicking. His eyelids fluttered, but he couldn't focus.

He heard her exhale in relief.

Parallel fluorescent tubes flickered. He groaned, squeezed his eyes closed, and felt himself go a shade paler.

She unzipped the body bag the rest of the way.

Evan didn't move.

She leaned over him. So quiet. Then he suddenly felt something brush against his jaw.

"Evan?"

"Why are you doing this?" His voice was a croak. "You could be arrested. You could go to prison."

She touched him again. "I'm helping a friend."

"As soon as it's dark, I'm out of here." He could do it. He could recharge as long as he didn't move.

"I'm sorry. I tried to keep the sun from hitting you."

Don't cry. I'm not dying. I'm not dead.

"You look dead." He felt her touch the back of his hand. He felt her fingers slide under his. "Your skin is like ice."

"I'll . . . be o-kay."

"What can I do?"

Just leave. Just leave me alone.

"Go a-way."

He felt her recoil and immediately regretted his choice of words. And what was that? In her eyes? Fear and self-doubt.

Chapter 20

When no one answered the door, Seymour gave the signal for the accompanying officers to break into Evan Stroud's home.

Inside they quickly searched the rooms, guns drawn, but the house was empty. The time between the call from the DNA lab and the warrant had been a little under three hours.

"I didn't think he could go out during the day," one of the officers said. He was young and blond and so healthy he gave off a glow. A nice kid, Seymour had always thought.

"Check the garage," Seymour said. One of the officers disappeared.

"Are you sure he isn't sleeping in a coffin in the basement?" another officer asked with a laugh.

They may have been joking around, but Seymour could tell they were spooked.

It wasn't much past noon, but the house was dark as a tomb. Upton, the young blond officer, went around turning on lights but it didn't help much. The bulbs were weak.

The officer who'd disappeared returned. "Car's in

the garage," he said breathlessly. "Maybe he has a secret compartment." He started going around the room, knocking on walls. "You know, like in the wall or something. Or a space under the floor some-where."

Seymour frowned. What a dumb-ass idea.

"Should we open the curtains?" Upton asked.

Seymour nodded, then brought a fist to his mouth, stifling a cough. His hand automatically reached for his pack of smokes, but he stopped him-self. Couldn't smoke here.

He wanted to go out on the porch and light up, but he didn't want to leave these guys alone.

Upton fumbled behind the heavy black drapes, looking for a cord. He finally gave up and tugged the dark fabric open by hand. All of them momentar-ily shielded their eyes as sunlight poured in the pic-ture window.

The intrusion of light robbed the room of mystery. Dust particles drifted in the shafts that cut sharply to the wooden floor and thick Oriental rug. The light invaded and exposed areas that had spent years hid-den and unswept.

Just a crazy bachelor's house.

Seymour knew how easy it was to let things go when nobody stopped by. And if you couldn't even *see* the layers of dust . . . what did it really matter?

He would have been content to wallow in his own filth if Rachel hadn't talked him into hiring someone to come in and stir up the dust once a week. And he had to admit that a fresh set of sheets was pretty damn nice. Since the weather had warmed up, Patricia had been hanging them outside.

"Isn't that the woman who's been coming around the station?" Upton asked, looking out the window.

Seymour followed the direction of his gaze.

Lydia Yates stood just beyond the gate, talking on a cell phone and gesturing wildly. Another woman was with her, and Seymour seriously doubted they were calling for pizza delivery.

Behind him, the dark-haired officer let out a shriek. That fit of girliness was followed by the sound of something heavy hitting the floor.

The officer bent over and picked up a book bound in soft leather. "Listen to this." In his other hand he held a scrap of paper, which he now read. " 'This book cover was made from the skin of Father Francis Xavier after his beheading in 1743.' "

"Then treat it with extreme care." Seymour moved toward the door. "I'm going out to see what our friend Ms. Yates is up to."

It also gave him a chance to have a smoke.

On the porch he parked himself in front of the picture window so the officers inside would know he was nearby and not be inclined to misbehave.

The person with Lydia Yates was Bonnie Stark from the *Tuonela Press*. By tomorrow morning everybody in town would know about the DNA match and the warrant for Evan.

Lydia closed the cell phone and passed it back to Bonnie, who tucked it in her pocket. "What's going on?" Lydia demanded.

Oh, how Seymour did not want to discuss this

here and now. He let out a heavy sigh. He'd hoped to keep it out of the papers for at least another day. "We have a warrant for the arrest of Evan Stroud on the suspicion of murder."

Both women gasped.

"Yeah, it surprises the hell out of me too."

"So where is Stroud?" Bonnie asked.

Seymour pulled a cigarette from his shirt pocket, lit it with his silver Zippo, and slipped the lighter back in his pocket. "Well, he's not home."

Bonnie pulled out a writing tablet and clicked her pen. "You mean he's run off?"

"Don't go jumping to conclusions," Seymour said. "He's not home at this moment. That's all. Not home."

Lydia held out her hand to Bonnie. "Can I borrow your phone again? I need to call the state attorney."

Ah, yes. Graham. The time they'd bought him was gone. Wasn't a judge in the world who would turn the kid over to his father now.

Chapter 21

Things were going to be okay. That thought had been creeping into Graham's head lately.

Isobel turned around in her desk and smiled at him over her shoulder. They were in American history, and the teacher was droning on about the Civil War. Even though his voice was a monotone, Graham got the idea he was excited about it.

Kids were still giving Graham weird looks, and some even acted scared of him, but he didn't care.

Things are going to be okay.

He gave Isobel a little wave.

They were both staying after school. The play was in a week, and Alba was pushing all the kids to get their lines memorized. And they'd hardly started on the stage set. This weekend he and Isobel were going to hit a few thrift shops to see if they could find some props. Later today he was meeting with Alba to work on the set design.

Someone knocked lightly on the door; then Principal Bonner came in the room and whispered something to the instructor.

"Graham Yates," the history teacher announced.

"Please gather up all of your things and join Principal Bonner in the hallway."

Graham's heart flip-flopped, but then he immediately thought that maybe it was good news. Maybe the judge—or whoever—reviewing his case wanted to talk to him about his mother.

They were heading toward the office when the principal indicated they should turn down another hallway. "You need to empty out your locker."

Graham stopped. "What?"

"Get everything out of your locker."

"What's going on? What's this about?"

"Everything out."

Okay, she wasn't going to tell him. But he knew the answer. He'd been here before.

He spun the combination lock, then opened the locker. He shoved his jacket and knitting and notebooks in his backpack.

"I'll take the books."

He tried to read her as he placed them into her outstretched hands. She looked nervous. Suspicious. A little disappointed in him, but more than that—annoyed at being put in this position, especially when Graham had never really been one of them to begin with. He was an outsider she'd been forced to allow into her school. And for what? Hadn't it ended up just like she thought it would?

He knew that look. He'd moved around enough, been to enough new schools to recognize it.

He slammed the locker shut and they walked to the office, past the receptionist's desk, through the orange door that closed behind them.

His mother sat in a chair, glaring at him.

It was a long time before he noticed that someone else was also in the room. His old buddy Police Chief Burton.

Burton was holding his hat. Graham didn't know what you called that kind of hat. It was like a cowboy hat, but not as big and not as Western. Whatever it was called, Burton was clinging to it with his old hands. The guy looked miserable, and for a second Graham felt sorry for him.

Burton came over to Graham and placed a hand on his shoulder. Time got all weird, and the room started to shrink. Graham knew what Burton was going to say, and he wanted to run. Burton's lips began to move, but Graham couldn't hear anything past the shouting in his own head.

No!

It didn't matter what Burton was saying. Graham knew he was telling him he was sorry, and that Graham had to go back to his mother.

Then the fear and terror fell away. Suddenly a warmth and a hollow numbness washed over him, and he felt safe.

Nothing could touch him. Nothing could hurt him when he felt this way. It was that same state of total calm Graham had called upon when he'd pressed Evan's gun to his head and pulled the trigger.

"That's okay, Officer Burton," he heard himself saying.

He must have smiled, because Burton smiled back. But Graham could tell the old dude was ashamed of himself for letting Graham down.

Suddenly he and his mother were leaving the room. She may have said something; he didn't know. By that time he'd shut himself down completely.

A bell rang, but the sound was muffled, seeming to come from another dimension. The halls erupted. He thought someone shouted his name, so he slowly turned to see a girl with blond hair waving frantically to him. He didn't respond. Instead he followed his mother from the building.

At the car he looked in the backseat and saw his big canvas travel backpack. She'd already picked up his stuff from Stroud's.

With a familiar feeling of futility, he opened the creaky front door and slid into the passenger seat. She started the engine, threw the car into gear, and they were off.

On a new and amazing adventure.

She was talking, her words coming fast and angry. It took him a little while to realize Evan Stroud was the subject of her rant.

"He murdered a girl," she said. "The girl they found in the park. Do you want to stay with somebody like that? A murderer?"

A murderer or the woman beside him . . . *Hmmm.* That may have seemed a tough one to anybody else, but to Graham the answer was easy: He'd take the murderer.

They flew through town. The car was an extension of Lydia's anger, the way it turned too fast and stopped too fast. The way the tires spun when it took off.

He was surprised she didn't get pulled over by a cop. But maybe they'd been warned about her.

Maybe they'd been told to let her get the hell out of town.

He thought about his friends in Arizona. "Where are we going?"

"Shut up!" She tried to slap him, but he leaned away. "Don't talk to me. Don't you ever, ever talk to me!"

Graham didn't have many old memories of his mom. She'd just been this person who came and went, sometimes giddy, sometimes mad. Occasionally, when she was drunk, she would hug him and tell him how much she loved him.

A steady stream of men moved like shadows through their lives. He finally figured out it was the strange men that kept her happy.

When you were little, there was no confusion over how you felt about someone. Maybe the reason for that response was unclear, but the emotion itself was well-defined. You loved. You distrusted, you even disliked, but you never wondered if you liked a person or not.

Maybe instincts were sharper in kids. Some kind of primitive survival thing.

His life hadn't been bad, not really, until his grandmother died when he was in the third grade. She'd basically raised him, with Lydia hovering on the periphery. His grandmother had died of what was called a salon stroke. Something to do with the neck arteries and how a person's head was tipped back when the hair was being washed.

It was her birthday, and she'd decided to treat herself. Graham had gone along. When she was finished her hair had looked fake and alien, her face strange. At the register she dropped to the floor, and six hours later she was dead. Without his grandmother around to keep Lydia in check, his mother spiraled out of control.

As the setting sun turned the sky a brilliant red, he thought about his grandmother. He thought about how much he'd loved her, and how much he missed her . . . .

Graham realized it was getting dark. There wasn't much traffic on the road, although occasionally the headlights from a car behind them illuminated the interior.

How long had they been driving? Time always got messed up when he shut himself down.

At least she wasn't talking. Just sitting there in silence, staring straight ahead. He wanted to turn on the radio, but that would draw attention to him and jolt her out of her silence, so he remained very still.

The car slowed and she leaned forward as if looking for something. Suddenly they veered to the right, shooting off the two-lane into a rest area.

She pulled to a stop in front of a low brick building with a green metal roof. Weird blue lights flickered and buzzed. Moths circled, and hard-shelled beetles dive-bombed the cement sidewalk in confusion.

"I have to pee," she announced, removing the keys from the ignition. They both got out of the car.

"Lock your door."

He pushed the button; then they walked toward the public restrooms.

The site was deserted except for a couple of semis parked in the distance, their diesel engines rumbling softly, their yellow parking lights on as the drivers slept. Graham hardly noticed the car that pulled off the highway and parked at the opposite end of the lot.

He and his mother split off into separate restrooms.

He peed. When he was done and zipped, he looked at himself in the mirror above the sink. Under the fluorescent lights his skin was green and his veins were dark blue.

Graham couldn't make himself leave.

He glanced up at a block-glass window. Too small. The door was the only way out. How long could he stay here before she came looking for him? Before she came and dragged him to the car?

From the women's room came a heavy, muffled noise followed by the slam of a door.

She was done. She was waiting.

He ran the water. He flushed the toilet so she would think he was busy. He ran the water again. Buying himself a few extra minutes in a public restroom.

He heard footsteps behind him. Ducking his head, he turned and shot for the exit. Someone grabbed his arm.

"Dude."

Graham looked up.

Travis.

"Come on," Travis whispered, tugging at him.

Baffled, Graham followed. How could Travis be here? In this world? The world of his mother?

Outside, Travis motioned for Graham to follow him under the cover of huge evergreens. Graham looked around, didn't see his mother in the car or outside the restroom. He took off after Travis. They both ran like hell, ducking under sprawling branches to arrive at the road where the semis were parked.

Not far off was the little green car belonging to Travis's blond friend. Craig. And the other kid? Brandon. Graham had finally figured out his name was Brandon.

Graham didn't have time to think about what had taken place last time he'd been in that car. He dove into the backseat. Doors slammed and tires squealed.

Once they were on the two-lane heading back to Tuonela, they all let out a loud whoop. Brandon shoved a fifth of vodka into Graham's hand.

"How did you find me?" Graham asked, his heart hammering, feeling something close to euphoria. He lifted the bottle to his mouth and took a swallow.

"We saw you leaving school, dude," Travis explained, holding out his hand for the bottle. Graham passed it to him. "So we followed you."

They all laughed.

Graham looked over his shoulder at the road behind them. No lights yet. This was so fucked. So wonderfully fucked.

Then he started thinking logically. "She'll find me. She always finds me." Maybe they should go back. "When she does, I'll be in so much trouble."

"She won't find you, dude," Travis said. "We have

the perfect place for you to hide. Nobody will find you there."

The bottle of vodka was in his hand again. In the dark, he didn't question it's stickiness. "Cool." But Graham wasn't feeling overly confident. After all, this was the same guy who'd sent him to the perv.

Chapter 22

Rachel headed to the basement morgue with food and supplies. Halfway down the steps her cell phone rang and she paused to answer it.

Her dad.

Upon hearing his voice, her inclination was to blurt out what she'd done and tell him about Evan. She'd never kept anything from Seymour, and now she wanted his advice, his help. She felt physically sick. Her loyalty should be to her dad, not Evan.

"Graham's been turned over to Lydia Yates," Seymour said. "There was nothing we could do about it."

It took Rachel a moment to shift from her own guilt to what her dad was saying. "How did he take it?"

"Fairly well, all things considered. Maybe his relationship with his mother isn't as bad as he's made it out to be. They left town this afternoon." Seymour let out a heavy sigh. "I suppose you've seen the news?"

The news about Evan. It was everywhere. Television. Papers. Probably hitting the national press soon.

Tell him. You have to tell him what you've done. "I've seen a little of it," she said.

"People go nuts when this kind of thing happens."

"Dad, I—"

"I don't think we have enough manpower to protect Evan Stroud if he shows his face in this town. People want him dead."

She'd almost told him. *I'm sorry, Dad.*

They said good-bye and disconnected.

A minute later she found Evan under the desk in her office, knees drawn up to his chest.

"I brought you a sandwich and some of your tea."

His face was ashen, his eyes red-rimmed and glassy.

The few cases of porphyria she'd heard of had to do with skin sensitivity, which caused blisters, even cancer, if the skin was exposed to sunlight too often. Evan's case seemed to involve a full-body reaction on the cellular level, something that maybe even changed the composition of his blood.

He closed his eyes and tipped back his head. "Just hafta wait," he whispered. "Ride it out."

She spread a blanket over him. One tiny sliver of sunlight had done this. His present state underscored her reason for hiding him, but it did nothing to alleviate her guilt.

With long, shaking fingers, he grasped an edge of the fabric and pulled it to his chin. "Thanks," he whispered. "W-where's Graham? D-did you pick him up from school?"

"I have some bad news."

Two dark pits stared out at her from a white face as he waited for her to continue.

"Graham's back in his mother's custody. They left town not long ago."

Evan squeezed his eyes shut.

"I'm sorry. Dad did all he could." Rachel pushed the plate and tea close and left him alone. She had to go away. She had to think about what she was doing. She had her own demons to deal with.

The musty scent of the tea drifted to Evan.

He forced himself to crawl out from under the desk. Head throbbing, he grabbed the cup and took a swallow.

He ate the sandwich, finished the tea, and fell into a deep slumber.

He didn't know how long he slept. A moment. A day. A year.

A hundred years . . .

He awoke to a thundering heart and the sound of blood rushing through his veins. He shoved himself to his feet. In the darkness he staggered to the autopsy suite, went straight to the coolers, and opened the center drawer.

Richard Manchester.

Evan stared at the mummified remains, his nerves humming.

An odd sensation of homesickness washed over him. Reverently he fingered the edge of the monogrammed scarf and imagined wearing it, standing in the center of Old Tuonela.

He pulled the scarf from the mummy's neck, lifted the cloth to his face, closed his eyes, and inhaled deeply.

Chapter 23

Craig and Brandon waited in the car while Graham followed Travis through the dark woods, his feet snagging on tangled vines.

"Keep the flashlight pointed at our feet," Graham complained after getting tripped for the second time. He hadn't eaten since noon, and the vodka he'd downed in the car made his head buzz and his fingers tingle. "Where're we going?"

"You'll see." The flashlight cast a pale circle of light with a dead spot in the middle.

They kept walking. For a little while Graham forgot they had any destination until Travis stopped and Graham bumped into him.

They stood in front of an old stone building that looked like it had once been some kind of church. The images Graham received were more like snapshots as Travis swept the flashlight beam up and down. In those snapshots, Graham managed to determine that the structure had a heavy wooden door that was pointed at the top and set deep in stones.

The building was smothered in vines.

In Arizona there wasn't a lot of green, viney stuff.

Here everything seemed alive. It *was* alive. A mass of oozing, growing, breathing vegetation coming out of the ground, shooting up buildings—even reaching into the sky. It was like some weird, messed-up fairy tale.

"Do those vines have thorns?" he heard himself ask.

"What?" Travis sounded confused.

Graham waved his hand. "Never mind." He hadn't meant to speak the words out loud anyway.

Maybe he could live here. Nobody would ever find him in his secret home in the woods. Maybe the vines would grow and grow and finally cover everything up. Hide him. Protect him.

What about winter? It gets cold here in the winter.

That was months away. Spring had barely started. He could figure something out by the time winter came. He could build fires. He could drag dead branches up to burn. He started to get excited thinking about it. Living off the grid. Was that what it was called?

The door was ajar. Travis shoved it open several more inches, the bottom dragging on the stone threshold. He squeezed himself inside, and Graham followed.

"What's that smell?" Graham put a hand to his nose and breathed through his mouth.

"Coon shit," Travis said. "Raccoons hang out in empty buildings like this. They can really tear things up with those little hands of theirs. You ever seen how they hold stuff? Pretty cool."

"Gimme that light."

Travis passed the light and Graham panned the

weak amber beam around the room. It *was* a church. Or had been at one time. A few pews were still left, and an altar with some half-melted candles. The walls had been sprayed with graffiti. Above their heads the roof had collapsed in places. Below the gaping holes, rotten beams littered the floor.

Something scuttled behind them. Graham swung around, aiming the flashlight toward the sound in time to see a bushy brown tail vanish through a crack in the wall.

"Coon," Travis said.

Graham paused the light in the corner, focusing on a gross, stained mattress. He felt sick to his stomach. Felt an old, abstract dread he'd experienced many times in his life.

"Nobody will ever find you here," Travis told him.

"What is this place?" Graham asked. "What's an empty church doing in the middle of nowhere?"

"Old Tuonela. It's a ghost town. A real ghost town. It's supposed to be haunted with the people that were killed. Anyway, nobody comes here." He swung around. "You believe in ghosts?"

"I don't know. I've never seen one."

"How about the Pale Immortal?"

"You mean, do I think he was a real vampire?"

"Yeah."

Graham let out a snort. "Right." But he didn't feel as confident as he sounded. Standing in this weird place, he could almost believe vampires really existed.

"What about your old man?"

"What about him?"

"People say he's a vampire."

"He has a disease that keeps him from going out in the sun."

"How do you know for sure? Maybe he's really a vampire. Maybe he just tells people he has a disease."

Graham thought about how Evan had scared him a few times.

"Did you ever see him drink blood?" Travis asked.

"N-no."

"What about mirrors? And crosses? Does he have any in the house?"

"There's a mirror in the bathroom. And as far as crosses go . . . I mean, who has crosses in their house?"

"My parents do."

"I'll bet everybody in Tuonela does. And garlic too." Graham gave himself a mental shake. "This is stupid." Again, he sounded more certain than he felt.

"Whatever." Travis shrugged. "I gotta go."

Graham suddenly felt bad. He appreciated how the bunch had come to his rescue. He didn't want Travis to think he didn't appreciate it. "Hey, thanks, man."

"That's cool. One of us will try to make it back tomorrow after school." Travis put out his hand for the flashlight.

"Wait." Graham walked to the altar. Using the flashlight, he looked around for matches, but all he could find were empty books. "You got a lighter?"

Travis patted his coat. "Musta left it in the car."

"Let me keep the flashlight then."

"No way. I gotta have it to find my way back."

Graham reluctantly returned it.

Graham had a hard time keeping himself from leaving with him.

Once Travis was gone, Graham stood in the dark listening to his own heartbeat. Gradually the structure began to awaken. He heard small sounds that might have been the tiny claws of mice scrambling across beams. And then louder sounds of an animal as it thumped over a wooden floor to escape the building.

Nice.

How was it that he seemed to be so good at going from a bad situation to one that was even worse? Like he was equipped with some kind of chaos magnet.

What'd you expect? A damn hotel with clean sheets and a hot shower?

In his head he visualized the stained mattress in the corner. Clean sheets would be nice. Clean sheets would be really nice.

He was tired. And hungry. So hungry his stomach hurt. The kind of stomachache where, if you did finally eat something, you'd probably get sick.

Ghost town.

They had a lot of ghost towns in Arizona, but they were dried-up old shanties, not some wet, moldy building in the middle of the woods. Not someplace where animals ran across the rafters above your head and shit all over the place.

It will seem better in the morning.

His mind shifted.

Where was his mother? She would be pissed, that's for sure. She would be so incredibly pissed. And she was capable of doing some evil stuff when she was in a full-blown rage.

Travis walked really fast back to the car. He would have run, but it was hard to see even with the flashlight.

No way would he have wanted to stay back there by himself. Every kid in Tuonela had grown up hearing stories about the old place. Travis didn't like being alone in the dark anywhere, but being alone in fucking OT was enough to give a guy a heart attack. And after the deal with the weird lights . . . What the hell was that all about?

Don't think about the lights. Don't look back. Just keep moving.

Graham was gutsy. He'd give him that.

By the time Travis reached the car, the hair on his scalp tingled and he was breathing hard. Brandon and Craig were sitting in the front seat, staring straight ahead, smoking like a couple of professionals.

"What'd ya do with the body?" Travis asked. "Did you drain it?"

"Nah." Craig rolled down the driver's window and flicked out his cigarette butt. "We don't want some old bat like that."

"Seems like a waste to me," Travis said. "I mean, we're always looking for blood."

"Not from some old whore."

"If you drank that," Brandon said, "it would probably make you old and stupid."

Travis wanted to tell Brandon he was already stupid, but he kept his mouth shut. Brandon was a sheep. He always did whatever Craig told him to do. He dressed like Craig, talked like Craig. It was pathetic.

Craig threw the car into gear. Instead of leaving, he drove deeper into OT before pulling to a stop. "Body dump."

They piled out of the car and hefted the body from the trunk, then let it fall with a heavy thud. The three of them dragged the deadweight across the ground until they came to an open well lined with stones. They rolled and shoved until the dead woman vanished into the dark hole, rocks and pebbles skittering after her.

Lydia had the vague idea she should be in pain, but she didn't feel anything. Oh, she'd been aware of being dragged from the trunk of a car. Aware of being dumped down a deep hole in the ground. Rocks had followed, hitting her on the head, knocking her out.

When she came to she felt no pain, and for a moment she thought maybe she was dead, or maybe she'd died and gone to hell. But then sounds came to her. Male voices, talking and laughing.

The voices drifted off, and she began to struggle, working her fingers between the rocks.

Stupid boys. Stupid friends of Graham's. They thought they'd bludgeoned her to death.

If you're not going to do a job right, don't do it at all. That's what her mother used to say. First of all, the idiots hadn't killed her. Then they'd been too damn lazy to throw more than a few pebbles on top of her.

She would get out. She would get out and find them.

She struggled with a stone, finally managing to dislodge and shove it aside. That led to another one. She dug, scraping the dirt with her nails as she tried to free each new stone.

She would track down those assholes and kill them.

Kill not only them but Graham too.

She'd heard him. When she was in the trunk of the car, she'd heard him talking just inches away. Maybe he was her flesh and blood, but it would have been best if she'd had an abortion. She'd wanted to, but her mother had talked her out of it. Said they could maybe make some money out of the deal.

They'd chosen Evan because his father was a cop and he seemed the most likely to feel he should do the right thing by her, but the plan had backfired on them, because Evan got sick and nobody paid attention to her after that.

The kid had ruined her life; that's what he'd done. He was a constant reminder of what things could have been like if only he'd never taken a breath.

She had to rest.

She leaned her cheek against the wall of the well. Her sexy summer dress was torn. She felt something trickle down her leg. Blood? Probably. Somewhere along the way she'd lost her shoes. Didn't matter.

Her fingers came in contact with the surface of the ground.

Just a few more feet.

She looked up and caught a swirling glimpse of tree branches. Past them, stars were shining. She grasped a tuft of grass and pulled. The grass ripped from the soil and she slid back down the well, her leg snapping with a crunch.

Graham woke up with a jerk.

He was lying on the bare, filthy mattress, his knees pulled up to his chest, struggling to keep warm. He shook violently, so much it would have seemed like a joke if he could see himself.

Who knew you could freeze to death when it was fifty degrees? People used to live outside. He thought about movies he'd seen where Indians trudged through the snow just wearing some deer-skin. Here he was, wearing a shirt and sweatshirt, his teeth chattering and his fingers numb.

Sunlight cut through the broken walls, revealing the church for the dump it was. Like something the woods not only covered up, but also devoured. Something that was returning to nature. Something that didn't belong there.

Chapter 24

A male voice shouted Rachel's name.

Evan came awake with a start, bumping his head on the bottom of the desk.

"Rachel?" the man shouted again. "You there?"

The voice was far away and hollow, sounding as if the owner were yelling down a stairwell. Evan scrambled to his feet, started to bolt, paused and snatched up the blanket, shoved it in a nearby cabinet, and ran.

In the adjoining room he opened an unoccupied cooler drawer and swung himself in feetfirst, leaving the heavy door open a crack.

Somewhere beyond the refrigerated box, the soles of street shoes echoed across linoleum and cement. The owner moved closer, then stopped. The handle behind Evan's head jiggled. Evan held his breath and squeezed his eyes shut.

Rather than opening the door, the person slammed it firmly shut.

Evan lay in the dark, listening intently, trying to control his breathing. Footsteps moved back and forth, then finally faded. Evan waited a couple of minutes, then reached above and behind. He pushed.

The door didn't budge.

He shoved again.

Nothing.

There was no internal release.

How much time did he have? Ten minutes? Fifteen?

Rachel turned at a red light, then headed up the hill toward the morgue. She'd run some quick errands, picking up a few groceries, filling up the gas tank, all the while trying to avoid people for fear that Evan would be the topic of conversation.

As she made a left to take the final climb home, she spotted her father's faded Cadillac crawling up the hill and disappearing around the corner.

She gripped the steering wheel tighter. Had he been at the morgue? Had he gone inside?

She pulled into the level area near the back door. As the van rolled to a stop she shut off the engine, jumped out, and dashed for the building. Her dad had a key. He didn't stop by often, and he almost always called first.

Inside, she ran down the hall leading to the autopsy suites, coattails flying. She pushed through the double doors, the metal bar clanging, and headed for her office. Evan wasn't under the desk, where he'd been sound asleep two hours ago. The blanket was gone.

She swung around and checked the autopsy suites and storage areas. Had he left the building?

But it was daylight. He couldn't go anywhere. Upstairs. Had he gone upstairs? Or had her dad found him? Another thought: Had Evan called her father and turned himself in?

She was moving toward the stairs and elevator when, for some inexplicable reason, she hesitated, then returned to the autopsy suite and cold storage. She pulled open the drawer containing the mummified remains of Richard Manchester. She closed it, then grabbed the handle of the next drawer. Rather than sliding open easily, the way it would if it were empty, the drawer took strength to pull out.

Evan was lying on the slab, skin ashen, lips blue.

She pressed her fingers to the carotid artery in his neck.

No pulse.

Oh, my God.

No, no, no.

Her father had just left. Maybe Evan hadn't been hiding long.

CPR.

For a fraction of a second she forgot how to perform it; then her memory kicked in. She made sure his airway was clear. She listened. God, her heart was hammering so loudly, how could she possibly hear anything?

Look, listen, feel.

He still had no pulse, and when she placed her face near his, she felt no air move past his lips.

She tipped back his head, grasped his nose, and blew five quick breaths in his mouth.

He responded immediately. His heart kicked in and he drew a gasping breath.

Back from the dead.

"Oh, Jesus."

Bending over him she placed a shaking hand to his jaw. Cold as marble. As she watched, blood pumped through his veins and the blue faded from his lips. His eyes, when he opened them, were unfocused. They slowly cleared until he was looking at her with recognition and lucidity while the chill of the refrigerator curled around them.

He'd been dead—*dead*—moments ago. A man with no pulse. No heartbeat.

Maybe he was another apparition, like Chelsea becoming Victoria.

Maybe he's still dead.

She pressed her fingers to his neck. He had a pulse, a strong one this time. She rounded up a gurney and parked it next to the drawer. She locked the wheels. "I'm going to slide you over, but you have to help." Normally a sheet would have been placed under the body, and she would have tugged the cadaver from one bed to the other.

She grabbed his arm and leg and counted to three. Once he was on the gurney she pushed him from the room, through the double doors, to the elevator, hoping like hell she didn't run into anybody.

Upstairs in her third-floor apartment, she pulled the bedroom shades and curtains tight, then helped Evan into her bed, covering him with a heavy down comforter. She filled a hot-water bottle and slid it near his icy feet.

*   *   *

Evan lifted the mug of tea to his mouth while willing his hand to stop shaking. The red stoneware with evergreen trees and reindeer knocked against his teeth. He gave up, put down the mug, and slumped weakly in the curved vinyl back of the chair.

It was early evening. He and Rachel were sitting in semidarkness at the small kitchen table in her upstairs apartment. She'd coaxed him out of bed with a wheelchair and the promise of a look around.

His near-death experience had created a somber, silent bond between them. She'd saved his life. More than once.

"This is nice." He ran his fingertips across the red Formica surface of the table. It was cool and smooth to the touch. The table was from the fifties, with a wide strip of shiny metal trim. A tremor ran through him; he made a fist and hid his hand on his lap.

"It came with the morgue." She pulled up her feet and wrapped one arm around her knees. Green socks poked out from the hem of her jeans. Her V-neck shirt was some kind of loose black tunic. Her short hair was tousled, her face pale and free of makeup.

Wouldn't she be surprised to know that he'd had sex only a few times in his life? Sex was a casualty of his exile. Just another something he lived without. And he wasn't exactly the kind of guy who attracted women you took home to mama. Most of the women who came on to him usually ended up having a penchant for black eyeliner, role-playing, and bloodletting parties.

He tried the tea again. This time he was able to take a small sip. The exotic flavor flowed over his tongue as he swallowed. A warm, almost electric sensation ran through him, all the way to his fingers and toes.

"You should try this." He offered his mug. "It's extremely rejuvenating. I'll have to find out where it came from so I can get more."

She took the mug, lifted it to her mouth, then handed it back. "No, thanks. I can't get past the smell. Would you like to look outside?" She unfolded herself—all long, graceful legs—and stood up. "The view from the living room is amazing."

Without waiting for an answer, and before he could take another swallow, she removed the cup from his hand and set it aside. She unlocked the wheelchair, turned him around, and pushed him from the small kitchen to the adjoining living room.

The colors. They were so vivid.

The room was done in deep hues. Greens. Reds. Blues. An orange scarf had been draped over a small table lamp to mute the light. The wooden floor creaked as she pushed him across the open space where moonlight fell through a curtainless window in the turret.

She was right: The view was amazing.

The old bridge with its rows of lights reflected off the Wisconsin River, which was smooth as glass. There was the courthouse, and the clock tower. Main Street with small white lights decorating trees that lined the streets. The art deco theater with its missing marquee letters.

Rachel sat down nearby. He couldn't see her, but he felt her presence as they both took in the beauty of the town.

He felt drowsy and sweet and melancholy.

This was an interlude. A tease. A sample of real life. This wouldn't happen again. He didn't know how he knew, but he knew. Very soon things would never be the same.

A change was coming.

As he stared below, his thoughts turned in another direction.

He'd always believed the old cliché that where there's smoke, there's fire. And there was a hell of a lot of smoke around him.

"I lose time," he confessed. "I'll look at my watch and it will be a little past midnight. When I look again, it's hours later. And now my DNA has been found at the scene of a brutal murder."

She didn't answer. At least she didn't give him some false spiel about believing in him and trusting him. She was suspicious, as well she should be. *He* was suspicious.

When she finally spoke, her words were measured and cautious. "You have no memory of what happens during that time?"

"No. Maybe I do bad things. Maybe I blocked out murdering that young girl."

"Kind of a Jekyll and Hyde?"

Yeah."

"If that's true, evidence will be found at your house."

"But in the meantime you could be in danger. Everybody in this town could be in danger."

He'd had a taste of prison. His life was a prison. But he couldn't imagine being unable to walk the streets at night. Couldn't imagine being unable to watch the light reflecting off the river from the bluff.

He reached up and behind and found her hand without looking. He brought it to his face, touching it to the stubble on his jaw. "I should turn myself in so they can lock me up."

He felt her stiffen, and sensed her shock and confusion. He was tempted to press her palm to his mouth, but he restrained himself.

His mind settled where it had been settling every time he let it go.

He stared blindly out the window, not seeing the buildings this time. He'd been a father for only a short while, but it felt much longer. Months, maybe years. It seemed Graham had always been there, that Evan had always known of his existence even though he hadn't. It was so obvious now. He'd felt him lurking in the depths of his soul; he just hadn't understood where the longing had come from. Now he knew. The fact that Graham had always been out there brought Evan comfort. His son had existed in the past and he would exist in the future.

"Do you think he'll be okay?" No names. He couldn't bring himself to speak his name out loud. "With her?"

Graham would go on without him.

Chapter 25

Isobel dug a half-eaten veggie sandwich from her backpack, unwrapped it, stared at it a minute, then tossed it in the trash. It hadn't been good earlier, and it looked even more disgusting four hours later. Why had she bothered to save it? Now everything in her backpack smelled like onions and green peppers. Even her locker smelled like some old deli.

She'd found a secluded corner in the carpeted lobby of the old downtown movie theater and was trying to study her lines, but she couldn't concentrate. She sat on the floor, back to the wall, legs out in front of her, black boots below yellow tights crossed at the ankles, trying not to think about Graham.

Just quit thinking about him.

But she couldn't. She kept replaying yesterday in her head, seeing Graham loping off down the hallway. When she'd called his name, he'd turned, looked right through her, and kept going.

Lalalala.

Now he was gone. Checked out. Locker empty.

Moved away. Back with mommy, and he hadn't even said good-bye.

He'd been using her to hang out with until his real life started up again. She'd just been somebody to mooch from and bum rides from and talk to so he wouldn't have to be alone. But she obviously hadn't meant anything to him, even after she'd stood by him when other kids shunned him.

She closed her eyes and leaned her head against the wall. Everything sucked.

"Bad day?"

She looked up, and her heart took a little nose-dive, the way it always did when Mr. Alba spoke directly to her. He was one of the coolest teachers, and he had a sad, tragic past that made him even more appealing.

She held up her playbook of *Macbeth*, open to a highlighted page. "Just having a hard time concentrating."

"Dress rehearsal is in two days," he reminded her gently.

"I know."

She heard he'd been going to graduate school and had been on a field trip to Mexico when the bus they were on plunged over a cliff. Everybody had died, even his girlfriend, but he'd walked away without a scratch.

He crouched down in front of her. "Want to talk about it?"

Other girls in school were always trying to guess Alba's age. He couldn't be that much older than they were. Isobel knew a man and wife who were twenty years apart, and she knew another married couple who were ten. Mr. A was probably in his twenties. He was still young enough to know how to dress cool, with his sweaters and dark ties, wavy hair that almost touched his shoulders.

"I'll be in my office until late tonight if you do. Stop by anytime."

She swallowed and tried to give him a natural smile. *Until late tonight.* What did *that* mean? Just what it sounded like? Nothing more?

She'd been to his office a few times, but always with other students. The way she understood it, Mr. Alba wasn't a regular teacher. He'd been hired on a part-time basis and was paid by a group of parents who had screamed when art, music, and drama were cut from the school budget. So poor Mr. A didn't even have a room. His classroom was the old theater, and his office was some hole in the corner of the basement that was no bigger than a closet, and had probably been an actual closet at one time.

Her heart was beating fast. Did he like her? Did he *like* her, like her?

Stop!

This was wrong. Nothing about his body language said she was any more to him than any other student with a problem. He wanted to help her so she could focus on the play. That's all.

But she was seventeen. Eighteen in eight more months . . .

He straightened. "Stop by after rehearsal if you feel like it."

"Okay." Would she? "I might be busy. I might have to get home."

That was lame. She would know right now if she had to get home, and Holly sure didn't give a damn when she came or went. Her cousin was in her own little world, always on the phone to someone or crying about the guy who'd dumped her.

Isobel had always sworn she would never grieve over a guy. A girl had to have more pride than that. But just five minutes ago she'd been doing exactly what Holly had done for the past six months. Losing herself. Letting go of what had been important to her before Graham walked into her life. Getting dumped, by a friend or boyfriend, was no reason to self-destruct.

Maybe she would ask the Ouija board what it thought about her talking to Mr. Alba.

Phillip Alba checked the clock on the wall. A little after nine. Rehearsal had ended an hour ago. He'd waited in his office for Isobel to stop by, but apparently she wasn't coming. Although he'd always been good at reading people, sometimes he got it wrong.

He packed up his briefcase, tossing in notes and play posters, then snapped the case shut. His fingers were wrapped around the black leather handle when a timid knock sounded on his door and Isobel peeked shyly through the opening.

He leaned back in his chair, hands splayed at his waist. "Isobel." He gave her a warm smile.

Phillip was careful to keep his body language casual and friendly so he didn't scare her off. He could tell she was attracted to him, but she was also leery and suspicious.

Women had always been drawn to him, even when he was a small child. They would come up to him in grocery stores and stroke his hair while they made crooning noises. What was it about him that drew them? He'd been cute, with curly hair and dark eyes. As he got older he learned it wasn't just about looks. There were lots of good-looking kids out there. He had something those other kids didn't have. The corny word for it was charisma.

Isobel lingered in the doorway, one hand gripping the molding. "Come on in," he told her.

A wooden straight-backed chair was propped against one wall. He jumped up, pulled the chair near his desk, and motioned for her to have a seat. Such a gentleman.

What was she wearing today? That was always what he looked for when it came to Isobel. Her sense of style. She would have denied being that shallow, but she gave her wardrobe a lot of thought. The outfits she put together didn't just fall out of the closet. And they couldn't be bought at the local mall. She probably didn't think of it in those terms, but not only was she constantly making a statement; she was a walking piece of art.

"Nice sweater," he said.

As if having forgotten what she'd put on that day, she looked down and touched the pink cardigan edged in bright red flowers. "I got this at the thrift shop on Jefferson. They have a lot of cool stuff."

He sat back down in his swivel chair. "I get some of my costumes there."

He didn't think of himself as a predator. He would have been pissed if anybody had accused him of such a thing. No, he became what people needed in their lives. He filled a void. He listened. He was a good listener.

Was that predatorial? No, unless shrinks were predatorial. He *helped* people. He was a replacement for absent fathers and mothers who were off working. That's what was wrong with the United States. Everybody worked. Nobody stayed home with the kids. And vacations? *Fuck it.* Why, the Swedes took off months in a single year, no question. Americans worked. And worked. So much that they didn't know how to relax. Didn't know how to spend time with their children.

Phillip was here for those kids. The kids who would be lost otherwise. They needed him. Isobel needed him. Maybe he was an opportunist, but what difference did it make? What successful man wasn't?

He made his voice soft, serious, and warm. "What's bothering you, kitten?"

He could see that she liked being called kitten.

Giving off a faint scent of stale onions that he tried to ignore, she sat down on the hard chair, legs together, and let her backpack slide to the floor.

"It has to be tough with your parents on tour."

"Yeah." She slumped closer, tucking her hands between her knees.

"And I know you were hanging around with

Graham Yates. I heard he moved back home. That's the best place for him. With his mother."

"I'm sorry I got him involved in the set design at the last minute. I mean, it was great of you to give him a break, but . . ." She pressed her lips together and shook her head.

"Not your fault. You were just trying to help a friend. Never be ashamed of that."

"Even if that friend stabs you in the back?"

"Want to talk about it?"

Nobody listened anymore. So many people, adults and kids alike, just wanted somebody to listen. "Don't tell me if you don't want to. Don't let me talk you into revealing something that makes you uncomfortable."

"He didn't really stab me in the back, I guess. That's stretching it."

Phillip got up from his chair and came around to sit on the corner of the desk so that he was closer to Isobel, so that he could reach out to her if the moment presented itself.

"He left without saying good-bye." She raised and dropped her hand. "There. That's all. It sounds so stupid now that I'm saying it out loud. It was no big deal. Not anything to get upset about."

Phillip leaned forward, hands on his knees. Shaking his head, he said, "That's not stupid at all."

She looked up at him, tears in her eyes. "I stood by him when other kids called him the freak's son."

"Sometimes we make people into who we want them to be rather than who they really are. Let me ask you this: When you were with Graham, did you get the feeling that you two were alike? That you had a lot in common?"

She nodded.

God, she was beautiful. Those green eyes. That flawless skin. Was she a virgin? He knew she didn't have any close friends, and she'd never had a serious boyfriend as far as anybody knew. Loners tended to remain virgins longer than party girls. Isobel was a person other students liked, but often couldn't relate to. She kept people at a distance, because she tended to think for herself a little too much.

And if she vanished, her disappearance probably wouldn't be reported for a long time . . . .

"Did you ever wonder if maybe you were making him like you? I mean, making him seem similar to you, at least in your mind?"

She frowned in puzzlement, and he continued. "When we don't know something about someone, we fill in the blanks. And what we use to fill in those blanks is usually something we can relate to in ourselves. When we don't know all the facts, we tend to make people like us."

Her face cleared as she got what he was saying. She was a smart girl.

"That's kinda embarrassing," she said with a self-conscious smile.

"It's human nature. So the person you miss never really existed. That's what I'm telling you. And how can you miss somebody who never really existed?"

He wanted to touch her, even just the skin of her arm, but he restrained himself.

She picked up her backpack and got to her feet. "Thank you, Mr. A. You've been great. You *are* great."

He smiled at her, and she mirrored his expression. "Stop by and talk anytime," he told her. "My door is always open."

Chapter 26

Phillip Alba drove through the darkness to his home five miles from Tuonela. Clouds blacked out the stars. The only light came from the orange glow of the dashboard.

At the house he stripped to his underwear, then carefully hung up his slacks, shirt, and tie in the bedroom closet before slipping into a pair of old jeans and a cotton work shirt. Downstairs in the kitchen he put on a canvas Carhartt jacket that wouldn't snag on the underbrush, and laced up his hiking boots. At the last minute he decided to grab a cheap wool blanket. Then he wrapped a slice of bread and slipped it into his pocket, picked up the lantern along with a small flashlight, and headed out the door.

The gate was closed, but the heavy chain had been linked incorrectly—evidence that the Pale Immortals had been there. Oh, the drama. But kids were like that. So over-the-top. They loved that shit. At least they hadn't named themselves Dracula's Death Squad or something equally stupid.

Their group had already been established when

Phillip returned to Tuonela after the accident. But they'd lacked direction and purpose. He'd been able to give them that.

Everybody was looking for something to believe in, especially kids their age. And once they connected with you, once bonding had been achieved, everything else was easy. If the Pale Immortals were the Manson family, then Phillip was a kinder, gentler, and much better-looking Charles Manson. Plus, he was *sane*.

Once Phillip was deep into the woods and away from the house, he lit the lantern and tucked the flashlight in his jacket pocket. Holding the lantern high, he continued through the woods.

Until the bus crash, Phillip had glided through life with no real plan or purpose. The accident turned him around. It got him thinking about immortality and cheating death, wondering if it was possible.

He'd always been special. Anybody who had contact with him would say so. And he'd lived through a horrendous massacre in which everyone else had died while he'd walked away unharmed.

A sign?

For a while he'd felt as if nothing could touch him, not even death. But that feeling faded, replaced by a nagging worry. If he as much as caught a cold, he thought it must be something more serious. Maybe tuberculosis. Maybe cancer. A trip to the grocery store brought visions of tangled metal and wreckage, his body impaled.

And so he had to have a way out. He had to find

a way to stop death, to become immortal. He didn't want to die. He couldn't allow himself to die.

He *was* special. He'd always known that. And he'd always been able to get whatever he wanted, if he wanted it badly enough. If anyone could achieve immortality, it would be him. And how very fortuitous that he lived in a town where a vampire had once roamed. A flashing neon sign couldn't have been any more obvious.

This is for you.

Suddenly he found himself at the old church. He'd been so lost in thought he'd hardly noticed the walk. It almost seemed as if he'd transported himself.

Maybe I did.

He squeezed through the church door and heard a gasp, followed by scrambling. The kid, Graham Yates, was huddled in the corner, knees drawn up to his chest, eyes wide.

"Hi, Graham," Phillip said softly.

"Mr. Alba?" Graham slowly uncurled himself and shot to his feet. "Am I glad to see you!"

For a horrifying moment Phillip thought the kid was going to hug him. He took a step back. Graham didn't seem to notice.

"W-what are you doing here?" Graham asked.

He was a mess. At school Graham had come off as fairly in control, cool, and aloof. Now he looked like a junkie in need of a fix, wide-eyed, paranoid, breathing funny.

"I live nearby," Phillip said. "My family owns this

ground. Here . . ." He pulled out the slice of white bread.

Graham snatched it, unwrapped it, and stuffed the bread in his mouth.

His fingers were filthy. He had tear tracks down his face. He was shaking.

Even though the temperature reached the sixties during the day, it still dropped at night.

"I haven't had anything to eat or drink since yesterday," he said once he'd gulped down the slice of bread. Phillip hadn't wanted to give him protein or anything that could give him a burst of strength or fire up any brain cells.

Starvation, sleep deprivation, and isolation. Those were the three most important factors in breaking somebody, and this kid was on his way. Add plain old physical discomfort, such as being dirty and cold, then remove external stimulation like music, books, and television. . . .

A kid could lose his mind.

Persona breakdown it was called. For some people it could happen fairly quickly. Others took longer.

And when you added fear to the equation . . . Most people would agree that it was scary as hell being alone in the woods, any woods, especially without a light source. But to be alone in *these* woods . . .

Phillip pulled the blanket out from under his arm and offered it to Graham.

With trembling hands, Graham took it and draped it around his shoulders.

Phillip had to be careful not to make the kid *too* miserable. So miserable that going to the police would have more appeal than staying where he was.

"We need to talk." Phillip walked over to a pew and sat down.

Graham followed. "Do you have anything else to eat?"

"No." He dismissed the question; he didn't want to talk about food. "Listen, I know this is rough, and I'd like to help you." He made his voice sound as if his help might not be possible. "But you have to understand that I could get into a lot of trouble for letting you stay here. I'm really sticking my neck out. I could lose my job. I could even be arrested."

"Are you saying I should leave? I can do that. I don't want to get you in trouble." He seemed to like the idea of getting out of there.

"Where would you go?"

Graham shook his head. "I don't know."

Phillip let out a heavy sigh and pressed his lips together. "I'll tell you what," he finally said, after pretending to give the situation some thought. "You can stay here for a few more days, but if anybody comes around looking for you, you have to hide."

Make him want to stay. Make him afraid of losing what little security he has. Make it seem like his choice.

"You can't let anybody know you're here. Understand? I want to help you. I *will* help you. We'll figure something out. Okay? How does that sound?"

"Thanks, Mr. Alba. That's cool of you."

"Do you want to talk about anything? Because I'm a good listener." When Graham didn't answer, he continued: "Your mom? Would you like to talk about her?" He paused. "Or your dad. Would you like to talk about him?" Because Evan Stroud was the person Phillip really wanted to hear about.

"I've done enough of that lately. I had to see the school counselor almost every day." Graham was calming down a little. He was looking more normal.

"Yeah, but she does that for a living. She has to listen to you. Not that Mrs. Beale doesn't do a good job. I'm sure she does. But counselors often reach a saturation point where they have to shut themselves off or risk a meltdown. They have to keep a distance, so there's always a lack of real connection."

"Yeah." Graham nodded while clutching the blanket under his chin. "That's how it was. Like her responses were something she memorized from a book."

"Exactly."

Graham was warming to him. But when it didn't seem he was going to share anything personal, Phillip got to his feet and headed for the door. Graham followed.

Phillip swung around. "You can't come with me."

Graham halted. "I can't stay here. Not in this building. Not in the woods."

"You have to."

"I can't."

"You don't have any choice."

"What about your place? Didn't you say you live around here? Couldn't I stay with you?"

Phillip gave him a long look. "I'm already risking everything by letting you stay here."

Graham backed off. "Okay."

"Just another day or two," Phillip told him. "Until we figure something out."

"I need food. I'm gonna start eating dirt pretty soon. And I need water. I'm so thirsty."

"I'll see what I can do."

"What about a light? Can you leave the light?"

"How will I get back?"

"I need a light. You don't know how it is here in the dark. I hear things."

"It's just mice. Just raccoons. They won't hurt you."

"No, I heard a voice earlier. A woman's voice. Like it was coming from far away. Like it was coming from underground."

Phillip stepped closer and put a steadying hand on Graham's shoulder so he could give him an earnest look. The kid was losing it. "What were the voices saying?"

Now that he'd confessed his fear, Graham's eyes teared up and he bit his lip to keep from sobbing. "Not voices—voice. One voice." He shook his head. "It's kind of a wailing. Like somebody who needs help."

"Ever heard coyotes before? They sound like people crying. And now, in the spring, they're having pups, and those pups can make a lot of noise."

"Coyotes? You think . . . ?"

Phillip lifted the lantern higher in order to get a better look at Graham's face. He was scared shitless. Phillip bit *his* lip to keep from smiling.

"I don't know...." Graham's mouth turned down at the corners. He'd already lost it.

Don't smile. Don't laugh.

"It's probably because of everything that's happened, but the voice...." Graham said in a trembling breath. "It sounded like a woman. It sounded like my mother."

Chapter 27

The sun was coming up as Seymour Burton swung the squad car into the rest area on Highway 21. He'd gotten a call telling him an abandoned car registered to Lydia Yates had been discovered there. It wasn't Seymour's jurisdiction, but he certainly had an interest in the situation.

State patrol was already at the scene, plus a couple of county deputies. Seymour took a swallow of coffee from his insulated refill mug, put it on the dash, got out of the car, and headed for the cluster of people.

One of the state patrol officers separated himself from the pack and strolled over to Seymour. "Maintenance personnel called it in," the officer said. "Saw the car there yesterday, but didn't think anything of it. Travelers pull off the road to sleep. But early this morning the car was still in the same place."

"Which means the car has been here"—Seymour did a quick mental calculation—"twenty-four to thirty-six hours."

"No sign of a struggle. No sign of robbery."

"Maybe the car broke down and they caught a ride with somebody."

"That was one of my first thoughts, but there are too many personal belongings left behind."

Seymour circled the car, peering in the windows, careful not to touch anything. He could see Graham's large pack in the backseat, his smaller one in front. Nearby was a CD player.

A feeling of dread washed over him. Kids didn't go anywhere without their music.

He thought about the photos that had just been discovered on the computer they'd confiscated from the pedophile. There had been about fifty digital images of Graham. And what they hadn't seen from the one full-frontal eight-by-ten print was the secret he'd been harboring. Scars. Scars old and new that crisscrossed his shoulders and back. If only they'd known. Maybe they could have kept him.

Why hadn't he told them?

He'd been ashamed. Seymour had seen it before. Victims often felt shame.

A young male deputy walked over. "Alien abduction," he said with a laugh. "No other explanation."

The state patrol officer made an annoyed face before practically agreeing. "The occupants do seem to have vanished into thin air."

"Not really thin air," Seymour said. "What you have is simply a cold, contaminated scene."

Wisconsin crime scene investigators were poking around in the grass, but it was probably pointless. "The car?" Seymour asked.

"We're sending it off to the state crime lab," the

patrol officer said. "Should be a truck here to load it anytime."

"Anything touched? Any chance of getting prints, even though it's rained?"

"It's possible. But I have to tell you that the local deputies rooted through the car already, hoping to find some ID."

Seymour sighed. "I figured that might be the case. Mind if I look around?"

"Have at it."

The restroom had been cordoned off, but that was more of a pretense, meant to look like the scene was being processed. Scores of people had been through there since the disappearance, and the building had been cleaned more than once.

He looked in the women's restroom, then the men's. Outside, a dark-haired, middle-aged woman in a gray uniform leaned against the wall, smoking a cigarette.

"Are you the one who called this in?" Seymour asked.

"I should have noticed earlier," she told him. "But cars park out here all the time. I mean, that's what the place is for. So people can pull over and sleep."

"That's perfectly understandable," Seymour reassured her.

Witnesses often felt guilty when they couldn't come up with helpful information. Which was why they sometimes subconsciously recalled incidents that had never really happened. They wanted to help so badly.

"Did you notice anything unusual? Anything out

of the ordinary in the restroom itself when you cleaned it?"

"I see a lot of weird stuff here. I mean, people are pigs. They do things they wouldn't do in their own homes. You have to have a strong stomach to clean these places. They shove things down the toilets. They go to the bathroom in the sink. They toss used tampons against the walls. It's not unusual to see blood. Especially in the women's room, although I've seen it in the men's too."

"Did you see blood yesterday morning?"

"Yes."

"Where?"

"On the floor. Near the sinks."

"And you cleaned it up?"

She suddenly looked as if she might cry.

"It's okay. You didn't do anything wrong."

"I mopped the floor. When I work someplace, I do a good job. Nothing half-ass. I scrubbed it down with the industrial-strength stuff we use. It'll kill anything. I did it twice, just to make sure I got it all."

"What about the trash containers?" he asked. "How often do you empty them? Even the ones along the road?"

"Twice a day."

"Ever skip it if they aren't full?"

"Never. That's just part of the shift. Doesn't matter how much is in it."

"Thank you."

Seymour walked away and found the officer in charge of the scene. "You might want to get some luminol and a black light in the women's room," he said, explaining what he'd been told about the possible bloodstains.

"We'll look into it."

Maybe they would, maybe they wouldn't, Seymour thought as he walked away. Some cops didn't like other cops putting in their two cents.

He made a perusal of the grounds. He walked up and down the lanes and checked the trash containers. He could see that the officers on scene thought he was just some old geezer sticking his nose where it didn't belong. It didn't bother him.

When he was finished looking around, he got in his car but didn't drive away.

He had to let Rachel know about the new development. She'd be upset. Graham was probably dead. Lydia was probably dead. That was how these things usually went down. Sickos preyed on rest areas. Rachel wouldn't be happy to hear about this. She'd never said it, but she'd liked the kid. Everybody had liked the kid.

Then there was the issue of Evan Stroud.

Damn.

Seymour and Rachel had always been close, and he'd never been one of those parents who kept a tight leash on his child. He didn't believe in that. Kids had to learn to think for themselves and even question authority.

But he shouldn't have told her about Evan and the search warrant.

He pulled out his cell phone, stared at it a moment, then forced himself to make the call. When she answered he closed his eyes and took a deep breath.

*   *   *

Rachel slowly hung up the phone, dreading what she had to do next.

From down the hall she heard the shower shut off. Five minutes later Evan appeared, dressed and clean-shaven. He'd put the same clothes back on—jeans and an untucked gray shirt over a black T-shirt, all badly wrinkled. "What's wrong?"

"Something's happened." But he already knew that. How he knew, she wasn't sure. "It's Graham."

From her years as a coroner, she'd learned it was best to say what had to be said clearly and concisely, packing as much information into that first sentence as possible, because once the ear heard the bad stuff, the brain shut down.

"You'd better move."

The shades and curtains were drawn, but sunlight crept in through cracks and around edges. With her hands on his shoulders, she walked him backward down the hall, where there were no windows. Behind him, several photographs had been grouped together on the wall. Of her mother, her father. There was even one of both their families, taken on a camping trip up north.

"Graham is missing," she told him. "Lydia's car was found at a rest area northwest of here."

His reaction was familiar. First came the shock. It was a physical thing—almost like the body taking a blow. Then came the shutdown. For Evan, that lasted only a few seconds before he came around and began thinking once more. She watched him pull himself together, watched his mind reach for information. "Signs of foul play?"

"Nothing obvious, although my father said he talked with the janitor who called it in. She scrubbed what looked like blood off the floor of the women's restroom."

"And the men's?"

Where Graham would have gone. "Nothing. The abduction could have been random," she continued. "Random victims are often attacked at rest areas."

What she didn't say—and maybe he didn't know—was that those kinds of attacks were the hardest to follow, because there was no acquaintance trail to trace back to the perpetrator.

"But they can't be sure it was an abduction," he pointed out.

"It's the most likely scenario."

"What about an Amber Alert?"

"They only do those if they have a lead. If they know the abductor's car. But they're getting the Missing Children's Network involved. They cropped—" She stopped, then continued. "They cropped the recent photo of Graham and are printing flyers."

"The first twenty-four hours are the most important," Evan said. "That's what you always hear. It's been over twenty-four hours."

"Yes." It was true. She'd rarely seen a good outcome after the forty-eight-hour mark.

Evan turned toward the wall. He was trying to maintain control. "It seems strange that they're both missing, don't you think?" He stared at a photo of Rachel and her father that had been taken at Lake

Tuonela. She was tiny, holding a fishing pole while her dad baited the hook. "If someone wanted to abduct a teenager," Evan said, "they would just take him. They wouldn't also take Lydia."

"I've seen abduction cases where witnesses were also abducted." Rachel left out the part about witnesses almost always being killed.

"What about Chelsea Gerber?" Evan straightened from the frame and turned around. "How long was she missing before her body was found?"

He was a researcher. Not the same as an investigator, but their minds worked in similar ways. They asked pertinent questions. They looked for connecting threads.

"Gerber was killed almost immediately," Rachel said. Not what a father would want to hear. Not what anybody would want to hear.

"Who's on the case?"

"Division of Criminal Investigation."

"Same people involved in the Gerber case." They both knew how little progress DCI was making. "I can't turn myself in now. I have to find Graham."

"Find Graham? *How?*"

"You'd be amazed by what I can get done at night," he said. "When everybody is asleep."

Chapter 28

Graham came awake with a jerk, his heart slamming.

Don't sleep. Can't fall asleep.

Last thing he knew, he'd been sitting on the mattress, his back against the wall, eyes open wide as he tried to make out any movement or sound. Now he was lying down.

He shoved himself up.

Still dark. Still night.

The night lasted forever. You never thought about that when you slept through it. You went to sleep and you woke up and that was that. But it went on and on and on.

He'd already lost track of how long he'd been there. Two nights? Three? He thought it was three. A little food. No water. No sleep. Freezing his ass off.

What was he doing here? He couldn't even remember why it had seemed important.

To get away from his mother. Yeah, he knew that. But he'd rather have her beat his ass every day than have to stay here any longer.

Alba had assured him he'd fix things, that he'd

figure something out. Like maybe find a decent place for Graham to hide. Maybe a place for him to start over with a new identity. He was almost an adult. He could do that. He could take care of himself.

But Alba hadn't been around.

And this was fucked.

That's all Graham knew.

Something small scurried nearby, and Graham imagined little mouse nails on the floor.

He'd been hallucinating. Yesterday he stepped outside in the woods and thought he saw some people walking around in the graveyard next to the church. Graham had quickly ducked behind the trunk of a tree, and when he looked again, nobody was there.

And hadn't they been dressed kinda weird? In old clothes?

One man had worn a black coat with tails; a woman was in a long, dark dress.

And hadn't somebody been crying?

Yes.

Wasn't somebody crying right now?

He listened intently.

There it was. That high, keening wail. That sobbing.

A woman. The woman he'd told Alba about.

The coyote.

He tried to picture the word in his mind. How did you spell that? He couldn't remember. He couldn't think. He hadn't been able to think clearly for a long time.

"Help me!"

The voice didn't come from Graham's head, but from somewhere outside.

A tremble shot through him, and his scalp tingled. Had he really heard that? Or was he dreaming while he was awake? People did that. He'd read about it. If you went without sleep for too long, you started dreaming when you were awake.

"Help me!"

He let out a terrified sob, then slapped a hand over his mouth.

Oh, God.

He scrambled up off the mattress. Arms outstretched, he moved forward through the blackness, taking high, awkward steps, trying to recall where the holes in the floor were.

He made it to the door and paused, his heart hammering.

She was out there. The crying coyote woman.

Don't leave. Stay here, where you're safe.

Safe?

He was losing his mind here. He was starving to death here.

He squeezed through the narrow opening. As soon as his feet touched soft ground, he took off. To the right was the way out. He remembered that. To the right, past the graveyard, down a lane.

His eyes were open so wide he thought his eyeballs would fall out. His legs ripped through tangled vines, and his boots broke dead twigs. He could make out some shapes that were dark and low to the ground. That were darker than the rest of the darkness.

Bushes? Or cloaked, crouched people?

His arms and legs pumped; his chest rose and fell, and his lungs burned. His foot caught and he was hurtled forward, slamming into the ground, the breath knocked out of him.

"Help me!"

She was closer now. She was following him.

Shit. Oh, shit.

He scrambled to his feet.

Suddenly, off in the distance, appearing and disappearing between tree trunks, a light caught his attention.

He ran for that light, his lungs raw, his legs shaking.

Alba's house. Must be Alba's.

He didn't take his eyes off the light.

He fell. He got back up. He fell again. And got back up.

Don't stop. Don't look back. Just run. Run like hell.

He came to a gate.

Locked.

He climbed to the top, swung both legs over, and dropped to the other side.

He heard a sound—like the release of a spring—immediately followed by a solid metal snap.

Raw, tearing pain ripped through his ankle.

Run. Keep running.

His eyes refocused on the light, which he now recognized as a kitchen window. He launched himself toward it. His leg was jerked out from under him.

He screamed.

She was grabbing him. The coyote woman had him by the foot and was pulling him back. He screamed again and dug his fingers into the ground, trying to wrench himself away, trying to kick himself free.

Clang.

Like the rattle of a heavy chain.

The pain in his ankle was intense. Worse than anything he'd ever felt before in his life.

He curled around and reached for her hands, her claws—and touched cold metal. Something metal was wrapped around his ankle. Something metal with jagged teeth.

A trap. The kind of trap hunters used. Attached to the trap was a chain, the chain attached to the fence.

The inside of his boot felt slick and warm. It took him a moment to realize that it was filling up with blood.

"Alba!" he screamed. *"Alba!"* And then, *"Help me!"*

Working blindly, he tried to separate the locked teeth of the trap. Dizziness washed over him, and he blacked out.

When he came to, he was lying on his back, the pain in his ankle so intense that his muscles were bunched, his teeth gritted hard enough to snap his jaw.

In the distance a light flashed.

The house. A porch light. A flashlight.

Thank you, Jesus.

Somebody had heard him. Someone was coming.

He could see the light wending its way toward him, bouncing, getting brighter and closer.

He wanted to go home. Even if it meant going home to his mom. He wanted a bed. A shower. Food. Sleep. He didn't want to die, not like this.

"Who's there?" the man with the flashlight demanded. It sounded like Alba.

"Here! I'm here!" Graham shouted, his voice snagging on a sob.

The man with the light closed the distance between them, until Graham could see that it *was* Alba.

"Oh, my God," he sobbed. "Am I glad to see you. My foot! I caught it in a trap. I'm bleeding all over!"

Funny that he'd tried to kill himself not long ago and he hadn't been scared for a second. But this was different. A trap. A trap meant for an animal.

When Alba didn't hustle, Graham grew impatient. "Hurry! You have to get me out of here! You have to get me out of this thing!"

Who would have put it there? Who would have left something like that there, right out in the open? Right by a gate where anybody could step on it?

He was already imagining being taken to the hospital and having to come clean about running away. He didn't like hospitals, but that was okay. Better than losing his fucking foot.

What was Alba doing? Standing there, looking at him.

"Help me!" Graham shrieked. "Get this off me!"

He was freaking out.

Still Alba didn't move any nearer. Finally he spoke: "I put the trap there."

"W-what?"

"I'm not that strong, and it was hard to set."

"Are you crazy? What were you thinking? Anybody could have stepped in it. I stepped in it. What were you trying to catch?"

"You were supposed to stay at the church," Alba said. "But I was afraid you might get tired of it. I was afraid you might decide to leave."

Graham stared into the blinding light, unable to see Alba's face. But Alba could see his, and Graham's expression had to reflect the sick horror he was feeling, even though his mind was still denying what he'd just heard.

"Last night I caught a feral cat," Alba said. "The night before, a raccoon. But I set the trap for you."

Chapter 29

Graham was having a really fucked-up dream.

One of those dreams that seemed more real than real life. One where you could actually feel pain. A lot of pain. In his dream he'd been running and he had gotten his foot caught in a trap. Right now his foot and ankle hurt like hell with a deep, heartbeat throb.

Wake up. Wake up so the pain will stop. So the nightmare will end.

He kept repeating the command until he finally woke up.

Or so he thought, but it ended up being one of those trick dreams. One of those dreams where you thought you were awake, but you were really in another stage of the dream.

His foot and ankle still hurt; he was still asleep.

Open your eyes. Maybe that'll work—just open your eyes.

He did.

Broken rafters above, filthy mattress below.

The church at Alba's place.

Home, sweet home.

But something was wrong. Really, really wrong.

He was bound up tight in some kind of Harry Houdini thing. A chain had been wrapped around his body over and over, his arms left free. The heavy links trailed away to encircle the leg of a nearby pew attached to the floor.

Travis jumped up from the back of the building. "Hey, man. I was startin' to think you was never gonna wake up."

The nightmare was real, the pain in Graham's leg intensified now that he was awake. "Unchain me." His voice came out a hoarse croak.

He tried to sit up but couldn't. Even the slightest movement made the pain a million times worse. Dark spots floated in front of him.

"You pissed him off," Travis said in a voice that was too casual for the situation and made Graham wonder if maybe he was still dreaming. "You can't ever piss him off."

"Who? What are you talking about?"

"Alba."

Graham closed his eyes and let his head drop. He tried to calm his breathing so maybe the pain wouldn't be as bad. It didn't work. If your pain was a ten and it fell to a nine . . . that wasn't much of an improvement. "Unchain me," he gasped with drama that would have been embarrassing as hell if he had given a shit about that right now.

"Sorry, dude. I can't."

Graham's mind was a mess, but not such a mess that he couldn't figure out what had happened. "You abducted me."

"No. No, man."

"Yes, you did. And now I'm a prisoner. Isn't that right?"

"No! No, you weren't! Not until now. Not until you pissed him off."

"Don't you mean until I tried to leave?"

Anger surged through him, and he momentarily forgot about the pain. "Come on!" He strained against the unforgiving metal. "Unchain me, asshole! Can't you see how fucking lame this is? How fucking stupid?"

"He told me to watch you and make sure you woke up. I guess you lost a lot of blood. But I gotta get outta here before dark. I can't stay here after dark."

"Why are you doing this? What's in it for you? I mean, I thought we were friends." Bullshit, but it seemed like a good tactic. And Graham had liked Travis more than he liked Travis's buddies.

"We're going to become immortal," Travis said.

Graham always knew Travis was stupid, but he'd never guessed how stupid.

"What does Alba want with me? I don't get it."

"He said you're bait."

Like ransom? Graham wondered.

His mom didn't have any money, but maybe Stroud did. How much did writers make? He'd never really thought about it. The famous ones probably made money, but he didn't think Stroud was famous. He'd never once run into anybody who'd ever heard of him. But then, he didn't hang out with people who read books.

Travis pulled out his cell phone, punched his

thumb across some buttons, then lifted the phone to his face. "Yeah, he's awake." A pause. "He seems to feel okay." He turned to Graham. "You feel okay, don't you?"

What the hell?

"Here." Travis crouched down and held the phone to Graham's ear. "He wants to talk to you."

"Sorry I can't be there," came Alba's voice over the small phone. "But today's our dress rehearsal for the play."

Graham's stomach dropped.

Over the past few days Graham's world had become incredibly small. He'd almost forgotten about school and the play. About Isobel.

Alba was roaming around playing cool drama teacher when he shouldn't be allowed near those kids.

"How do you feel?" Alba asked.

Graham had always thought he'd had some experience with insanity—spending his life with a sick woman he sometimes refused to think of as anything more than the Uterus—but Alba took craziness to a new level. The calm normalcy of it all was too much.

Graham blew up. "You crazy son of a bitch!" He wanted to say more, but the rage and frustration exploded in his head and made him dumb and confused. Suddenly he wondered who the real crazy one was here.

"Sorry, Graham," Alba told him. "You seem like a nice kid."

Graham let out a loud sob, distantly aware of Travis hunkered over him, the hand with the phone next to his face. "My fucking foot is going to fall off, and you're critiquing my personality? I'm going to lose my foot!"

"I have to go," Alba said, his voice casual and unchanged. "Someone is here. Hello, Isobel. No, come on in. I was just signing off." Then, back to Graham. "Talk to you later, dude," he said in what he probably assumed was coolspeak.

It obviously worked. Everybody seemed to be falling for it.

Travis closed and pocketed the phone, then stood up. "It's getting dark. I gotta go. Need anything?"

"What do you think?"

"Sorry," Travis said. "I really am." He looked around, picked up a blanket, and tossed it over Graham. "Things'll be okay. You'll see."

"I might die," Graham said. "Did you ever think about *that*?"

"It won't happen."

But Graham could see the idea made Travis uncomfortable. "I'm probably dying right now."

"You just need to rest, that's all."

"My foot got cut half off by some rusty piece of metal." He didn't know if it had been rusty or not, but it sounded good. "I need a tetanus shot. I probably need antibiotics; otherwise I'll get gangrene. Otherwise my foot will rot and I'll get blood poisoning and die."

He didn't want to look at it. He didn't want to see what damage had been done, but he made himself unlace his boot. "Pull it off," he said, extending his leg.

Travis shook his head and took two steps back.

"Come on. Don't be a chickenshit."

Guys like Travis didn't like to be called chicken. Travis stepped forward and grabbed the boot with both hands.

"Easy," Graham said.

"What if your whole foot comes off in the boot?"

"Come on. Pull it."

He gave it a slow tug.

Sweat broke out on Graham's upper lip. A second later his entire body was drenched, and the pain had him squeezing his leg with both hands and clenching his teeth until they should have shattered.

"Oh, man," Travis said once the boot was free.

The sock that used to be white was burgundy.

"Pull off the sock."

Using a finger and thumb, Travis peeled off the sock and dropped it to the floor. "That's some nasty shit, dude. I think I see a bone." He leaned closer. "Two bones." He looked up at Graham, who was breathing fast and hard through his mouth, still gripping his leg. "That is awesome," Travis said. "I mean, I can't believe you're not screaming your fucking head off."

"Okay, so now don't you see why you need to let me go? You need to take me to a hospital. Just dump me at the door of the emergency room. I won't say anything to anybody. I swear."

Travis's gaze left the foot he was still holding, went to an area near the door, then returned. "I can't do that." He let go of Graham's foot and began to back up. "Do you know what kind of trouble I'd be in if I did something like that? Man." He shook his head. "That would suck. That would suck so much."

Graham lowered his foot to the filthy mattress and propped himself up on his elbows, trying to concentrate through the pain-induced stupor. "Think about what you're doing." But Graham knew it was a lost cause. Travis had made up his mind a long time ago.

Travis spun around, grabbed a small paper bag from the church pew, and slid it across the floor, where it bumped against the mattress. "I brought you some stuff. A little something I ripped off from my mom. I'll be back tomorrow."

"I'll be dead tomorrow," Graham said, staring into Travis's eyes, hoping to draw out some spark of compassion. All he saw was nervousness and fear.

"I didn't bring a flashlight. I gotta go."

Travis slipped through the doorway. Graham listened to the sound of his feet pounding over the ground. Then he gave in to the pain and collapsed against the mattress.

Later, as darkness crept in through the cracks and around the corners, Graham forced himself to open the bag Travis had left. The brown paper was soft from being handled so much. Inside Graham found a beer, a candy bar, and a prescription bottle.

No water?

No real food?

In the dim light he read the prescription. Vicodin. No secret what that was for.

He twisted off the cap, shook the single pill into his palm, and downed it with beer.

He'd planned to take only one swallow, but he

was so damn hungry and thirsty. He emptied the bottle in less than a minute. Next came the candy bar, unwrapped and finished off in five bites. Chocolate and peanut butter. He'd never been crazy about candy, but it tasted amazing.

His stomach must have shrunk, because suddenly he felt stuffed. He'd managed to forget about his foot for a few minutes.

He bent his leg to look at it. Thank God it was almost dark. Otherwise it probably would have scared the hell out of him.

Dizziness washed over him, and he broke out in a cold sweat.

Fainting.

He let go of his foot, straightened his spine, then tumbled over backward against the mattress, losing consciousness.

Graham drifted in and out of sleep. There were times when he awoke and knew his head was screwed up. His thoughts were weird, and they floated off in directions that had nothing to do with his present situation.

Other times he would wake up with a terrible start, his leg raw fire, his heart pounding. He was going to die here like this. Rotting on some filthy mattress in the middle of nowhere.

He floated. . . .

And dreamed that animals were eating him, chewing on his leg. He could hear them munching. In his sleep, in the throes of his nightmare, he let out a scream that woke him up. He sat upright, staring into the darkness.

He'd never felt so alone in his life. The loneliness of this new existence was driving him crazy. From the corner of his eye he saw a movement. He gasped and turned.

Blackness. How had he seen anything when it was pitch-black?

From outside came a wail. He squeezed his eyes shut even though it didn't change anything, and he begged for morning to come. The pain in his leg was worse now. The Vicodin must have worn off. He grabbed his leg and rocked back and forth.

What time was it?

He couldn't even guess. Maybe early. Maybe before midnight. Or late. Almost dawn. He tipped back his head and let out a cry of frustration and rage and pain. And then he began shouting, crying for help. Maybe somebody would hear him. Maybe somebody would come.

Suddenly he heard a bird. Then another. With his eyes wide-open, he began to make out the vague shapes of pews, the altar, windows.

Morning was coming. *Thank God.*

And then he heard a new sound. Something closer than the wailing. Something right outside, scratching at the door.

His breath caught, and he focused in the direction of the sound.

Scratch, scratch, scratch.

A raccoon, he told himself. He exhaled, then inhaled raggedly.

Black had turned to gray.

More scratching, followed by a moan.

A human moan.

The door couldn't be closed or opened all the way. It was always ajar. In that opening a hand appeared. Low to the ground, very near the floor.

A hand.

Followed by an arm and long, tangled hair.

Jesus.

A woman in a torn dress came crawling across the floor toward him, dragging a pair of lifeless, bloody legs behind her.

The fabric of the dress seemed vaguely familiar.

No. No, it couldn't be.

He had to be dreaming. He had to be asleep.

The woman tilted her head and looked up. He could just make out a single eye peeking between two curtains of matted hair that was tangled with twigs and moss. She lifted a hand—a broken-nailed, bruised, and bloody hand—toward him. In one long exhale, she gasped: *"Graham."*

How many times had he had this dream? This nightmare?

Only this was real.

His mother.

Alive, her flesh rotting and falling off her bones right before his eyes. He didn't know why she was here, and why she was a stinking, bloody horror. It didn't make sense, but nothing made sense.

He tried to scramble away, moving off the mattress, his back to the wall, the chain pulled tight.

She was coming for him.

Chapter 30

Her clawed, bloody hand latched around Graham's injured ankle.

He screamed. Then fainted.

When he came to, she was hovering over him, her hair hanging on either side of her discolored face as she stared at him with glassy eyes.

"Gra-ham." She spoke his name on a broken exhale.

This can't be real. This can't be happening.

It was a twisted parody of everything he'd always feared. It was like somebody had crawled into his brain, discovered his biggest nightmare, and presented it to him.

She lifted her hand. With a ragged nail she touched his cheek, scratching him. "You gotta get outta this place."

What?

Those weren't the words he'd been expecting. He hadn't expected her to be on his side.

"What are you doing here?" He pulled his head back into the mattress as far as he could, trying to get away. "How did you get here?"

"Your friends . . . tried to kill me. They attacked me." Her sentences were short and broken. "Put me in the trunk. Thought I was dead. I could hear you." She pulled in a breath. "Talking. In the backseat."

Graham struggled to put it together, to make sense of what she was telling him.

She'd been in the trunk. While they were laughing and drinking vodka, she had been in the trunk. That was *so messed up.*

"They dumped me. In a well. I finally got out. Couldn't walk. Didn't know what direction to go. I think . . . I kept going 'round in circles." She touched his face again. "Then I heard you scream."

She was the person he'd heard crying and sobbing and calling for help.

He put a hand on her shoulder. That felt weird, so he took it away. "You're right. We have to get out of here. Now."

She looked down at the chains wrapped about his body and around his good leg. She looked at the lock. "The key? Where is the key?"

"I . . . I don't know." Alba probably had it.

Graham had a sudden flashback of Travis's reaction when he'd begged him to let him loose. He'd looked in the direction of the door.

"Maybe the key is stashed over there somewhere. I saw somebody lookin' that way." He pointed. "On a ledge, or under a stone or something."

Remaining on the floor, she pushed herself upright with both arms, swiveled around, and began dragging herself toward the door. That's when it dawned on Graham that both of her legs were broken. Somehow she'd managed to pull herself out of the well using only the strength of her arms.

For so many years he'd been terrified of her, resentful of her. Now, as he watched her struggle, tears burned his eyes and he had to blink them away.

Between ragged breaths she tugged up the flat stones of the entryway one after the other, occasionally collapsing while she waited for the weakness to pass.

"No," she finally sobbed. "Nothing."

"What about the wood floor?"

She shifted her body, then felt around between the broken boards. She pulled up a loose slat. "I see something." She stretched herself out to reach inside the gap. "A key!"

Graham's heart soared. Maybe they would get out of here. Maybe they would make it.

She dragged herself back across the floor.

"Here." He reached for the key.

She put it in his palm, her hand trembling violently. Once he had the key, she collapsed.

He was shaking almost as much as she was, and for a moment he thought it was the wrong key, put there as a trick, as a twisted mental game. It slid into the lock, but he couldn't get it to turn.

No! It had to be the key.

His heart was slamming in his chest. He pulled out the key and jammed it in again, turning it back and forth.

The lock fell open.

He let out a laugh of exhilaration.

He unhooked the lock, then unwrapped the chain, letting it drop to the floor with a heavy crash. He didn't know where they would go, but they would run. They would get away and hide, then figure out the next move.

"Go!" she gasped. "Hurry! Before somebody comes!"

He looked at her in question. "What about you?"

"Can't."

"You have to!"

"I've been a bad mother. I want . . . to make it up to you. Let me . . . make it up to you. Here. Now."

"You can take me out for pizza."

She laughed. She actually laughed. He'd never had much luck getting that reaction out of her.

"I wasn't supposed to be . . . a mother. The idea . . . of being a mother made me sick. I resented it. I took it out on you."

"You hated me."

She stared at him for a long time. "Yes."

It was no secret. He'd always known. It had been hard growing up with that kind of hatred. He waited for her to tell him that she loved him. That deep down she'd always loved him.

"Go," she said. "Get the hell out of here."

He grabbed his boot. His foot was swollen, and he had trouble getting the boot on. The pain almost made him pass out again.

"Don't think about how much it hurts," she said. "Focus . . . on getting away."

He stood up, keeping most of his weight on his

good foot. "You can't stay here." He couldn't leave her for Alba to find.

He grabbed the blanket and spread it on the floor next to her. He somehow managed to drag her onto the blanket. She was light, but it wasn't easy. Then he grabbed two corners of fabric and began limping backward, pulling her across the floor, stopping at the door.

"You have to help me get you outside." He shifted out of her way. "I'll hide you in the woods, then come back for you."

She gave him a familiar look that was full of exasperated annoyance and disgust. Then she rolled to her side and started to squeeze through the doorway.

Halfway through the opening, she froze.

"Go! Go!" Graham urged from inside.

"Turn around," Lydia said quietly in a way you might talk if you were afraid of stirring up a mean dog. "Turn around . . . and run."

Graham looked through the gap.

Alba stood a few feet away, his arms crossed at his chest. Beside him were Travis and the blond kid, Craig.

Graham turned and ran.

Ignoring the pain in his ankle, he skirted a pew and dodged across gaping floorboards to pull himself onto a window sill. Feet braced in the opening, he jumped, crying out and folding when he hit the ground.

On his feet again, he scrambled through the

ragged underbrush, limping heavily. Behind him, he heard a scream.

He paused and turned in time to see a massive rock, held in two hands, coming at him.

Chapter 31

"Isobel."

Isobel let out a startled gasp, then peered intently into the darkness of the alley, where light from the street lamp didn't fall. She was about ready to jump into her truck when a man stepped out of the shadows.

Evan Stroud. Graham's father. He was dressed in a long black coat, his skin almost translucent. Crow black brows slanted beneath hair of the same shade.

She'd met him only once, but she sure remembered him. And knew all about him. She didn't believe in vampires, but damn! Where had he come from? How had he appeared so suddenly like that? So soundlessly? Like he'd stepped right out of the night. Or had she just been preoccupied?

"You should be more careful," he told her. "You should park your truck closer to the theater under a light."

"It wasn't dark when I got here."

"You have to think about those things. Especially now."

What he meant was, now that teenage girls were

being murdered and somebody was drinking their blood. People said it was vampires.

People said it was Evan Stroud. She couldn't help but notice the dark bruises under his eyes, the combined sense of fragility and power.

"This place may look tranquil on the surface," he said, waving long white fingers, "but that's an illusion."

She moved toward her truck. He took one step out of the deeper shadows of a tall building.

"I have to talk to you. About Graham."

She gripped her keys tightly. "I've already talked to the police—Officer Burton and some state cop."

"I know that. I'm sorry." He shifted back into the shadows so that he was only a vague shape with a deep, low voice. "Come closer."

In all of her confusion over her concern for Graham and the shock of having Evan Stroud jump out at her, she'd completely forgotten that he was a suspect in the Chelsea Gerber murder.

There was even a warrant out for his arrest. They were looking for him. The whole damn town was looking for him.

Her heart pounded in her throat, and she braced herself to turn and run. He must have read her mind, because suddenly he shot forward. He pressed a hand to her mouth and dragged her deep into the alley, into an alcove that had once been a loading dock.

She could feel his breath against her cheek. "I just want to talk," he whispered. "I haven't hurt anybody.

I'm not going to hurt you. Graham could be in danger. I have to find him, and I need your help."

He sounded sincere. A father concerned for his son. And she wanted Graham to be found too.

"Okay?" Evan asked, his hand still pressed to her mouth, but looser now.

She nodded; he slowly released his grip.

Last night she'd cried herself to sleep over Graham.

"Do you think he's dead?" *Oh, jeez!* Why had she said that? But it's what everybody was thinking and just not saying.

"If he's alive, he could be in danger."

"Maybe he ran away. Maybe he's just hiding somewhere."

"That would be my first guess if his mother weren't also missing."

"Oh, yeah. That's really weird."

"You knew him as well as anybody around here. Has he tried to contact you?"

She sensed that he was holding his breath, the next moment hinging on her response. "No." She hadn't even considered that Graham might try to get in touch with her.

"Are you sure? You have to tell the truth."

"I am telling the truth. I swear. I knew him, but we really didn't have that kind of relationship. I mean, we hung out at school and at play rehearsal, but he didn't come to my house or anything."

"I believe you."

She felt his disappointment; it was heavy and dark.

"I-I'm sorry," she said.

A sound crept into her awareness. A *ping* that at first she couldn't place. As the sound became more frequent, she realized it was rain—falling on the bricks in the alley, on metal trash can lids.

"I have to go," she said.

"Wait!"

He grabbed her once more, and for a moment she was afraid all over again.

"If you hear from him, get in touch with the coroner. With Rachel Burton, okay?"

She nodded, even though he couldn't see her. Unless he could see in the dark. "Yeah." Graham wouldn't call her. He wouldn't come to her house. He hadn't even told her good-bye. "I will."

"Isobel?" a male voice shouted from the street. "Is that you?"

"It's Mr. Alba," she whispered. "I gotta go."

Stroud released her arm and dissolved into the shadows. She turned and ran up the alley.

"What were you doing down there?" Alba asked, his voice full of concern. He held a black umbrella over his head.

"I thought I saw something."

"What?" He tipped the umbrella toward her, and she stepped a little closer, her arms hugging herself as the cold rain increased.

"An animal. A kitten, I thought."

She didn't know why she lied. She should call the police so Stroud could be put in jail. But what if he was telling the truth? What if he was innocent? Not only innocent, but also the only person who could find Graham?

"You'd better get home," Alba said. "You don't want to get sick before the play."

Using the remote on her keychain, she opened the truck door and jumped inside. Engine running, she coasted down the street and lowered the passenger window when she was even with Alba. Her left arm looped over the steering wheel, she leaned toward him. "Want a ride to your car?"

Without hesitation he ran for the truck, closed his umbrella, and jumped in, settling the point of the umbrella between his feet. "Thanks." He flashed her a smile that made her stomach feel funny.

With his back pressed into the alcove, Evan waited until he heard the truck pull away. Then he stepped into the middle of the alley and lifted his face to the cold rain.

It was coming down hard now. The bricks had absorbed the heat of the sun, and they released a scent Evan associated with summer and sudden storms. It took only a minute for the rain to soak through his coat and shirt, cooling skin that was so hot he thought he must have a fever.

In case Isobel had called the cops, Evan took off, running down the alley in the opposite direction from the street where he'd found her truck. Ending up in the warehouse district, he crossed a series of railroad tracks, then cut behind freight cars and through a tunnel that opened onto a walkway that edged the bluff and overlooked the river.

Once he was out in the open, wind whipped his saturated coattails, and cold rain pelted his face. He jammed his hands into his pockets, tipped his chin down, and walked into the deluge. At the crest of a hill he came to an area where he could view the curve of the river and the steeples of downtown Tuonela.

He braced his hands against a wrought-iron fence and gazed over the river. Even though it was dark, he could make out the curve of the water, and the softer, darker form of trees on the opposite bank.

He felt so strange. Exhilarated. Blood thrummed through his veins. The wrought iron beneath his palms was wet and cold and solid.

Back in the diagnostic stages of his illness he'd had a series of transfusions. Sometimes, even years later, he would wake up from a deep sleep with the feeling that someone else was living inside him, or that he was in some way linked to the new blood that had been pumped into his veins. He knew the blood system rejuvenated itself and that the foreign blood had long ago been replenished by his own, but someone else still lingered in the dark areas. He could feel a stranger sometimes. It was an unnerving sensation.

This feeling was like that, only much more intense.

He opened his coat and pulled out a small, insulated container he'd found in Rachel's kitchen. One of those metal hot-drink holders, the kind they sold at coffee shops. He opened it and took a long swallow of tea brewed from the mixture in the antique tin. The dark liquid was lukewarm, but that didn't matter. He drank.

Deep in the shadows, coroner assistant Dan Salsberry watched Evan Stroud drop to the ground.

Dan had been following him for quite some time. He started to move closer, then paused when Stroud staggered to his feet and straightened—like a man reborn.

Rachel woke with a start. She lay in bed, heart pounding, ears straining for the sound that had dragged her from deep sleep. Had she dreamed it? What was it called when you thought the sound in a dream was real, when it came from something in the room? In a movie it was called diegetic.

She tossed back the covers and swung her feet to the floor. Blue light from the street cut through a crack in the shades, creating a narrow path to the hallway. She followed the light, pausing outside the bathroom door, which was partly ajar. From inside she heard a faint splash.

"Evan?"

When no one answered, she slowly pushed open the door.

Someone was in the claw-foot tub. Someone with long, dark hair.

Victoria.

Unlike last time, this was no morphing of Chelsea Gerber's face into a vision from Rachel's past. What was the woman doing here? In her apartment?

What do you want from me?

Rachel couldn't move. She couldn't look away or even close her eyes. All she could do was stare in horror.

Victoria turned, long hair hanging down either side of her face.

She lifted a hand and reached for Rachel. Something dripped from Victoria's fingertips.

Blood.

Rachel finally moved. She ran down the hall to the living room. "Evan!"

She could have sworn he was nearby.

When she didn't find him in her apartment, she dashed down the stairs to the morgue, to the autopsy suite and the coolers.

She felt compelled to open the two empty drawers, then the one containing the remains of Richard Manchester. She stared at the hollow pits where eyes had once been. As she watched, the mummified face changed. It grew flesh until the apparition before her was no longer a mummy, but Evan Stroud.

Chapter 32

Standing on the small overlook, Evan occasionally spotted headlights in the distance. Whenever that happened he stepped behind the trunk of a tree and waited until they were gone. The night air, the cold rain, the smell of the earth, all reminded him that he was alive.

He needed to be reminded of that. He always needed to be reminded of that.

He stayed until the rain slowed to a drizzle. He stayed until frogs began to croak in a nearby marsh, and fog began to roll in. Morning would be coming soon.

He flipped up the wet, limp collar of his coat and strode back down the hill, retracing his path through the tunnel and along the railroad tracks. Instead of taking another slope to Main Street, he kept to the tracks, following them through the heart of town to where the bluff resurfaced and houses clung to the steep hillside.

It was easy to spot the morgue, with its turret rising from the landscape. He imagined Rachel asleep and warm. He recalled the time he'd spent in her bed, enveloped by her scent.

He closed his eyes and inhaled. He could smell her now. Like sage and lavender.

He walked toward the turret and the hill and the light. A steep set of broken cement steps, darkened by years of mildew, led straight up from what had once been a riverbed. He didn't have any trouble seeing in the dark, and he took the steps as they turned left and right, then left again, always moving up. He was hardly out of breath when he reached the curved street that led to the house on the bluff.

He crossed and ducked under the heavier shadow of the morgue. With a key he'd found in Rachel's kitchen, he unlocked the delivery door and slipped inside.

He heard a movement and turned to see Rachel standing barefoot in the long hallway, wearing a T-shirt and plaid pajama bottoms. The dim overhead lights cast the room in a retro-green, Ektachrome haze. One hand on the wall, one to her throat, she hung back. "Evan?" Her voice was tremulous. "Is that you?" She shot out of the shadows, running to him. She grabbed his arm, then let out a shudder of relief.

"What's wrong?"

She immediately looked flustered, and he could see her attempt to pull herself together. "I thought maybe you'd been arrested." She pressed a hand to her mouth and turned away.

He touched her lightly on the shoulder and she swung back around.

The fog seemed to have followed him inside. The dim lights had a haze around them. His heart thrummed in the strange way it had taken to doing lately.

He was relieved to see she was acting more like Rachel now, but there was something else going on here, something he didn't understand.

"Where did you go?"

"I had to talk to Isobel."

"Isobel?"

"She hasn't heard from Graham. I really thought she would have heard from him." *If he's still alive,* were the words not spoken.

"You were gone a long time."

He read the concern in her face, the worry.

The suspicion.

"What did you do? Where did you go?"

Where did you go?

Where had he been? Before Isobel? He didn't know . . . . He couldn't remember. "To the park. To the river."

Rachel went to the shower room adjacent to the autopsy suite and grabbed a couple of towels. Once she was out of his sight, she kept up a mental dialog, telling herself to calm down.

Her head was full of thoughts of Victoria and the Pale Immortal. Of Isobel and Graham. Of Evan and someone else—a stranger. When she returned, Evan was in the same spot.

"You need to get out of those wet clothes."

"I'm okay."

"You're soaked."

Peripherally, everything faded. Her chest felt tight, and she couldn't look away. The room seemed to narrow and darken and blur—until he was all she saw. Her eyelids fluttered, closed partially, and she inhaled, smelling tea and musty books and the scent of outdoors. Rain and a kind of peaty, boggy soil. He was so beautiful with his dark, mussed hair, his pale skin that sunlight hadn't damaged, lips that hadn't faded. He was perfect.

Perfect and diseased.

She could feel his energy, his *soul.*

Does he feel the same thing? Or was it all coming from her?

You're scaring me.

But was it fear? Really? Or was it something ineffable masquerading as fear?

He was reading her mind. He could see she wanted this. Now. Here.

His eyes were so strange, going from a light brown on the outside of the iris to dark near the pupil. She'd never noticed that before. And his lashes—they weren't extremely long, but they were black, which created a faint outline.

He's different. Evan, yet not Evan.

She felt his fingers gripping her arms. She felt him pulling her to him. Just as suddenly his mouth pressed to hers, cold and wet, gradually warming, softening. She touched his hair; she urged him closer. His jaw rubbed against her cheek; his skin smelled like a damp, warm night.

From far away thunder rumbled, rattling metal autopsy instruments in a nearby drawer. A ceiling light flickered. On the other side of the block-glass windows, the world grew dark and still.

The storm was returning.

Time and mortality didn't exist.

Don't stop touching me.

Without removing his lips from hers, he reached between them and tugged down her elastic pants and panties in a few simple movements. She heard the sound of a belt buckle, then his zipper.

He swooped over her, pressing her to the wall, his saturated clothes cold against her hot skin.

"Hurry," she whispered against his face, afraid that he would suddenly stop, suddenly realize what was happening. *Don't think*, she telepathed to him. *Don't think.*

And then he was inside her.

She felt a sweet, cramping tug that ran through her center all the way to her chest.

He was stealing her soul.

For a long, long moment, the only movement was their chests rising and falling, the air filled with ragged breathing.

"Rachel." It was a statement, but also a question.

She felt herself slipping, and a tremor ran through him.

She reached up and grabbed a water pipe above her head.

"Let go. Come closer."

She looked at him. His pupils were dilated. He seemed like someone else. Like a person she'd caught glimpses of in the glass, only to turn and see no one there.

He's not real. He's another figment of your imagination.

"You aren't close enough," he said breathlessly.

She let go.

They tumbled to the cement floor. He ran his hand over her body, touching her everywhere, shoving up her T-shirt. And then he let out a groan and was moving in her and against her so hard that she slid away and he pulled her back. He stroked her deep, all the while holding her, murmuring words she couldn't distinguish, that didn't matter anyway.

He pressed his mouth to the pulse in her neck, his lips pausing there, lingering while his hands framed her hips and lifted her to him, while her fingers dug into his shoulders.

"Don't run away."

"I'm right here."

"Don't run away."

She didn't know what he meant. She didn't care.

"You and I are linked," he said. "You know that, don't you? We've always been linked."

"No."

"Yes."

"You have to let go."

"I did."

"Really let go."

He was right. She didn't know how she knew that, but she did.

He wants your soul.

He rolled to his back, taking his weight off her, his long coat falling open. "It's up to you."

She sat upright and closed her eyes, her breathing

shallow, her hands pressed to his stomach hidden below layers of cloth.

She wanted to get closer, wanted skin-to-skin.

That won't be enough.

She opened her eyes and looked at him.

Let go.

She shook her head.

He smiled a little, but she could see the pulse beating rapidly in his neck. She could feel his skin trembling. Her hearing seemed to fade and become hollow. As she stared, a tightness coiled inside her and moved upward, as if an invisible finger stroked from the point where they were joined all the way to her throat.

She heard a strange, odd noise, and realized it came from her.

This is madness.

This isn't real. Just like Victoria isn't real.

I'm still in bed. I'm dreaming.

She felt drunk and stoned and on the verge of passing out. Like she'd been inhaling belladonna, or drinking some strange brew.

This wouldn't be enough. This would make her want more. This taste of him.

Evan's smile faded and his eyes darkened.

He rolled her to her back, his black coat covering them both. He clutched her, his face buried in her neck until he shuddered to finally collapse in her arms, sweating and shaking and spent.

They always take your soul. That's what he wants. That's what he needs.

She opened her eyes to say something and saw a monogrammed scarf around his neck.

It was a scarf she recognized, a scarf that belonged to Richard Manchester. The Pale Immortal.

Chapter 33

A fly landed on Graham's face.

Without opening his eyes, he lifted a hand and tried to wave it away. It worked for a minute, but the fly came back.

He could hear more flies gathering and buzzing in the distance. At first there were just a few, but they musta sent out their fly messengers to recruit more, because it was beginning to sound like some damn construction site, a wall of noise that was so loud and constant he sometimes became desensitized and stopped hearing it altogether. But when one of those filthy bloated fuckers landed on his face and tried to crawl up his nose, he would jerk awake and the buzz would start all over again.

At one point he realized he must have a fever. He was sweating and shaking and dreaming weird dreams. When he opened his eyes, things were still weird and he was having trouble figuring out if anything was real.

Underneath, a smell was forming. Like the buzzing it sometimes went away, even though he was sure it never really left. He just quit noticing it.

But then he would turn his head or swoosh a fly, and the air would shift and the smell would waft over him.

Like roadkill. Rotten and heavy and sweet and nauseating.

In Arizona, animals hit on the road didn't last long. Vultures ate them. What was left dehydrated in the desert heat and sun. They didn't swell up and bloat and drip like they did around here.

Don't open your eyes.

Don't open your eyes and look at her.

He drifted off—into oblivion, where he'd been spending a lot of time lately. He liked it there. Sometimes he would dream about Isobel, about sitting in the sun knitting. That was fun. He'd been happy then.

"Graham."

He ignored the voice and went back to thinking about Isobel.

But it came again. An insistent whisper. *"Graham."*

It was a voice he'd learned to obey over the years. A voice he had to listen to or there would be shit to pay.

"Open your eyes. Look at me. Listen to me."

Graham opened his eyes.

Just a crack.

He thought he remembered blood running down his forehead, dripping into them. Yeah. That's what had happened. Somebody had smacked him in the head and knocked him out. Somebody had dragged him back to the church, back to the mattress and the chains and the lock.

They didn't need the chains and lock. He couldn't move. He was one fucked-up dude. And anyway, it almost seemed right. Almost seemed like he belonged here. They should put one of those lame signs over the door with his name burned into the wood. He laughed just thinking about it.

He heard a flutter outside; then a breeze gusted through the broken windows with no glass. Above his head, something creaked.

He'd heard that sound before. He'd heard that sound a lot.

Don't look.

"Graham."

Don't look.

Out of the corner of his eye something fluttered. The fabric of his mother's dress.

He turned his head—just a little. Then a little more—until he saw a hand dangling a few feet from the floor.

The arm was swollen—like an Easter ham. The hand was triple the size it should be. Yellow juice dripped from the fingertips, leaving a puddle on the floor and a feast for the flies.

Creak.

"Graham."

She moved. She turned slightly, gracefully. *"You have to listen to me."*

Maybe she was alive. Maybe he'd just dreamed that other stuff.

His eyes tracked up and he squinted through his lashes.

A rope had been tied around her ankles. It was now buried deep into the folds of swollen flesh. They'd hung her upside down from the rafters, punctured a couple of arteries, and drained her blood.

He wouldn't have known it was her. Her head was the size of a basketball. Except for the dress and hair, it could have been some fat guy. Some sumo wrestler.

"You have to join them," she told him. *"Otherwise they'll kill you. That's the only way to get out of here alive. You have to make them think you're one of them."*

She was right.

Even though she was dead, she was right. Dead right.

His leg didn't hurt anymore.

"That's probably bad," she told him.

Okay, now she was reading his mind.

He opened his mouth. His lips were cracked. "I have a fever," he told her. Was that his voice? That weird, raspy thing? "My head hurts."

"You need water."

"I need a doctor."

"Remember when I used to sing to you?"

"You never sang to me."

"Sure I did."

"What'd you sing?"

"Bob Dylan."

"I don't like Bob Dylan."

"You never gave him a chance. You hated him because I liked him."

"I don't like his voice. He sings through his nose."

"It grows on you."

"Sing somethin', then."

She started humming, then singing. It was a song Graham recognized. "Girl of the North Country." After a moment he joined in.

Travis and Craig paused outside the broken door of the old church.

"Whew!" Travis shuddered and put a hand to his nose.

Craig tipped an ear toward the door. "Who's he talkin' to?"

Travis listened. "He's singing. I thought maybe he was dead, but he must be better."

They squeezed through the opening one at a time, then stopped.

"He ain't better."

Graham was staring at the body that hung from the ceiling. He was smiling to it. Singing to it.

"He's dying, isn't he?" Travis asked.

Craig pulled out a digital camera. "We need to get a picture of him before he croaks."

"Shh! Don't say that in front of him."

"What? Croaks? He doesn't even know we're here. Look at him."

"We better tell Alba he needs a doctor."

"Are you worried about him?"

"Kinda. Yeah. What's wrong with that? Graham's okay. He never squealed on us about the mummy."

"Graham!" Craig snapped his fingers.

Graham's head slowly came around. He somehow managed to prop himself up on one elbow. His forehead was bloody, one eye caked half shut. He gave them a little smile and a wave.

Craig stepped closer and began snapping the camera. Once they had prints, Dan, the coroner's assistant, would deliver them to Stroud.

Graham gave him a thumbs-up.

"Don't do that," Travis said to Graham, trying to breathe through his mouth and not his nose. "You can't look *happy*, you dumb shit."

"Jesus Christ," Craig said. "He's out of his fucking head." He stepped forward and raised his hand to slap Graham.

"No, wait."

Travis put himself directly in front of Graham so he could have his full attention. "Graham. Graham. Look here. Make this face." He let his mouth fall slack and tipped his head. Graham complied and Travis stepped away. "There. Take the shot. That's perfect." Craig fired off a few more rounds, then stuck the camera in his sweatshirt pocket.

"Wait!" Graham shouted after them as they hurried to leave.

"Can't stay," Travis said, thinking he might vomit.

"Take me to your leader," Graham said in an exaggerated, drunken voice. "I need to talk to your leader."

The guy was probably dying, but he was still being sarcastic. That was pretty fucking cool.

"Our leader?" Craig asked.

"Alba."

"Why?"

"I wanna become a Pale Immortal. Tell him that, 'kay? A Pale Immortal. I'm ready to take the pledge or drink the blood or whatever the hell you guys do. So tell him that, 'kay?"

Craig looked at Travis and raised one eyebrow, then shrugged. "Sure. We'll pass that on."

Graham fell back against the mattress, his eyes closed. Travis thought maybe he was dead, but then Graham muttered, "Cool."

Graham had never felt so weird before, not even when he'd smoked pot. Floaty and out-of-body. He could no longer tell the difference between reality and the crazy stuff going on in his head. And it didn't matter. That was the great thing: Nothing mattered.

Through a heavy-headed fog he thought he saw Alba float in and out of his field of vision. But maybe he was just dreaming the visitation.

Chatting with him. Talking to him. Feeding him his bullshit like he did everybody. Because the guy was most definitely full of bullshit. Only nobody seemed to know it. Nobody seemed to see it.

It was like one of those reality shows where the asshole always won. And not only did he win, but almost every fucking person rooted for him to win.

Survival of the fittest. Graham had learned all about that in school. Didn't matter how nice or how fair or how *right* you were; you had to have survival skills.

He opened one eye and saw Alba hovering over him like some mother hen, looking all concerned and worried. He was washing Graham's face.

Oh, this had to be a dream.

Then he was giving him a drink of water. Dream or not, Graham grabbed the bottle.

"Wait." Alba held out his hand. "Take this."

A pill in his palm.

"It's an antibiotic. For your leg."

Graham popped the pill in his mouth, then swallowed the rest of the water.

"I have something else." Like some magician, Alba pulled out a granola bar. Graham shook his head. Now that he'd finished off the water, his stomach felt weird. Like he might throw up.

"Yogurt?" Alba held up a container of yogurt. Where was he getting this stuff? Pulling it out of his ass?

"No." Graham dropped back on the mattress, an arm thrown over his eyes.

Alba continued to hover. He lifted Graham's bad leg and began doing something to it.

"What's going on down there?"

"I'm cleaning your ankle." Another bottle of water materialized. Alba opened it, then poured it over Graham's wound. Graham let his eyes close again. He heard someone rummaging around in a plastic bag. He heard a cap being unscrewed. More liquid hit his leg.

Graham shot upright.

"Peroxide," Alba said.

The searing pain gave way to a steady throb, and

Graham fell back against the mattress again. Alba kept fiddling around. He wrapped Graham's leg in gauze, then rested the leg on a pillow. He tucked another pillow behind Graham's head, and covered him with a warm, soft blanket.

"I'll be back to check on you later."

"Thanks," Graham said without opening his eyes.

His leg felt better already. The blanket felt amazing. Overwhelmed with gratitude, he opened his eyes and grabbed Alba's hand. "Thanks, Mr. Alba."

In that moment he loved the man. Loved his generosity and the care and attention he'd just shown. If he wanted to ignore the rotting corpse hanging from the ceiling, he could do that. "You're a humanitarian."

In the back of his mind Graham remembered how he came to have the injury in the first place, and he knew Alba had been behind his mother's murder, but the kindness he now showed erased all the bad stuff. This was a new world. A new, skewed, and messed-up world, and the rules were different. It all boiled down to viewpoint. You could look at anything and make it right or wrong. Because there wasn't any right or wrong. Just the rules set down by society.

And anyway, this wasn't the real world. It was some kind of alternate universe existing in Graham's head. If he wanted to like Alba, he could. If he wanted to ignore the rotting corpse hanging from the rafters, he could do that too.

He had a warm blanket. And a pillow.

Everything he needed.

Chapter 34

Coroner's Assistant Dan Salsberry pulled up outside the morgue. He grabbed a manila envelope off the passenger seat and climbed out of his gray Honda Accord.

He entered through the delivery door, pausing just inside. The building was silent. The cleaning woman wouldn't be there, and he knew Rachel wouldn't be home for at least another hour. Dan had made sure of that.

He took the narrow stairs, staying to one side so they didn't creak, walking on the balls of his feet, the soles of his sneakers barely making a sound. But then, somebody like Stroud could probably hear through walls.

Dan's heart was pounding hard by the time he reached the third floor. He paused and listened once more, then moved down the hallway on the strip of Oriental carpet.

At the apartment door he bent and slipped the envelope under the crack. He knocked loudly, turned, and ran like hell.

*   *   *

Inside the apartment, Evan stared at the envelope on the floor. His name was written across it in large letters.

Who hadn't viewed this scene a million times in movies and on TV? Feeling sick with dread, he picked up the envelope and ripped it open.

It contained several eight-by-ten color photos of Graham.

For a fraction of a second Evan allowed himself to dissolve, to let fear take over. Then he flew down the stairs, one hand on the railing, skipping several steps as he sailed through the air, reaching the basement level, down the hall with its low ceiling, and out the door.

Nothing. No one.

The waning light sent Evan stumbling back inside.

With the envelope still in his hand, he collapsed to the floor. Sitting cross-legged, he examined the photos.

Graham was lying on a stained mattress, his clothes filthy, his hair falling in greasy clumps. There were a couple of close-ups of his face. Graham's eyes were glassy and fevered.

He looked as if he'd lost his mind.

Evan forced himself to move on to the next photo.

It partially explained why Graham had such a disturbing expression in his eyes. This photo was of a body—hung upside down. A bloated, fly-encrusted body with hair that looked familiar.

Lydia?

The face was twice its normal size, the lips curled

and tongue protruding. It was hard to tell, but Evan was pretty sure it was Lydia.

A note from an ink-jet printer accompanied the package. A quick glance told Evan it was written from Graham's viewpoint, but hadn't really been written by him.

Dear Dad,
   Having a wonderful time. Wish you were here.

That was it. No request for ransom money. Nothing.

What was this about? Who was behind it? What did they want? And how had they known he was at Rachel's?

The photos and note could be sent to a lab for analysis. The paper and envelope could probably be traced. But that would take days. Graham didn't have days.

Evan's immediate reaction was to call Rachel. In case someone was keeping tabs on his cell phone, he went into her office and used her landline to dial her mobile number.

Voice mail.

"Call me when you get this," he said, then hung up.

He could call Seymour. But Seymour would feel duty-bound to arrest him.

State patrol. Bad idea. They would arrest him without question, while screwing up the search for Graham in the process.

Evan went back through the photos, this time

concentrating not on Graham but on anything that might provide a clue. He found it in the photo of the dead woman.

Blurred in the background was something that looked like an altar. He'd seen enough old prints to recognize the church in Old Tuonela.

"A death?" the nursing home director asked, her expression puzzled. "No, we haven't had a death. Not today."

Rachel backtracked to the conversation she'd had with Dan. He'd taken the nursing home call and relayed the message to her. "We had a report . . . " Rachel said.

The director shook her head. "Not us. Not today. Maybe one of the other nursing homes in town."

Confused, Rachel thanked her and left the building. In the parking lot she discovered that her van had a flat.

She stared at the tire, hoping it wasn't as bad as it had first appeared. Worse. Too flat to drive on. She pulled out her cell phone and called AAA. After ten minutes the agent came back on the line to inform her that someone would be there in two to three hours.

It was getting dark. Dark meant Evan would be able to leave the morgue, and she wanted to make sure that didn't happen.

She'd changed flats. Years ago.

"I'll do it myself."

She disconnected, located the tire iron, and loosened the lug nuts. She dragged out the spare, dropped it on the ground, and began jacking up the van chassis.

What had happened last night between her and Evan seemed far away, like a dream she couldn't quite remember. A few hours after the event her memory had been foggy. She wasn't ashamed, but just the same she'd managed to avoid him, not quite sure how to handle a face-to-face and feeling the need to further process their encounter before they spoke.

She got the spare in place and lowered the jack.

The spare was flat.

She let the iron slip from her fingers and fall to the ground.

Tired. She was suddenly so tired. She closed her eyes and leaned her forehead against the glass of the driver's door.

She would just rest a minute, then figure out what to do.

A sound penetrated her exhaustion.

Scratching.

One long, squeaking scrape.

She lifted her head and opened her eyes.

Sitting in the driver's seat was Victoria.

As Rachel watched, frozen in horror, Victoria dragged a nail down the glass between them.

Rachel staggered backward. She braced herself to bolt, then paused for one last look.

She could no longer see Victoria's face. Just the hand, just the fingernail scraping down the glass.

*   *   *

Rachel hadn't returned his call, and Evan couldn't wait any longer.

He hovered in the doorway of the morgue. When the last glimmer of light left the sky, he slipped out the delivery door and moved quickly down the alley, sticking to the shadows and avoiding streetlights. Whenever a car drew near, he stepped behind a tree or wall until he gained cover of a wooded area that wound through town. He followed streams and steep embankments, which eventually led to his property.

Once there, he remained hidden in the woods, watching his own house to make sure no one was around. He spotted a suspicious car down the block. Someone sat in the driver's seat.

A stakeout.

They'd probably had undercover agents watching his place since he'd taken off. Waiting for him to come back.

It felt a little strange and even satisfying to be doing something so predictable. The human animal. It was instinct to return to your comfort zone.

Everybody eventually wanted to go home.

Chapter 35

It was relatively easy for Evan to get past the under-cover cop.

The poor guy had probably been there all day. After a couple of hours, Evan imagined the mind would begin to drift and the eyes glaze over. You would start thinking about being uncomfortable, and how you had to take a piss. You'd start wondering why radio stations played the same twenty songs over and over.

Evan slipped in the basement door, closing it behind him. He paused and listened for the sound of possible alarms that may have been put in place after he'd left.

Nothing audible. No telltale clicking. Not that a lack of sound meant very much.

He moved through the dark house, bent at the waist, keeping his head low. He found a flashlight in his desk. His Smith & Wesson was gone. No surprise.

He made his way to the windowless library, closing the door behind him. He clicked on the flash-light, then quickly scanned a shelf of books until he came to the leather-bound volume of Shakespeare's plays. He opened it and fished out his Glock from its hiding place.

It was no way to treat a book; that was for damn sure. But Evan hadn't been the one who'd actually done the damage, and when he'd come across the oddity in an antiquarian bookstore, he'd noticed it would be the perfect fit for a handgun.

Also included was a tray of shells.

Load it.

Pocket the extra shells.

For a moment, standing there surrounded by the smell of books, he longed for his old life, his life of a few weeks ago. Now those days seemed comforting and safe. But back then there had been no Graham. No Rachel.

He dug out a huge, dusty antique plat book. With the handle of the flashlight in his mouth, he thumbed through the crisp, yellowed pages until he came to a map of Old Tuonela. He tore it out, folded it, and shoved it in the back pocket of his jeans.

In the bedroom he found a shoulder holster hanging from a hook in the closet.

Evan had grown up around guns. His dad had made sure Evan knew how to shoot and take care of a gun before he was old enough to ride a bicycle.

He removed his coat and slipped on the holster, sliding the Glock into place. The extra clip went into the front pocket of his jeans, extra shells in the deep pocket of his coat, which he shrugged back into.

Ready for part two.

This wouldn't be as easy.

With keys in his hand, he moved through the

house and down the stairs to the basement. Out the door, then pause and listen.

Silence, except for cicadas and croaking frogs.

He moved through the darkness to the garage. He unlocked the walk-in door and slipped inside, smoothly closing it behind him. His car was still there. He'd been afraid the police had confiscated it, but that would have been extreme.

He settled behind the driver's seat.

Key in ignition.

Two deep breaths.

Turn the key.

The engine rumbled to life.

He gave it one second, then pushed the remote-control box clipped to the visor. The garage door creaked open.

Slow. So fucking slow.

Evan pressed down on the clutch and put the car in gear, his right foot on the gas.

Come on, door. Come on.

When the space looked big enough, he tromped down on the gas and shot through the opening.

The car roared up the sharp incline and bottomed out on the sidewalk in front of the undercover cop. Sparks flew and tires squealed as Evan made a sharp right turn onto Benefit Street.

The cop's headlights came on. A second later a red light was flashing and a siren blared.

Leaving his headlights off, Evan shifted into second and increased his speed. He'd mapped out the route in his head before he'd even stepped from the house.

He cut up one alley, then another, with the guy in the stakeout car staying with him. Evan was impressed and getting a little worried.

He didn't want to go too fast through town, so he had to rely on sharp turns. He also knew the longer the chase went on, the more likelihood there was of backup being called in and his ass being caught and tossed in jail. He couldn't let that happen.

Down into the valley and the heart of Tuonela. Over railroad tracks, behind warehouses, back up the hill, and a quick right to hit City Park.

He checked the rearview mirror.

Headlights appeared, along with the strobe and siren.

Focusing on the street in front of him, Evan accelerated and took a quick right that plunged him down a steep cobblestone lane.

Lover's Leap.

A hairpin curve, then another quick right.

The road fell out from under him. Low branches scraped the sides of the car as the tires regained contact with the ground.

Evan cut the engine.

He tumbled out, shutting the door behind him. The narrow lane was a dead end used by maintenance workers. If he was spotted, there was no escape by car.

Ducking, knees bent, he ran for cover of the stone wall that circled the end of Lover's Leap. Above his head twin headlight beams bounced off tree trunks. The beams shifted as the car made the hairpin curve, tires squealing.

Keep going. Just keep going.

Evan crouched lower, hands pressed to the stone wall as the siren and flashing light invaded the quiet.

Evan listened intently, waiting for any hesitation or indication that the driver was backing up or turning around. The vehicle stopped, then sped away.

Evan waited a full half hour. Then he returned to the car, backed up the hill, shot onto the narrow lane, and headed out of town.

Chapter 36

A distant rustling and murmur of voices coaxed Graham out of a semiconscious state.

It was dark. Pitch-black.

He turned his face toward the vicinity of the door. A circular glow appeared in the blackness, followed by a rustling of movement.

Alba entered the church, a lantern in hand. His footfalls echoed across the floor as he set the light on a nearby pew.

"How are you feeling?"

Travis, Craig, and Brandon trailed after him.

Graham struggled to get himself upright, elbows pressed into the mattress. His head felt thick, and the movement made him dizzy.

Alba dug into a plastic shopping bag and pulled out candles, which they all lit. Then Alba crouched down by Graham, produced a key, and unlocked the padlock.

"Whew," Travis said, raising a hand to his face and leaning back. "He stinks."

Alba smiled at Graham as he unwound the chains. "Look who's talkin', huh?"

A shared joke.

Graham nodded and smiled back as much as he could. Once the chains were off he felt light, so light he would have to be careful or he might float all the way up to the ceiling and out a hole in the roof.

He was thirsty. Not hungry anymore. He hadn't been hungry in a long time.

Alba must have read his mind. Or had Graham been thinking out loud? Anyway, Alba pulled out an insulated mug that said PEACHES on the side.

God, that didn't even seem real, thinking about that place. This. *This* was real.

The girl . . . What was her name . . . ?

Alba unscrewed the lid and held the mug out to Graham. It was one of those tall, thin ones, the kind that didn't have a handle.

Alba laughed. What was he laughing at? He lifted the cup to Graham's mouth. "Come on, drink this. You'll feel better."

As soon as the cold metal touched his mouth, Graham's body responded by swallowing.

Thick. Cold. Salty. Metallic.

He recoiled and looked down. "What the hell?"

"Just drink it."

Graham wiped his mouth, then checked out his fingers. *Red.* "What is it?"

"You know what it is."

"Blood?"

Graham glanced up to where *she* had been.

"We took it down, remember?" Alba asked. "This morning. And I wouldn't give you her blood. What kind of person do you think I am? That's sick."

Graham thought about the blood he'd heard had been stolen from the hospital. For some reason that didn't seem so bad. Already packaged and on a shelf. Kinda like grocery shopping. Maybe the blood in the cup was that blood. Maybe he wouldn't even ask.

"You want to be a Pale Immortal, don't you?" Alba asked.

Graham looked past Alba's shoulder to Travis, who was standing there taking it all in. He gave Graham an exaggerated nod, then went through a drinking pantomime.

Graham lifted his hand and wrapped his fingers around the mug. That single swallow and he could swear he already felt stronger. And it hadn't tasted that bad, he tried to convince himself. It had just been a surprise, that's all.

He looked down at the container. It wasn't full. It wasn't even half-full. That was good. He looked up at Alba. "Do you have a straw?"

Everybody laughed. All of them. Travis doubled over, bracing his hands on his knees.

Yep, I'm a fucking clown. Just give me some balloons to twist into a wiener dog.

He really *had* wanted a straw.

He lifted the mug to his mouth and downed the contents in two takes, pausing between each hoist of the cup to gag slightly. When he was finished he returned the container to Alba and wiped the back of his hand across his mouth.

He could feel the blood lying cold in his belly. Maybe it had been cow's blood. Maybe it hadn't been human blood at all.

"Where'd you get that?" he asked, unable to stop himself, even though he didn't want to know.

The blood was beginning to warm up, beginning to digest. He hadn't eaten in so long that his stomach felt huge. It was rumbling, kicking into gear as it struggled to figure out what to do with this shit. "Was the blood from a person?"

"Oh, yeah." Travis smiled a huge smile. "Can we bring her in now?"

Her? The donor was with them? Graham didn't like that. He didn't like that at all.

Travis disappeared out the door. Graham heard feet shuffling through dry weeds and grass. Then a movement in the opening caught his eye as someone stumbled into the room.

The girl.

The girl whose name he couldn't remember.

Isobel.

Her mouth was covered with silver duct tape, her wrists bound in front of her with the same stuff. She was wearing a black skirt and a pink sweater he remembered from that other life of so long ago. Her knees, above black boots, were caked with blood. And her face . . . Her face was gray; she had dark circles under her eyes.

She stared at him, freaked out.

He was glad the dead body wasn't still hanging from the rafters.

Oh, Isobel. If you'd seen that thing.

It would have sent her over the edge. It would send anybody over the edge.

He started to move, to jump up and run to her.

Pain shot up his ankle, and he crumpled back down on the mattress.

"Pretend you're one of them," his mother's voice whispered. *"Make them think you're one of them."*

He looked back up at the beam above his head. The rope was still there, but the body was gone.

The only way to fool them is to go all the way. To become one of them, because they're smart. They'll see through you otherwise.

Now he realized her voice hadn't come from inside the room at all. It had come from outside, sounding echoey and distant.

"I believe you two know each other," Alba said, watching Graham intently.

The really weird thing was, now that he'd finished off the blood, Graham's thinking wasn't as fuzzy. His vision was even clearer. He suddenly understood that this was a test, and if he passed he would be a Pale Immortal.

"Yeah." Graham ran his tongue across his lips. "I know her."

What were they going to do with Isobel?

Once again his eyes were drawn to the rafters. He knew what would eventually happen. He knew where she would end up.

Alba motioned toward her. "You can take the tape off her mouth."

Travis, who was holding her by one arm, reached up and ripped off the duct tape. She flinched, but remained silent. Graham was impressed.

"If you make a sound, we'll put it back," Alba said. "And anyway, if you scream, nobody will hear you out here." He turned his back to them and bent over the pew near the lantern. He rummaged around in the bag and pulled out a small plastic box.

"Stand up."

Graham stood, much more carefully this time, favoring his good leg.

Alba held something small and metal in his hand.

A single-edged razor. The kind carpenters might use to scrape paint off windows.

"Take it."

Graham took it.

"I think you know what I want you to do."

"Become one of them."

Graham looked at the razor in his hand, then up at Isobel. "Yeah." He stepped toward her.

Her mouth was colorless, trembling. Tears glistened in her eyes. He wanted to tell her he was sorry, at least with his expression, but Alba wasn't dumb. He *would* read him.

So Graham remained emotionless. For a moment he thought about turning and attacking Alba, but that was a stupid idea. He could hardly stand, let alone bring down three guys.

"Why are you doing this?" Isobel stared directly at him, separating him from the pack. Graham wanted to look away, but Alba would see that as weakness.

"I thought you were different." Her voice was tired. Breathless. Good thing he was so fucked up himself. Otherwise he might have given away how worried he was.

"I *am* different."

"You think you're a vampire? There's no such thing as vampires." She looked from him to Alba, to Travis, to Craig. "There is no such thing as vampires."

Graham reached down and lifted her bound arms. Her elbows were bent, her upper arms pressed against her breasts in a cramped position. Now he could see a bandage wrapped around one of her crossed wrists.

"Not too deep," Alba warned.

You could take the teacher out of the school, but you couldn't take the teacher out of the nutcase.

Isobel ignored him. She continued to stare at Graham as if they were the only people in the room. "I trusted you," she whispered. "Out of everybody, I trusted you."

He bowed his head so she couldn't see him swallow. "You shouldn't have."

"I stood up for you when other people called you a freak."

He brought the blade down.

A line of blood appeared on her white skin. Beads formed. Blood quickly pooled, then began to run down her arm and drip on the floor. Alba put out his hand, and Graham returned the blade. Then he lifted Isobel's arm to his mouth and sucked.

"I hate you," she said quietly.

With his head bent, blood on his lips, Graham looked up at her. "I know."

They passed her around.

Like a can of beer or something. When she made

it back to Graham, he saw that she was bleeding quite a bit.

Had he cut her too deeply? Had he hit an artery?

This time she didn't speak. She didn't even look at him. He was lifting the exposed wrist to his mouth once more when whatever color in her face washed away and her eyes rolled back in her head.

She folded; he caught her before she hit the floor.

Travis helped drag her to the mattress. Alba was already pulling out a roll of gauze, which he wrapped deftly around her wrist. "Don't want her to bleed out," he said. "Not yet."

It was coming. They would string her upside down from the rafters and drain all of her blood.

Alba crouched beside her and stroked her cheek.

Graham wanted to knock his hand away.

Alba put his arms around her and dragged her against him. Watching Graham, he pressed his lips to her temple, leaving a bloody smear. "You still like her, don't you?"

Graham's heart was hammering out a warning. "I never liked her."

"You were friends."

"Not close friends."

"Did you fuck her?"

Graham closed his eyes and breathed deeply.

He wanted to hit Alba and rip his hands away from her. He'd always been a fairly mellow person, slow to anger. This rage was something new, something he'd never felt before.

"Don't do it," his mother whispered from wher-

ever they'd dragged and stuffed her body. *"Don't lose control."*

"Well, did you?"

"No." He spoke quickly, biting out the word.

"You wouldn't be playing the gentleman here, would you?"

"Why would I want to do that? We may have hung out, but that's all it was. She was there, that's all. Just a girl." He shrugged.

Alba picked up a length of chain.

"No," Graham said.

"I'm sorry, kiddo."

"I thought I was a Pale Immortal now." Had this whole act been for nothing?

"You are, but I'm not ready to let you roam free."

He should have tried to fight. He should have tried to get away. He shouldn't have listened to Lydia. When had she ever given him good advice in his entire life? Why would he start listening to her now, when the bitch was dead?

It had been a trick. She was in with Alba. They were in this together.

Graham ran a hand across his eyes. His thoughts were muddled again, the moments of clarity getting farther and farther apart.

The adrenaline that had kept him going for the past ten minutes faded. He trembled. The room began to spin, and he dropped to the floor, letting out a cry as sharp pain shot up his leg.

Travis and Craig chained them together—Graham and the still unconscious Isobel—while Alba oversaw the operation.

Spooning.

That's what it was called. The way they were puzzled front to back, both facing the same direction, with Graham behind Isobel. She was curled up in a fetal position, her wrists still taped and crossed. They dragged the chain around them, across their chests, around their waists and hips, pulling it tight with each circle.

Was she dead? Graham wondered at one point, when Isobel didn't respond to any of the jostling or positioning. No, he could see her chest rising and falling.

While Travis looped the lock through the chain links and snapped it closed, Craig toyed with a thick strand of Isobel's hair. Her hair wasn't that long, and he got really close so he could put it under his nose like a mustache. Isobel's hair almost matched the hair on Craig's head. Graham found himself staring, trying to make sense of Isobel's blond hair as Craig's mustache.

Craig made the mustache bob up and down.

"Get away." Graham shoved him.

Craig dropped the hair and stumbled backward.

"Hey, asshole." Craig turned to look at the others, while keeping a finger pointed at Graham. "He pushed me. Anybody see that? Better tape his hands."

"No!" Graham panicked, then forced himself to calm down. "I have to be able to get a drink. I need water." He ran a tongue across his cracked lips. "Just one bottle of water."

Alba looked disgusted and annoyed by all of them. "Let's go." He and his gang blew out the candles and took the lantern and flashlights, leaving Graham and Isobel alone in the dark.

Chapter 37

In Tuonela, twilight never lingered and darkness always came quickly, like an extinguished flame or a dropped curtain. The sky was a deep blue velvet when Rachel checked her cell phone and found she'd missed a call from Evan—made from her number. Most likely while she was waiting for a response from AAA. She called her own number, then tried his cell but there was no answer.

Without leaving a message she pocketed her phone and made the final ascent up a sidewalk that was broken by steep steps. Once she gained street level, she paused to catch her breath—and spotted Seymour's patrol car parked in front of the morgue.

She hurried across the street, and around the back to the service entry. The door was unlocked. She stumbled inside to find her dad standing in the hallway outside her office, the green semigloss walls a backdrop, the ceiling light casting a dark shadow on his face below his hat.

"Isobel Fry has been reported missing," Seymour said. "She didn't come home last night."

Evan had seen Isobel last night.

"And remember the girl up north who vanished?" Seymour asked. "Just found out that Evan was in the area that night. Used his credit card at a gas station three miles from where the woman was last seen."

The circumstantial and physical evidence was mounting. Add that to Evan's lost time and strange behavior and he couldn't look much guiltier.

Rachel was also guilty. She'd helped him avoid arrest. If Isobel was dead, it was Rachel's fault.

She glanced up, toward her apartment.

"He isn't there," her dad said, easily reading her. "I already checked. He was at his house not long ago. Left in his car and lost the officer who was tailing him."

"You think I might know where he went?"

He looked at her with expectation. "I was hoping."

She moved quickly past him, almost running into the autopsy suite. She opened the cooler drawers. One, two, three. The only occupant was the mummified corpse.

"Lose something?" her dad asked, appearing behind her.

"Just checking."

"I'm heading to Evan's house right now to see if I can stir up any clues."

She shut the cooler door with a loud click. "I'm coming with you."

Seymour didn't speed and didn't use his siren. He drove smoothly and efficiently, relaxed in the seat, one hand on the wheel. They might have been heading to Dairy Queen. He would order a hot-fudge sundae and she would get a cone with sprinkles. They would sit at a picnic table under the oak tree and watch the hatched mayflies come shooting out of the river.

Seymour turned the final corner, drove up the hill, and stopped in front of Stroud's house. A single police car was already there, an officer standing outside. Seymour put the car in park and shut off the engine. "All the other patrol units are at Isobel's house," he said.

On the porch, Seymour pulled out his handgun. The door was already unlocked. He pushed it open and stepped inside. When he gave the all-clear, Rachel followed.

Stroud was everywhere. This place was Evan as much as any place could be a person.

She forced herself to move through the living room, looking for any sign of disruption, any clue to where Evan might have gone.

Had he killed Isobel last night, before he'd returned to the morgue? Before they'd made love? Or had sex? Whatever it could be called.

She'd moved through the day in a fog, as if deliberately trying to forget what had happened between them. Now she concentrated on last night, and a memory came rushing back. In her mind she saw Evan wearing the Pale Immortal's scarf.

Evan is the copycat killer.

Moments ticked by until she straightened and stared at her father. "Evan thinks he's the Pale Immortal."

"That's kinda why we're here," Seymour said.

"No, I mean Evan really thinks he's the reincarnation of Richard Manchester."

Seymour looked skeptical.

"It all makes sense." Rachel spoke in a rush. "Everything. His infatuation with Old Tuonela. Even his disease. Especially his disease."

"You mean his disease isn't real?"

"It's real. The disease brought all of this on. Think about it. People have been accusing him of being a vampire for years. They treat him like a freak. The disease had destroyed his life. So he lost it. In his own head he became a vampire. He became the Pale Immortal. The fantasy has replaced what's lacking in his own life. As long as he imagines himself a vampire, he can be stronger than Evan Stroud. More powerful than Evan Stroud. He can be more than he really is."

Last night he'd pulled her into his fantasy. Last night she'd believed it too.

"That's an interesting theory, sweetheart. But to be honest, I don't care about any of that psychological stuff. I don't want to get in Stroud's head and stroll around to figure out why he's doing what he's doing. I just want to stop him."

Seymour checked Evan's answering machine. Only a few messages, all old. Two were from his editor, one from his agent, another from his father, and a couple more from a lawn-care company. The editor and agent wanted to know the approximate delivery date of his next book.

How quickly things changed.

"They must have called before word got out that he was wanted for questioning," Rachel said.

She sifted through a pile of mail on the table, but nothing jumped out at her. "He came for the car, of course," she said. "But what else would he have gotten?"

"Money. Credit cards. Travel clothes. Passport maybe."

"So you think he's heading out of the country."

"That would be my guess."

"He can only travel at night."

"He'll go as far as he can, then stop for the day."

"I don't think he's leaving. Not with Graham still missing."

"He wasn't even aware of the kid's existence until two weeks ago. And let's face it, you know the statistics. Graham's been missing long past the crucial window. Evan would also know that."

Rachel pulled out her cell phone and tried to reach Evan again. No answer. His phone was probably turned off.

The next room they hit was the library.

On the way down the hall, Rachel managed to slip past the photo of the woman in the tub without so much as turning her head in that direction. Inside the library she spotted a large, thin book teetering on top of a stack of much smaller ones.

A plat book of Juneau County.

She picked it up and thumbed through it. A page had been torn out. After examining the maps on either side of the missing section, she looked up at her father. "I know where he went. Where all vampires go. To Old Tuonela."

Chapter 38

Isobel gradually returned to groggy consciousness.

So tired. Too tired to even try to open her eyes. As she lay on her side, her wrists bound in front of her, she gradually became aware of pain and hot spots on her hip, her thigh, her breastbone. She tried to move, to stretch, but couldn't; she was not only taped, but bound by a heavy chain.

Breathing.

Behind her.

She gasped in terror and her eyes flew open, her own breathing ragged.

Black.

She'd never seen such darkness. It was so close. It covered her. She struggled, fighting the bindings, terror and the need for flight taking over all thought.

She screamed.

A hand clamped over her mouth. "Shhhh," a voice rasped in her ear.

She struggled, and whimpered deep in her throat.

"Isobel!" The person holding her gave her a small shake.

She stopped fighting, but her breathing was still

rapid and shallow. Slowly he removed his hand from her mouth.

"Graham?"

"Yeah. It's me."

For a brief second she relaxed, then tensed again. He was one of them. A Pale Immortal.

"W-where are we?"

"In the church."

"What are *you* doing here?"

"I'm supposed to watch you. Make sure you don't scream or try to get away."

"Where's Alba?"

"Don't know."

"Is there anybody else around?"

"Don't know that either."

Maybe he wasn't really one of them. Maybe he was just an opportunist. "We have to get out of here."

That suggestion was met with a long silence. "Didn't you hear what I just said?" he finally asked. "I'm here to watch you. To make sure you don't get away."

A chain had been wrapped around them both, binding them together. "You're a prisoner too."

"Temporarily. This is a test. A test I'm going to pass."

She thought about the boy she'd known, and tried to connect him to this stranger.

You couldn't trust anybody. She felt like such a fool. She'd actually daydreamed about him. She went out of her way to avoid that conventional, mainstream crap, yet she'd daydreamed about him.

"You drank my blood," she said. "Do you realize how sick that is?"

"Depends on your perspective."

"Do you really think you're a vampire? Because you drank my blood?"

"Not yet. I'm not one yet."

"Vampires don't exist."

"Do you believe in God?"

"Yes. I think so."

"Do you have proof He exists?"

Alba's betrayal had hurt, but Graham's betrayal hurt more. "I was good to you. I helped you. I defended you. I taught you to knit." Her voice broke.

"It's nothing personal."

"You stink."

Behind her, he shifted. He touched her hair.

"You smell good."

"Vampires don't exist."

"Did you forget? My dad's a vampire. That makes me a vampire's son."

She wished she could see him. Wished she could look into his eyes. Maybe then she could reason with him. Maybe she'd be able to tell if he believed what he said.

"They're going to kill me. You know that, don't you?"

"Haven't you ever wished you were dead?"

She didn't answer.

"Everybody does at some time or another. I know you have. Alba will be doing you a favor, if you really think about it."

The air in the room was cold, but she suddenly

realized he was putting off a lot of heat. It radiated from him. And his voice was strange, kind of fervent and slurred at the same time.

She lifted her bound wrists to her mouth and began chewing the duct tape. Once she got a good rip going, it was easier.

"Stop that," he said.

With her teeth, she tore a narrow strip free. She spit it out, then wiggled her hands, finally pulling them apart. Her muscles were cramped, and at first she couldn't control her arms. Finally, with a slow, awkward movement, she raised one hand behind her—to touch Graham's temple.

"You're burning up."

She ran a hand down the side of his face.

She could feel whiskers, and once again she had the sensation that this wasn't Graham, that this was a different person, someone she didn't know. His jaw was sharp, his cheekbones pronounced. In her mind she pictured how he'd looked when she'd first seen him in the church. Like some homeless guy. Skinny, his kneecaps poking sharply through his jeans.

"I think I have a fever."

"You need a doctor."

He made an annoyed sound and slapped her hand away. "Quit trying to talk me into something that isn't going to happen. Let's change the subject." He paused for a new thought. "Do you read?"

"Read?" That was his new subject?

"Yeah, like books. Do you like to read books?"

"I'm not sharing anything else with you." And

she wasn't going to let him lead her off in a different direction. "Graham, listen to me. We have to try to get out of here. Before . . . someone . . . comes . . ."

Suddenly she didn't have the energy to continue. Her voice trailed off. Her chin dropped to her chest. She jerked awake, but immediately began to drowse again. "Sleepy . . ."

"You lost a lot of blood. That's what happens when you bleed to death. If you're worried that it'll hurt, it won't. You just fall asleep. And you never wake up again. It's no big deal."

No big deal. Her death would be no big deal. "You're an animal. Worse than an animal. I hate you. I *loathe* you."

"You said that before."

Nothing touched him.

She wanted to hurt him. She wanted to get back at him, at least a little.

"I listened to your stupid CD with all of those stupid songs. I didn't want to, but I did just to be polite."

She'd loved them, every single one. She would lie in bed at night and listen with earbuds.

"I hated them. Lame, happy, naïve crap. Stupid, stupid stuff. I mean, my parents are classical musicians. I know good music. The stuff you gave me was like something somebody who doesn't know anything about music would like. Like something a baby might listen to."

She wanted to say more, but her rant had worn her out. She tried to lift her arm, but couldn't. Her eyes fell closed again, and her body went limp.

Before she lost consciousness, she imagined she heard a strange sound. Like a sob.

Travis stood outside his house, hands in his pockets, shifting from one foot to the other while waiting for Johnson to pick him up. It was actually going to happen. The trap had been set. Everything was going just like they'd been told it would. Travis had to admit he'd been skeptical at first. He'd just gone along with the whole vampire thing because he liked that kind of shit. But this was the real deal.

He patted his waistband, making sure his dad's handgun was still there. The front door opened and his mother stuck her head out. "Honey, don't forget your jacket. You really need a light jacket tonight."

He walked to the house and took the jean jacket from her. "Thanks." He realized he might not be coming back. A car came barreling around the corner, then squealed to stop.

"I wish Craig wouldn't drive so fast," his mother said. "Tell him not to drive so fast."

Travis laughed and gave her a quick kiss on the cheek. "See ya, Mom."

He spun around, ran down the sidewalk, and jumped in the car. Johnson put the vehicle in gear and they roared away. Five minutes later they were speeding down the highway.

This was it. The night they would all become immortal.

Chapter 39

The green Toyota sped up the highway, sending the digital readout on the state patrol's radar gun to seventy-three mph. It was a fifty-five zone. Officer John Malcolm set the gun aside, flipped on his lights and siren, and peeled out, gravel flying.

He hated radar duty, but he loved this part of the job.

The pursued car didn't slow.

Not that unusual. Sometimes it took drivers a few minutes to realize they were being chased. But as John continued to follow, the car increased its speed. He radioed for backup, giving his location and the direction the car was heading. He shifted in his seat, sitting up straighter, both hands on the wheel. His patrol car had a lot of horsepower—he rapidly closed the distance between them until he was near enough to read the plate. He tapped on his high beams, pulled out his radio, and called in the number to Dispatch.

There were three heads inside the car. All appeared to be male. The person in the backseat turned around. Suddenly John's passenger windshield made a popping sound, then shattered in a sunburst.

John swerved and almost lost control as he whipped the car back to attention, at the same time backing off.

They were shooting at him. *Jesus.* He'd been a cop for five years and nobody had ever fired at him.

This was river country, and the landscape rapidly shifted from gently rolling hills to craggy cliffs and sharp turns. The road surface was black; the night was cloudy and dark. The only thing worse would have been rain.

He slowed for a hairpin curve. A back tire hit loose gravel, and for a second he thought he might roll. Once he was back in control, his heart hammering, breathing rapid, he realized he'd lost visual contact with the car.

He drove two more miles.

Nothing.

They couldn't have gotten away. At least, they couldn't have gotten *that* far ahead of him. He slowed, flipped off his siren and lights, did a quick three-point turn, and headed back in the direction he'd come.

He lowered his window and aimed his search light along the bluffless side of the road, following the guardrail's sharp curve until he came to a missing section.

Idiots.

He pulled over, withdrew his high-powered flashlight, got out, and walked to the section of broken railing. At the bottom of the ravine he spotted the green car lying upside down, one back tire spinning.

There was no sign of activity.

He radioed the dispatcher and gave his location. "We're going to need a couple of ambulances." He was afraid it was too late. A request for a coroner would probably be his next call.

Now what?

Someone could still be alive and in need of immediate medical attention. Yeah, and that person could have a gun.

He waited and listened, trying to come to a decision. Then he thought he heard a faint cry.

Drawing his weapon, he slipped and slid down the steep hill. When he reached the bottom he bent and shined the flashlight into the crushed car. The person behind the wheel looked dead. He circled the vehicle and shined the light in the passenger side. His stomach lurched and he had to look away. The head was crushed.

Definitely dead.

"Help," came a faint cry from several yards away.

He raised the light.

Lying on the ground, one leg bent under him, forehead bleeding profusely, blood running in his eyes, was passenger number three. The guy who'd shot at him.

John crouched beside him. "An ambulance is on the way," he said. "Hang in there." Just a kid. Probably only sixteen or seventeen. "What's your name?"

"Travis."

"Travis, somebody will be here any minute. I need to go back over and check on the others in the car." Make sure the driver was really dead.

"Wait!" Travis didn't want to be left alone. "How are they? Are they okay?"

"They're both in pretty bad shape."

"Are they dead?" Travis's voice rose. "They aren't dead, are they?"

John couldn't see much point in lying. "I'm afraid one of them didn't make it. I'm not sure about the driver."

"No. We can't die. None of us can die."

"Everybody dies."

"Not us. We're the Pale Immortals."

Ah. John had heard of them. Buncha idiot kids who pretended they were vampires. "You just need to lie there and keep still. Someone will be here any second."

"No! I have to get outta here. I gotta go. We all gotta go."

"Where? Where are you going?"

"Old Tuonela. We have to get to Old Tuonela right away."

John was sick of all the Old Tuonela, new Tuonela garbage.

Whenever he went to a law enforcement conference and people there found out where he was from, they teased the hell out of him and he was no longer taken seriously. He'd been thinking about getting a job somewhere else, in another state, but whenever he brought up the subject his wife got upset, saying she didn't want to leave her friends. But John figured it was better to get out now, before they had kids.

"There's nothing in Old Tuonela," he said. "Nothing but a bunch of decaying buildings."

"You're wrong. That's where we were heading."

"Were you going to a party?"

Underage kids liked to party there, but most teenagers were too afraid to go to OT during the day, let alone at night.

The injured kid reached blindly for him, and he gave him his hand to squeeze. John kept looking at his bent leg, wanting to straighten it, but knowing that would be a bad idea. It was probably a compound fracture. Straightening it could slice an artery.

John's ears picked up the faint wail of a siren. "There'll be other beer parties to go to," he told the kid.

"No, not a party. Not *that* kind of party," the kid said in protest. "First we . . . we were gonna bathe in the blood of a virgin. After that, we were going to eat the heart of a vampire."

John let go of the kid's hand and stood up. He could see the flashing lights now. Oh yeah, he definitely needed to look into relocating.

Chapter 40

Sitting in the passenger seat of the police car, Rachel leaned forward and strained to see through the windshield, watching for the narrow lane that led to Old Tuonela. The night was humid, and the wipers were on high. Wisps of fog hovered in ditches and clung to vegetation along the side of the highway.

Seymour had radioed the dispatcher to check on the availability of backup, only to find that all units were occupied—some at Isobel's, the rest at a fatal crash site.

"There it is," Rachel said. "Turn here."

Seymour guided the car down the lane that had once been a road. Over the years the gravel had been swallowed by mud until the only things remaining were parallel ruts with center vegetation that caught and scraped on the undercarriage. The headlights didn't penetrate very deeply. The beam reflected off birch and cottonwood trunks, illuminating the car's interior in uneasy flashes of light.

Seymour made a left, shot up a steep hill, and pulled to a stop not far from the main house.

"I heard the Pale Immortal was born here,"

Rachel said as they walked up the curved path of uneven bricks and weeds, her father training his flashlight in front of them.

"I heard the man who killed the Pale Immortal lived here," he said.

That's how it was. So many conflicting stories. The very stories Evan had hoped to sort out. But instead he had become part of the lore.

They climbed the steps to a sprawling porch surrounded by a wall of the same gray stone with supporting pillars that narrowed from a broad base.

Phillip Alba answered their knock, his face in shadow, his body backlit by a ceiling light. He wore black pants, black shoes, and a gray wool vest over a white dress shirt.

Seymour apologized for their late visit. Alba opened the screen door wide and they stepped inside.

The house had been beautiful once, with dark wood and high ceilings. Now piles of crumbled plaster littered the floor, and in some places water-stained floral wallpaper and bare one-inch wooden slats showed through. A massive staircase led to a landing with a boarded-up window, a turn, and another flight of stairs.

Even though the house had endured a few half-hearted renovations, it felt dead. Not a good place for anybody to live. Especially someone with a recent history of tragedy.

"We're looking for Evan Stroud. We have reason to believe he headed this direction."

"I heard he's suspected of killing Chelsea Gerber." Alba shook his head. *Very sad,* he seemed to say.

Alba had probably known her. Maybe she'd been one of his students.

"Have you seen him?" Seymour asked.

"No."

"Have you noticed any suspicious activity or people around here lately?"

Alba frowned in concentration. "The weather's getting warm. On weekends I sometimes have to run kids off."

"Would you mind if we look around? In Old Tuonela?" Seymour asked. "Just a quick peek."

"It's not safe to walk there at night." Alba stuffed his hands into the pockets of his vest. "It's hard to get through now. All the paths are overgrown."

"I was there not long ago," Rachel pointed out.

"Things grow fast here. I guess it's the soil." He shrugged. "But if you really want to go . . . " He shook his head, implying that he thought they were nuts.

"We'll manage," Seymour said. "I have a couple of strong flashlights."

Alba stood there a moment longer. "I'd better come with you. At least I can show you where the paths are. Wait; I'll be right back."

He vanished through the dining room. A light appeared in the kitchen; then Alba returned wearing a brown coat with deep pockets and carrying a lantern. He'd exchanged his shoes for brown leather boots.

All three of them left the house and headed in the

direction of the woodland that stood like a thick wall on the edge of the clearing.

"Looks like you've had a lot of traffic this way," Seymour noted as they strode down a well-worn path that led away from the house.

"Raccoons." Alba lifted his lantern higher. Up in a tree, two pairs of eyes reflected from the branch. "The place is overrun with them."

He removed a padlock from a gate and swung it open, stepping out of the way to allow Seymour and Rachel to pass.

Rachel and her father walked side by side, their flashlights trained to the ground as they swept them back and forth.

Tire tracks.

If it was so hard to reach Old Tuonela on foot, why were there tire tracks? "Who's been driving here?" Rachel asked.

Alba paused to stare at the ruts. "I don't know. . . . I keep the gate locked."

Seymour crouched down. "They're fairly recent."

"Today?" Rachel asked.

"Not sure."

Father and daughter resumed their walk, ending up in the graveyard with the rotten oak tree.

The ground had been disturbed.

An unmarked grave had been dug up and left exposed. Rotten, splintered pieces of wood littered the area.

"So he *was* buried here," Seymour said in a hushed tone.

Rachel put a hand on her dad's arm in silent communication. Who had known about the oak tree and the possibility of a secret grave? Her father. Alba. Dan.

Evan.

Evan could be nearby right now, with the girl. Seymour must have been thinking the same thing. He unsnapped his holster and drew his gun.

And the world exploded.

A deafening roar came from a few feet away. Her father jerked. His flashlight hit the ground and went out. There was a gasp of pain and the sound of exhaled air moving through clenched teeth.

Rachel struggled to comprehend the event.

Another gunshot.

Another grunt of pain from her father.

She felt his hand on her arm, his fingers like claws. She thought he was clinging to her to keep from falling, but suddenly he shoved her. Hard. More gunshots exploded and the ground dropped out from under her.

She tumbled down a sharp incline, smacking her flashlight against a rock, breaking it. Trying to stop herself, she reached blindly, slamming into a tree halfway down the steep slope, the wind knocked from her.

Within seconds she was on her feet. In the dark she struggled to maneuver, to find a foothold. She skidded until she hit level ground, loose soil and small rocks pattering around her.

"Rachel!" came a shout from above.

Alba.

His flashlight beam bounced off tree trunks.

Rachel ducked her head and curled her body, pressing herself against a washed-out hollow beneath the base of a tree.

Like a searchlight, the beam moved back and forth. "Rachel! Are you okay?"

She held her breath.

Far above, leaves rustled.

It took all of her willpower to remain where she was. She heard a scuttling sound—and realized he was standing at the top of the precipice.

There had been several gunshots. Had they all been from Alba? Or had her father fired his own gun?

Alba came sliding down the hill. His crash to the bottom was followed by silence. A moment later she heard him wading through leaves, heading in her direction.

She didn't move.

He walked past her. And kept going, the flashlight beam vanishing around a bend, the sound of his footsteps fading.

Rachel unfolded herself and quickly made her way up the hill, feeling in the dark, grabbing small tree trunks to pull herself out of the ravine.

She reached the top and dug into her pocket, retrieved her keys, and squeezed the light attached to the chain.

"Dad?" she whispered, casting the orange light around, trying to get her bearings.

She spotted her father sprawled on the ground. Beneath his head lay a pool of blood. Tendrils of red escaped the pool, crawling and searching out deep cracks in the earth.

Something cold and metallic pressed against her neck, followed by Alba's voice: "Hello, Rachel."

Chapter 41

Evan pulled off the blacktop road into a short lane lined with trees and brush that led to a nearby field. According to the page he'd ripped from the plat book, this ground bordered Alba's property.

His plan was to get close, but not so close that his arrival would be noticed. He had approximately eight hours of darkness left, but he hoped to find Graham long before morning.

He'd briefly thought of going directly to Alba's house, but Alba would probably contact the police, and a massive parade of sirens and cops was something Evan wanted to avoid.

Best to sneak in and scope things out. He had his cell phone. He could call if he needed help.

He leaned across the seat, opened the glove compartment, and dug out a flashlight. He tested it. The battery was low.

He shut it off, stuck it in his pocket, and got out of the car.

The terrain was dense woodland cut with steep, narrow valleys. The sky was partly cloudy, offering an occasional view of a yellow slice of moon, the Big

Dipper, and a hint of the Milky Way. Even though Evan could see fairly well in the dark, his vision wasn't anywhere close to daylight vision. The ground kept dropping out from under him, and he was forced to slow his pace.

He came to a sagging wire fence that most likely marked the edge of Alba's property. Placing a hand on top of a gnarled cedar post, he leaped over, landing solidly on the ground on the opposite side.

He stood there a moment, trying to get his bearings. Not easy. He looked up. The moon and stars were gone again. He had a good sense of direction, but this was like cave diving, where it was sometimes impossible to tell which way was up, let alone north or south.

In his mind, he mentally pulled up the image of the map. If he was going in the right direction, he should hit a valley created by a small vein of the Wisconsin River.

The vegetation had become thick and tangled. Vines wrapped around his ankles, tripping him, and multiflower rose thorns ripped at his skin.

As far as Evan knew, none of the ground was farmed or grazed, and Alba hadn't struck him as the type to get out and work on trying to keep down the unsavory, nonnative plants.

The topography was rougher here too.

He saw something—a dark shadow of movement, human size—out of the corner of his eye. He swung to face it.

Nothing. He blinked.

Still nothing.

He continued until he came to a sheer drop, stopping just before stepping into thin air. He got the sensation that a few inches of dirt and sod were all that kept him from plunging into the ravine.

Carefully, he moved back from the edge—and realized he was lost. As he stood there, hoping the clouds would pass and the moon would give him some indication of direction, he heard gunshots—rapid-fire, several in a row.

He turned and ran toward the sound, climbing down into a fissure and jumping across a stream. His feet landed in boggy soil, and he struggled up the opposite bank, grabbing small tree trunks to pull himself skyward, finally reaching level ground and a grassy lane.

He paused and a stench wafted toward him.

Death.

No mistaking that putrid odor.

Graham?

Suddenly he felt incredibly heavy and weak.

It could be a dead animal.

It could be a dead raccoon, or something bigger, like a deer.

He forced himself to walk toward the smell, his feet reluctantly moving over soft, bumpy ground and brushing up against dry, dead grass.

It didn't take him long. The sliver of a moon was out again, illuminating two white arms stretched above dark hair. Long hair.

Not Graham.

He clicked on the flashlight, put a hand over his nose, and stepped closer, immediately recognizing the fabric from the photo. Lydia. Most likely hung upside down, where she'd died and stiffened with her arms stretched to the ground.

Something strange and almost unrecognizable rose up in him.

Rage.

He'd never liked Lydia, but Jesus. And whoever had done this had Graham.

He felt something on the back of his neck—like a finger drawn up his spine, into his hairline, and up his scalp.

For most of his life he'd been warned to stay away from Old Tuonela. Unlike his classmates, Evan hadn't gone there for a thrill.

His had been a deeper fear. An unknown fear, embedded in his soul by myth and stories that grew with each telling. It was why he'd written about Old Tuonela and the Pale Immortal. To face those fears, to draw them out and examine them.

But fear couldn't be examined. When you shined a light on it, it ran and hid before you got a good look at it. All that was left was the sick dread, the feeling deep in your belly that there was more wrong here than humans could ever grasp. There was more to Old Tuonela than rotting buildings and tall tales.

There was evil here.

That's what he'd always known.

An evil that had been growing. Waiting for the right time, the right circumstances, the right person to come along.

Don't go there, his dad had always said. *You can't ever go there.*

Evan shut off the flashlight, straightened away from the bloated, stinking mass of putrid flesh, turned, and began walking in the direction that would take him into the heart of Old Tuonela.

Evan got his bearings fairly quickly.

There was the old graveyard. There was the church.

Hiding behind the trunk of a tree, he stared intently at the church and its broken windows. He could see no light, hear no sound that alerted him to a human presence.

But the smell of death was here too.

In his mind he visualized the photo, the layout of the church. He stepped free of the tree trunk. Keeping low, he moved forward, carefully placing one foot in front of the other.

Broken flagstones led the way to a door swollen from rain that could no longer be opened or closed. The structure had become organic, shooting up from the earth to shrivel and die like some winter-killed plant. Now it was returning to the soil.

Evan stood in the narrow opening, straining for any sound that wasn't of nature. He could smell the rot of wood and the breakdown of plants. He could smell the trail Lydia had left behind.

And blood. Fairly fresh blood.

He heard something.

Like a quickly indrawn breath.

He sensed fear.

Evan waited.

There it was again.

Someone inside the church. Someone else listening. Someone who was afraid.

He pulled out the flashlight, then reached inside his coat, quietly and slowly snapping open his shoulder holster. He slipped out the Glock and lined it up with the light. In one swift motion, he clicked the switch and swung into the room.

Two pairs of terrified eyes stared at him.

It took him a moment to make sense of the scene.

It almost seemed as if he'd interrupted some kind of weird tryst. But as his brain rearranged the pieces, he saw that the people were chained together. It took him even longer to realize that the scraggly, skinny kid with blood on his face was Graham.

Now it was Evan's turn to pull in a shocked breath.

The other person was Isobel Fry.

Graham raised his arm to shield his eyes against the beam of light. Evan dropped his hands and slipped the handgun back inside his coat. Caution forgotten, he ran across broken boards and swept down on them.

Isobel screamed.

Graham clamped a hand over her mouth. "Get back," he told Evan.

"It's me." Evan didn't quite know how to introduce himself.

"Evan?" The flashlight beam was fading fast, turning a faint orange. "She said you'd come. She told me you were coming."

"Who?"

"Lydia."

Evan frowned. "Lydia is dead."

"No. No, she isn't. She looks dead, but she's alive. She was here. Talking to me."

Graham's mind had slipped. It had taken what it couldn't tolerate and twisted it into something else. He'd probably watched them murder Lydia, and then she'd hung there and rotted right in front of him. Who wouldn't have gone crazy under those circumstances?

"I think you can take your hand from Isobel's mouth."

"Are you gonna be quiet?" Graham asked her.

She nodded.

Slowly Graham removed his hand.

"He's one of them!" she shouted. "He drank my—"

Graham clamped his hand back over her mouth.

"I am not one of them. She just thinks I am."

Isobel made a noise of protest in her throat and violently shook her head.

The flashlight died.

"Candles," Graham said in the darkness. "On the first pew."

Evan lit two of them using a book of matches he found nearby.

Back at Graham and Isobel's side, he ran his hands over the chain.

"Alba has the key," Graham said.

"Alba?"

"Yeah."

No time to think about that.

The chain was held together by a lock. Not a particularly strong lock. Evan could try to muffle his gun and shoot it off, or he could break it.

He hurried outside, dug his fingers into the ground, and pulled up two half-buried flagstones, then carried them back inside. He placed one stone under the lock. "Turn your faces away." He lifted the other stone high and brought it down hard and fast. Sparks flew, but the lock remained intact. "Again." He repeated the action. The third time the lock broke apart.

He unwrapped and unrolled the chain from around their bodies to drop it in a pile near the stained mattress.

Isobel shoved herself weakly to her feet, rubbing her arms and moving stiffly. "I'm telling you, he's one of them."

Graham managed to get himself upright, keeping his weight on one foot.

"Are you hurt?" Evan brought the candle closer.

"Animal trap."

Evan stared, the feeling of sick horror growing.

"He's one of them," Isobel repeated.

They both looked at her. Evan was ready to tell her Graham couldn't be involved when a sound caused them all to turn toward the door.

Phillip Alba stood in the opening, a gun in his hand.

Chapter 42

Graham swayed and blinked fevered eyes as events unfolded before him.

Alba stood in the doorway of the church, facing Evan. As Graham watched, Evan reached inside his coat.

Suddenly the shadowy darkness of the room exploded in a light so bright Graham could see nothing. He brought up a hand to block the intensity.

"Graham! Run!"

Like somebody who'd been shot, Evan dropped to his knees. Alba held a superpowered flashlight that was as bright as the sun.

Graham had seen this scene before. It was like the time Evan chased Graham from the house to collapse when sunlight hit him.

Just in case Graham hadn't heard him the first time, Evan turned and shouted again.

Now Graham could see his mouth moving, saw the anguish combined with urgency.

Go!

The command shook Graham from his trance.

He swung around on his good foot, grabbed Isobel's hand, and ran toward the window. At first she fought him, but then she must have realized he was the lesser of two evils.

Graham pushed her through the opening, then dove after her while rapid-fire gunshots filled the air and bullets shattered the window frame. He slammed into the ground below. Searing pain shot through his ankle. His breath caught, and he was momentarily stupefied by the agony.

"Come on." Isobel tugged at his sweatshirt, urging him upright. She wedged herself against him and wrapped her arm around his waist.

They ran.

Side by side, they crashed through the overgrown tangle of bushes and vines. Graham couldn't think beyond the pain. He was hazily aware of Isobel leading the way, urging him to keep moving. He had no idea how far they'd gone when they both collapsed. Graham rolled to his back, his eyes squeezed tightly shut, hugging his knee, his lips compressed, his lungs burning as he struggled to catch his breath.

His leg was rotten. That's what he was thinking. It was rotten, and if he lived through this it would have to be amputated.

In the dark, hands grabbed him by both arms and gave him a shake. "You creep," Isobel whispered harshly, inches from his face.

His damn leg was falling off, and she was yelling at him. Couldn't she smell the rotten flesh?

She slapped him.

He let out a breathless laugh. What was funny about getting slapped? He was delirious.

"You drank my blood."

"Sorry . . . 'bout that."

She shoved at him. But not hard. Then she collapsed against his chest and began to shake. Was she crying? He thought she was crying.

He put his arm around her. He wished he could do more. He wished he could hold her with both arms. He wished he could kiss her. But he smelled, and he was so weak he couldn't lift his head. And there was something he should do that was beyond their immediate situation. Something very important . . .

He thought maybe they both fell asleep, because there seemed to be an empty space between the time he put his arm around Isobel and the moment she shoved herself away.

"Sick," she mumbled. "Gonna be sick . . . ."

Once she was gone, he could still feel the outline of her body against him.

He heard her throwing up. *Poor kid.*

He opened his eyes.

Stars.

And a moon. The moon was like a cartoon moon, really big. Really close.

This was nice. Lying under the sky with Isobel.

He'd actually meant to say the words aloud, but he didn't think they came out that way. How long had it been since he'd talked? Really talked?

Isobel was moving around.

She screamed.

Then came a lot of weird, panicky noises.

She needed help.

Gotta help Isobel.

He rolled to his side, then to his hands and knees. He heard rustling; then her body slammed into his, knocking him down.

"Oh, my God!" She clung to him. "A dead person. I tripped over a dead person."

That was what he'd been smelling. Lydia. Lurking out there in the bushes. Not him. Not his leg.

Whew.

Lydia, who'd dangled from the rafters while her throat was slit and her blood drained and caught in a bucket.

Which reminded Graham of the important issue that had been nagging at him for quite some time.

Evan was in trouble. Evan needed help.

Chapter 43

Drip, drip, drip.

The repetitious sound spoke to Rachel. A warning, but also an invitation, coaxing her deeper. Choices to be made. Wake up . . . or go to sleep. Forever.

Sweet, soft, seductive whispers: *Join us. Stay with us.* So many mingled voices. Coming from inside her head, outside her head.

Nothing to be afraid of. Why had she ever been afraid?

She hadn't understood. People were afraid of what they didn't understand.

She opened her eyes for a final look.

A dark room. Flickering candles. She was naked. In a metal tub. Past physical discomfort, she didn't feel cold. She lifted her hand and, with the distance of an observer, watched the blood run down her arm and drip from her elbow, hitting the floor with a repetitious *splat*.

So, that's what's making that noise.

Interesting.

She tried to pull her arm back in the tub, but

couldn't. Her body wasn't her own anymore. Her hand fell, fingers brushing the floor.

Evan fought the weakness pressing him down. He looked at Alba, who sat cross-legged several yards away, hands resting on top of a high-powered LED flashlight, the battery box against his knee, the light directed away from Evan's face. Evan's confiscated Glock and cell phone were beside Alba on the floor.

"You may have most of the people in Tuonela fooled, but not me." Alba swung the light at Evan.

Evan's reflexes were slow; the ultraviolet brilliance connected with his pupils before he could raise a hand and turn away. A fresh wave of nausea and weakness washed over him.

"Nice that there's a disease to match your symptoms." With one hand Alba gave the word *symptoms* air quotes, then pulled the light away, aiming it at the floor. "I wonder how many people have used that before?"

"Come on, Alba." Evan swallowed and struggled to sit up.

Maybe if he acted even weaker, he could trick Alba into relaxing. "Your theory isn't anything new," Evan said breathlessly. "All the little kiddies in town have been threatened with me their whole lives. 'Go to bed; otherwise Stroud will get you.' 'Eat your breakfast if you don't want Stroud to come.'"

"But do they really believe it? I don't think so. I *know*." Alba nodded. "*I* believe."

"Okay, say I am a vampire. What then? I don't go around killing people." Evan glanced up at the rafters. "I don't hang them by their heels and drain their blood. We all have cravings and strange desires. Everyone has a demon inside him. We have to learn to control it."

"Why?"

Evan didn't know how to work this. Try to reason with him? Sympathize? Agree? He was playing for time, hoping Graham and Isobel could find help. "Why is it you need to gain immortality?" Evan asked.

"You're the expert on the subject. I think you already know."

He would try to engage Alba in conversation. He would watch for him to let down his guard.

"I'm guessing you're the one who dug up Manchester," Evan said. "For his heart. Maybe you already have immortality."

"His heart wasn't there."

So Rachel had been right.

"I made a visit to the old guy whose father buried Manchester," Alba said. "Someone else got there before me. Someone named Stroud."

Evan frowned. There were no Strouds in the area except his family.

"That's right," Alba said, reading Evan's thoughts. "Your old man."

Impossible. His father had always been adamant that they stay away from Old Tuonela. That they have nothing to do with the place. He would have had no interest in the body of Richard Manchester.

"You never knew, did you?" Alba asked.

"You are talking shit."

"You were sick. You were dying. And not far away was the possibility of eternal life."

"My father would never have done anything like that. My father is the most practical person in the world. He shops at Sears, for chrissake. He golfs."

"If you had the chance to save your son's life, even if a cure was remote, wouldn't you do it?"

Evan put a hand to his chest, where his heart was pounding, and imagined his father digging up the body of the Pale Immortal. It was ludicrous. Wasn't it?

"He made a broth of the heart, and you drank it."

When Evan was extremely ill, unable to walk, the pain in his head blinding, his parents had coaxed him to eat and drink many strange things. He never questioned what they were or where they'd come from.

The tea.

His mind recoiled from his own thoughts as he struggled to deny them.

The tin contained the ground-up heart of Richard Manchester.

The heart of the Pale Immortal.

Still he fought what was suddenly making too much sense.

Even if his dad *had* robbed the grave of the Pale Immortal, even if he *had* stolen the heart and fed at least part of it to Evan, that was the end of the story. Like someone who believed in charlatans in hopes of a cancer cure, that's all it had been. Ingesting a madman's heart had been his father's snake oil.

Yet Evan couldn't convince himself of his own argument. He was different since he'd recently begun drinking the tea from the antique tin. Changed. Not completely changed, but he was undergoing a transformation.

Could he really be part human, part vampire? Part Pale Immortal?

No.

Yes.

Which meant Evan was the ransom. "You want *my* heart."

Alba seemed to forget that they weren't buddies, and Evan wasn't somebody Alba had charmed. He relaxed. He began gesturing with one hand, orating. Evan was no longer the enemy, but Alba's audience.

"I'm not making excuses for myself, but this was meant to be. There was a reason I ended up here, in Old Tuonela." Alba looked away and smiled to himself, at something he was envisioning.

Evan moved with lightning speed, swinging his leg, kicking the flashlight to send it flying across the room, the lens shattering. In the candlelight he hurled himself at Alba, knocking him over backward.

He had to take Alba down quickly before his own strength gave out. In a fraction of a second he had Alba's gun. Alba knocked it from his hand. The weapon spun across the floor and vanished through a crack in the broken boards. Alba scrambled after it.

Evan dove for his Glock, grabbed it, and swung back around. Alba was frantically trying to locate his weapon in the deep crevice. "Get up," Evan said.

Alba slowly and reluctantly pulled his arm from between the boards and got to his feet.

Keeping the gun trained on him, Evan glanced around the room and spotted a length of rope that had probably been used on Lydia. He made a slip-knot. "Stand over there." Evan nodded his head at a rough-hewn support post.

Alba positioned his back against it. He was smiling. Why was he smiling?

Never taking the Glock off him, Evan used his free hand to lasso Alba's wrists behind the wooden pillar, pulling the rope tight.

Dried blood caked Alba's hands.

Whose blood?

Even slipped his weapon back into his shoulder holster, finished securing the rope, then retrieved his cell phone and punched 911.

"I need police and an ambulance," he said. He told the dispatcher who he was, where he was, then disconnected and looked at Alba. "You'll be in jail before morning." Now he had to find Graham, tell him an ambulance was on the way.

"I left a surprise for you back at my house." Alba was still smiling.

Fresh dread curled in the pit of Evan's stomach, and he thought of the blood on the man's hands. "What are you talking about?"

"I can't tell you; otherwise it wouldn't be a surprise, would it? You have to go there and see."

Rachel.

Instantly Alba became of little importance. Evan shifted his focus and stumbled from the church. He cut through the graveyard and snagged his toe on something solid and soft, falling to his knees.

A body.

Blindly, he felt the clothes and badge, the stickiness of blood, his fingers coming in contact with the neck. No pulse.

Evan straightened. With fresh urgency he jumped the low stone wall and sprinted down the lane. He could see Alba's house through the trees. The gate was chained and padlocked. He climbed the metal slats and dropped to the ground.

Up the front steps, turn the knob, throwing his shoulder into the door.

Locked.

He looked around, grabbed a chair from the porch, and smashed it against a window. With the chair legs he knocked out the glass to make an opening big enough to crawl through.

Inside, candles burned.

Blood on the floor. Blood on the walls.

A trail of white candles, dripping and smelling of wax, littered the room and led to the second floor.

He took the stairs three at a time, the candle flames sputtering out as he passed, the path before him lit, the path behind him dark.

"Rachel!"

Because he knew Rachel was the surprise. Rachel, who had saved him more than once. Who had put herself at risk. Rachel, whom he loved but could never have.

He hit the landing, and flew up the rest of the steps.

The area at the top of the stairs opened to three small rooms. The candles led to the right.

Evan's heart hammered madly, and he followed the flames, stepping into a large, sweeping room.

A path of candles reflected off the wooden floor. Moonlight fell through large windows.

The room was devoid of furniture except for a tub. An old-fashioned zinc tub, like the one in the photo he'd gotten from the estate sale.

In the center of the otherwise empty room, lying inside the tub, was a woman, her face turned away, one hand dangling over the side, blood pooled on the floor beneath her fingertips.

"No!"

He ran, skidding to his knees.

He picked up her limp hand. The wrist had been slit, long and deep. He turned her face to his.

Rachel.

Blue lips. Marble skin.

This couldn't be happening.

With a violently trembling hand he touched her face. "You can't be dead."

He wrapped his arms around her, pulling her body halfway out of the blood-soaked tub, gathering her to him. A sob tore from somewhere deep inside him—a loud, anguished cry of despair.

He was holding her close when he heard air leave her lungs. He pulled back and put an ear to her mouth . . . and detected faint breathing.

Another sound intruded. A sound that belonged to the world. A wailing siren, winding through the hillside, moving steadily closer.

Evan removed his coat, ripped two strips of cloth from the lining, and bandaged her wrists. Then he wrapped his coat around her, lifted her from the tub, and carried her down the stairs and out of the house.

Headlights bobbed as the ambulance jerked to a stop, leaving a vast space between the vehicle and Evan.

They were afraid of him.

Stepping sideways, averting his eyes, Evan moved out of the glare. "Get over here!" He kept walking with Rachel in his arms.

Two men stepped from the ambulance and approached with caution.

"She's alive, but she needs a transfusion. Do you have blood with you?"

"Plasma."

They got her in the ambulance. One of the EMTs started an IV. There was nothing more Evan could do.

Not here.

He turned and ran, back toward Old Tuonela, back to Phillip Alba.

His strength was increasing by the second, fueled by a rage his body seemed unable to contain. He had no awareness of getting from Alba's front lawn to the church. He burst through the door, flying across the room. He untied the man with two quick tugs. He grabbed Alba by the jacket, tossed him to the floor, then proceeded to punch him in the face again and again, finally pausing to survey the damage before he went in for the kill.

"I don't know why you're so upset." Alba wiped

at his bloody nose. He looked at his fingers. "When people die in Old Tuonela, they aren't really dead. Can't you feel them all around us? Even the animals?"

It was true. Evan could sense them. All the dead killed by the Pale Immortal. And more recent ones. A girl . . . The girl who'd gone missing from Summit Lake.

"When I kill you," Evan said, "I assure you, you will be dead." With both hands he dragged Alba to his feet.

Alba reached into Evan's exposed shoulder holster and pulled out his Glock.

Evan didn't care; he swung.

Alba jumped away and squeezed the trigger.

Evan felt a stinging in his shoulder. He stumbled back two steps, then went for Alba again. Another shot barely slowed Evan down. "That's no way to kill a vampire. You should know that."

Alba scrambled to his feet and ran out the door into the darkness. Evan ran after him.

Outside, away from the candlelight, Evan had the advantage. He could not only hear Alba crashing through the underbrush; he could see the evil bastard.

He heard his own rasping breath. Something wet and sticky ran down his arm, but the rage in his head hadn't subsided. If anything, beating the shit out of Alba and now pursuing him had ratcheted it up two notches.

He'd wanted to kill the bastard with his bare

hands, but he would settle for watching him die no matter how it happened.

Alba cut between decayed buildings, every so often turning to fire a shot in Evan's direction.

Birds sang out a warning of the coming dawn.

Alba ducked into a tall, weirdly shaped brick structure on the opposite end of town. It was listing to one side and looked as if a slight breeze would knock it over, leaving nothing but a pile of rubble.

The old flour mill.

Evan was on Alba's heels. Inside, Evan could see better, but Alba knew the layout.

In the distance, Evan caught the faint sound of more sirens.

He chased Alba upstairs and across a creaking floor.

Along the way Evan pulled up a piece of splintered board and continued after Alba.

Alba scurried like a spider up a ladder attached to the wall. Evan followed.

At the top Alba was waiting. He kicked Evan in the side of the head. Evan dropped his makeshift sword, grabbed Alba's foot, and pulled. Alba tumbled to his back.

Evan cleared the top of the ladder and threw himself on Alba. The men rolled across the floor. Evan couldn't get a punch in. Suddenly Alba was on top of him—and Evan felt the cold steel of his Glock pressed to his head.

Click, click, click.

Empty.

Evan laughed.

Both men scrambled to their feet. Alba slammed the gun against Evan's skull.

Evan cried out in pain and took a step back.

The floor shifted and broke under him. In a cloud of dust and debris, Evan tumbled backward through the air, falling to the floor far below.

Consciousness returned slowly, and Evan gradually realized one arm was caught under him. He was unable to draw more than a shallow breath.

Shafts of light cut through cracks. Dust wafted and drifted gently skyward.

A movement had him turning to see Alba picking his way toward him. Something glinted in his blood-caked hand.

At first Evan thought it was the empty Glock, but it was too shiny for that.

Chapter 44

Graham told Isobel to stay hidden, then shoved himself to his feet and began walking. It wasn't easy. It was dark, and he kept forgetting where he was going. When he did remember that he was heading back to the church, he had no idea if he was pointed in the right direction.

At least the moon was out.

Then again, maybe light was a bad thing—because Lydia appeared on the path in front of him. She was no longer hanging upside down, but her face was half-rotten, maggots crawling in her eye sockets. He took a step back and put a hand to his face. He breathed through his mouth, but that made him gag.

"Sorry," he mumbled behind his hand.

He didn't want to be rude, but . . . *Damn, Sam!* "Which way to the church?" he asked.

"I'll show you."

He wasn't sure how she could talk, because her mouth was a big gaping hole, but she seemed to be doing okay. She headed straight up a hill in a direction that seemed totally wrong. When he didn't follow, she paused and waited.

She'd been right before, so she was probably right this time.

Graham let out a heavy sigh. His leg wasn't hurting as much, but it felt swollen and heavy. He didn't want to look at it. It might look like Lydia's face.

He grabbed the trunk of a small tree and braced himself for the steep climb. "Lead on," he told his mother.

"Who are you talking to?"

He swung around to see Isobel behind him. "You can't come."

"I can do whatever I want. Who were you talking to?" she repeated.

He turned back around, but Lydia was gone. No surprise. She wouldn't want a young girl like Isobel to see her.

"Don't tell her about me."

No, he wouldn't. Isobel would think he was crazy.

He had a fever. He was dehydrated. They said the reason people in the desert hallucinated was because they were dehydrated. Being dehydrated really messed with your head.

He'd never done acid, but this might be what it was like. Not unpleasant. Kind of mind-expanding. "I knew a guy who did a lot of acid, and he was fried." Graham pushed aside a big branch, holding it so it wouldn't snap back and smack Isobel in the face.

"What are you talking about?"

"I don't remember his name, but there was a

delay to everything he said and did. Kinda like his thoughts were taking a detour through his brain."

He quit talking to concentrate on climbing. At the top of the hill he spotted a familiar scene and stopped in his tracks. Isobel bumped into him from behind.

"The church," he whispered over his shoulder.

Lydia had been right. The direction he'd taken had seemed completely wrong, but here they were. He could see the grassy, open area where the road had once been. He saw the peak of the church roof and the crumbled remains of a bell tower silhouetted against a velvet sky.

Out of nowhere, panic clutched his belly. What were they doing here? He didn't want to be here.

Then he remembered. Evan needed help.

Oh, yeah.

He felt Isobel behind him, then her hand gripping his tightly. "You aren't going back, are you?" she whispered.

"I have to."

It was quiet. He couldn't hear or see anything or anybody. But then, he *had* seen Lydia, someone who wasn't supposed to exist. "Wait here."

Isobel squeezed his hand harder. "Don't go. The police will come. Wait for them."

"We don't know that. Nobody has come yet. I've been here for days, and nobody came. I'll be careful."

He slipped his hand from hers. Crouching, trying not to drag his foot because of the noise, he moved toward the church. He limped across the open area that had been the old road, quickly dropping into deep, rustling grass and brush that scratched his arms. He was used to sneaking around. He'd done it a lot when he'd lived in Arizona. Sneaking out of the house at night, then sneaking back in.

He crawled to the window, then peeked inside.

One small candle sputtered on the floor, the flame tall and moving wildly even though Graham didn't feel any breeze.

He slowly rose to his feet, at the same time scanning the interior.

There was no sign of anyone.

Now what, Lydia?

A shadow fell across him.

For a second he thought he saw Lydia swinging from the rafters again before he shifted his eyes away. Or had she always been there? When he looked back up, she was gone. A trick of candlelight?

He strained for any sound, but there was a roar in his head like the inside of a shell, and it was almost impossible to sort the internal from the external.

Until he heard gunshots.

He was fairly certain those weren't in his head.

Chapter 45

Graham heard a crash that seemed to come from the other end of town. He limped in that direction, trying not to think about his injury, yet unable to keep from visualizing a boot filled with rotting meat. Some round stub that looked more like a ham hock than a foot.

He hopped to a stop in front of a cluster of crumbling buildings—and heard another sound coming from deep inside the tall stone structure. Dragging his foot behind him, he moved as fast as he could. When he reached a vine-covered doorway with no door, he looked through the barrier of stems and tangled greenery to see Evan sprawled on the floor.

He was hurt. Badly hurt.

Alba stood over him, a knife in his hand.

Graham looked around for something—anything—he could use as a weapon. He spotted a piece of wood that was narrow at one end, wide at the other.

He picked it up. "If you want to be a vampire, then die like one!" Graham charged, a horrible sound coming from him, a sound that was half scream, half roar of rage, meant to trick himself into thinking he could do what had to be done.

At the last moment Alba turned to face his new enemy.

The wooden stake went through Alba's chest wall and through his heart, stopping when it hit bone.

Alba didn't die immediately, not like on TV or in movies. That would have been a lot better—if he'd just closed his eyes and dropped to the floor. But no, he stared at Graham in shock and disbelief. He opened his mouth to say something. Instead of words, chunks of blood and stuff that looked like raw liver poured out.

His heart? Was that his heart?

Could a person live after the heart was destroyed? Apparently so. At least for a while.

Time froze.

Graham's ears started doing something weird, almost like they'd closed.

Just shut yourself off.

Yeah, he'd done this before. He knew where that switch was.

One last spurt of blood, and Alba folded as if the bones had been jerked from his body.

Graham tried to close his eyes but couldn't. It probably wouldn't have helped anyway. He would probably still see Alba's face, still see the horror in the man's eyes, the accusation and surprise.

Not you. You wouldn't kill me. I would never have expected that of you.

"G-Graham?"

Close your eyes.

Evan was talking to him, trying to get his attention, but he didn't want to deal with Evan right now.

He'd just killed a man.

He staggered backward, his gaze going from Alba and the awful, surprised look on his face, to Evan. He could see from Evan's expression that he understood the horror Graham was feeling, and that made it worse, made it more real.

He didn't want to be Graham anymore. He didn't want to be standing there, held together with Graham's skin.

"It'll be okay," Evan said. Each word seemed to require a struggle. Like he couldn't breathe.

And his effort did no good. It didn't ease Graham's despair.

He'd killed a man. He was sixteen years old, and he'd killed a man. How messed up was that?

He heard a sound and looked over his shoulder.

Isobel stood in the doorway, silhouetted against a sky that was growing lighter by the second. "Get out!" he shouted, and waved her away. "Get out of here!" He didn't want her to see what he'd done.

Sirens were wailing, very close now. He swore to God they were mocking him.

She extended her hand toward him. "Come outside," she said softly. "Come outside with me."

He stumbled forward, and when he reached her he threw his arms around her and pulled her close, hugging her to him, shaking all over, sobbing like a baby.

Chapter 46

Graham and Isobel sat on a quilt in City Park. It had been a hot day, but evening had arrived and things were cooling off.

Without saying anything, Isobel extended her hand as if she were holding an empty cup. Graham passed her the smoothie they'd picked up at Peaches. Isobel stuck the straw in her mouth, took a long drink, and passed it back. "This is gonna be so cool."

The event they were waiting for was called Music and a Movie. An actual band—a *real* band—was stopping on its way from Minneapolis to Madison. A relative of Isobel's knew the bass player, and had invited them to play. Everybody was shocked when they'd agreed, but then, who could turn down an overnight stay in the land of vampires?

The band planned to play while Chaplin's *City Lights* was projected on a screen. It should be pretty damn cool.

Isobel wore a black tank top and a floral skirt. Her feet, in black sandals, sported purple toenail polish.

Graham loved her skin and the way she smelled.

He might even say he loved *her*, which scared the hell out of him. Which was really weird, because they'd never even kissed.

Most people changed as you got to know them. Isobel had remained Isobel. She was exactly the same person she'd been that day she'd picked him up along the road as he'd run away from Evan's house. She was *real*.

Another weird thing was that she didn't seem all that bothered about what had happened in Old Tuonela. She'd seemed able to put it behind her, while Graham struggled with it daily. And nightly.

He had bad dreams. Sometimes he saw Lydia. He would wake up and see her sitting by his bed, and it would freak the hell out of him.

In Old Tuonela, the dead are never really dead.

He believed it. He didn't want anybody else to know he believed it, but he did.

The band was setting up, unloading equipment from a white van. More people were arriving, most with blankets and some with picnic baskets.

Graham finished off the smoothie and leaned back on his elbows. "You could almost pretend this place was normal."

His foot was still there.

That was a good thing, but it had been pretty messed up, and he'd been on IV antibiotics for a long time. And he was going to a shrink. Not the school shrink, somebody else. A guy Graham actually ended up liking, even though he hadn't wanted to. The man was helping him, but certain things Graham wouldn't tell anybody, not even his shrink. Like seeing Lydia. They'd lock him up if he told anybody about that.

When Lydia visited his room at night, the smell of rotting flesh was what woke him up.

Why was he thinking of her now? Why did she keep intruding on his real life?

Change the channel. Just change the channel.

He couldn't stop. She'd been his guide out there in OT. He would never have made it without her. Maybe none of them would have made it. Now he didn't know if she'd been the monster she'd always seemed. Maybe he'd needed for her to be worse than she was. Maybe he'd needed to hate her so her lack of love wouldn't hurt so much. So that he could tell himself he didn't care.

Evan's father was moving back from Florida. Turned out he missed Tuonela, and for some reason Evan thought it would be a good idea to have another adult around. That was cool. Graham liked old people. Too bad about Chief Burton. Graham had liked him. And now Rachel was sad. And maybe leaving town, he'd heard. But Graham had to quit thinking about that. He had his whole life ahead of him. And Isobel was right beside him on a blanket.

They were seeing a band together in the park. That should make him happy as hell. It did make him happy.

"Did you really hate that CD I gave you?" he blurted out.

Wow. He'd finally said it. He'd been trying for days, slowly working up to it, like the time he'd finally gotten up the nerve to dive from the high dive.

But now the question that had been dogging him for so long just popped out of his mouth with no prethought.

"What do you think?" She was lying on her stomach, running her palm over the grass at the edge of the blanket.

"I don't know."

If she really hated it, could he still like her? God, that was shallow. Or was it? When you were passionate about something, and the person you cared about hated what you were passionate about, that wasn't good.

She rolled to her back and smiled up at him, twirling a piece of grass in her hand. "I can't believe you didn't see through me. I listened to that CD every night when I went to bed. I still listen to it."

He nodded, trying not to smile. "Oh."

The band was doing a sound check, and the kid behind the movie projector was making sure everything was set up right.

Graham felt better. "Have you ever crocheted?" he asked. "Because I was thinking I'd really like to learn to crochet."

Chapter 47

Evan swept from the house and charged down the dark, steep hillside. He hadn't completely recovered from his injuries, but he moved quickly, ducking under low limbs and sliding on soft, muddy soil.

When he reached level ground he walked with long strides. Near the bluff, then down across the railroad tracks and beside the river. From there he took the decayed steps up through a maze of vines and bowed branches heavy with dew and summer leaves, winding to the street where Rachel lived.

He looked up to see a light glowing faintly through the turret window.

He closed his eyes and inhaled. He smelled the scent of sage and the sweet smell of her skin. An image flashed into his brain of her lying in the zinc tub. So close to death.

He needed to talk to her, but the more time that passed, the harder it got. Soon it wouldn't matter. Soon she would hate him.

He climbed the hill to the morgue.

*   *   *

Rachel rolled the coffin and cart from the autopsy suite and down the hallway, parking it near the door.

She missed her father. Sometimes she got confused and forgot he was dead. There were times when she heard his voice, and times when she thought she saw him. Just a glimpse from the corner of her eye. But whenever she turned, he wasn't there.

She wanted him to be there. Ghost. Illusion. She would take whatever she could get.

So far Victoria hadn't reappeared. And as time passed, Rachel began to think she hadn't really been a ghost at all, but a premonition, a warning she'd failed to heed.

Rachel had worked hard to convince the city they should buy back Old Tuonela, bulldoze the buildings, secure the fences, and let nature take care of what was left. The city council had almost agreed to the plan, only to discover that some unknown person had bought the property from the Alba family before they'd put in an offer.

Who would want it?

Travis had confessed that he and some of the others had broken into Evan's house, looking for evidence that would prove once and for all that he was a vampire. They'd hoped to find Evan himself, asleep in a coffin in the basement, or at least asleep in the middle of the day so they could steal his heart. When they hadn't found him at home, they'd taken personal items that had contained Evan's DNA. Chelsea Gerber's body had been transported in the trunk of Craig Johnson's car, where it had come in contact with that DNA.

The March girl had finally recalled being "rescued" from Evan by Alba and the Pale Immortals. They'd taken her to OT, where she would have died if she hadn't escaped. Travis's fate hadn't yet been determined, but many were hoping he'd be tried as an adult. He'd implicated Rachel's assistant, Dan, in the mess. They'd found the body of the missing Summit Lake woman jammed into a crevice in Old Tuonela. Apparently she'd been Alba's first kill.

Someone knocked on the delivery door. Rachel opened it to find Evan standing there. He slipped inside, smelling like night air—kind of damp and boggy. He unbuttoned his coat, jamming his hands in his pockets.

She'd seen him only a couple of times since the events in Old Tuonela. She knew he'd found her in Alba's house, but she had only a vague memory of it all. Since then there had been no personal conversation other than his voicing sympathy over the loss of her father.

He was keeping a deliberate distance.

"My father is coming home," Evan said. "He's going to help with Graham."

"That's nice."

"He misses Tuonela."

Rachel thought about how the mummy's face had turned into Evan's that night. "Would you like to say good-bye to Richard Manchester?" She swung open the coffin lid to reveal the remains of the Pale Immortal. "It's a shame I can't find his scarf, don't you think?"

There had been a lot of discussion about what to do with the Pale Immortal. Some residents thought he should be reburied in Old Tuonela, that his removal had unleashed a sinister evil. Some thought he should be put on display in their local museum. Rather than running from history, residents seemed ready to embrace their strange heritage, especially if it meant tourists and money. Rachel could see it now. The Pale Immortal Pancake House. The Pale Immortal Taffy Shop.

Celebrities and millionaires had offered staggering amounts for the mummified remains of a heinous monster who had slaughtered women and children.

Who owned the dead? That's what they were trying to decide. Normally it would be family, but half of Tuonela's inhabitants were descendants. Until a decision and agreement could be made, the Pale Immortal would be stored in an undisclosed location.

"I hate for him to leave here without his scarf." Rachel looked up, hoping Evan would admit to taking it.

His face was ashen.

"Evan?" In that moment she finally understood that part of her own longing for Tuonela hadn't been about Tuonela at all.

We are good at keeping secrets from ourselves.

He pressed long, pale fingers to his temple. "I have to go."

"You should sit down. You're doing too much too soon."

She wasn't herself yet either. The loss of blood had left her weak and anemic. She fell asleep at odd moments, and would wake up disoriented from strange dreams.

He whirled around. "I have to go."

She closed the coffin lid, sorry she'd used such juvenile tactics to draw him out. "Let me drive you."

"I'll be okay."

In a flurry of coattails, he was gone.

She reached the door in time to catch a glimpse of his dark, lonely figure moving down the street to finally vanish under the tree branches.

Alba had been a bad person, but would he have killed if not for the close proximity of ground that had been cursed and imprinted by the horrors of the past? And had the fresh murders, so reminiscent of the old, awakened evil?

They would never have all the answers. There simply weren't answers for such questions. But she knew people weren't supposed to know what happened to them after they died. Death was supposed to remain a mystery. The door to the next world, whatever the next world was, should remain firmly closed.

She'd always tried to tell herself that the stories surrounding Old Tuonela were wrapped in ignorance and superstition. Now she could finally admit the truth; that Old Tuonela was a place no human should ever go.

*   *   *

Evan headed out of town. He drove too fast, so lost in thought that later he had no recollection of the trip. He found himself in an overgrown lane, the headlight beams illuminating a FOR SALE sign. He got out of the car, removed the sign, and tossed it aside. Then he dug the antique tin from his coat, lifted the lid, and studied the remaining contents.

He'd drunk tea made from a vampire's heart. He wasn't sure what it had done to him, but he knew he was no longer completely human and that a part of the Pale Immortal now dwelled within him.

Nobody must discover his secret. Especially not Rachel and Graham.

He put the tin away, pulled out the mono-grammed scarf, and wound it around his neck. Then, his hands deep in his coat pockets, he walked up the lane to Old Tuonela, land of the dead.

Look for the sequel to *Pale Immortal*
from *"master" storyteller Anne Frasier

Coming from Onyx

It will make your skin crawl.

*Welcome back to Tuonela, a town haunted by
its horrific past where darkness lingers . . . a
darkness that speaks to the residents who belong but that terrifies visitors. Rachel Burton
is ready to escape her entanglement with
Evan Stroud and the evil that permeates the
town—until she's sucked back onto a murder
case involving the skinned body of a woman,
a visitor lured into the woods by what ap-
pears to be a lost child. But nothing is as it
seems in Tuonela. . . .*

*Minneapolis Star Tribune